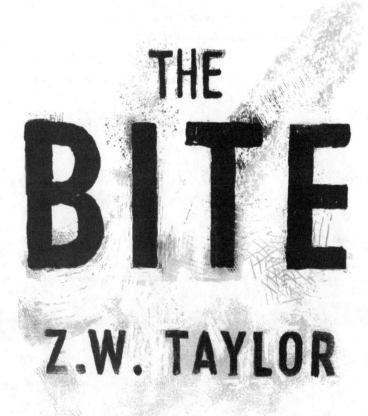

# THE
# BITE

## Z.W. TAYLOR

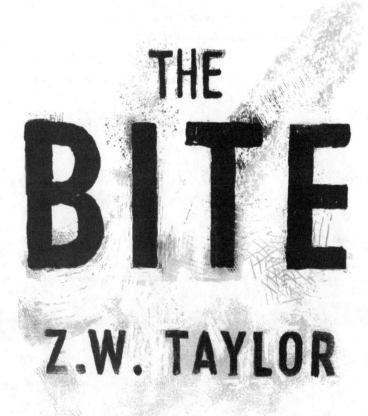 by **wattpad** books

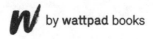

An imprint of Wattpad WEBTOON Book Group

Published in Canada by Wattpad WEBTOON Book Group,
a division of Wattpad Corp.

36 Wellington Street E., Suite 200, Toronto, ON M5E 1C7 Canada

*www.wattpad.com*

First W by Wattpad Books edition: February 2023

ISBN 978-1-99025-965-4 (Trade Paper original)
ISBN 978-1-99025-966-1 (eBook edition)

Library and Archives Canada Cataloguing in Publication information is
available upon request.

Printed and bound in Canada

1 3 5 7 9 10 8 6 4 2

Cover design by Laura Klynstra
Images © Trevillion, © Roxane via Adobe Stock

To my parents for believing in me, my dear friends for supporting me, and to the team working on this project with me to bring this to life. Without you all, this book would have only been a dream.

# CHAPTER
# ONE

I was done.

My foot pressed harder on the gas. My fingers clenched the steering wheel until my knuckles were white.

It was over. I was never going back to him. Never.

"I'm done," I commanded myself.

I checked the rearview mirror again, half expecting to see the headlights of Nate's cherry-red convertible tailing me. There was still a part of me that half wished he was. The shame and embarrassment of it had been riding shotgun since I'd merged onto the I-405.

It was just me and my beat-up 4Runner out on whatever highway this was now. I'd bought it as a trade-in for the sleek black Mercedes Nate had bought for me. He'd bought so many things for me that eventually my entire existence felt purchased. The diamond earrings in my cup holder? Anniversary gift. That tennis bracelet burning a hole in the side pocket of my Chanel bag? Birthday present. Even the French manicure and my overpriced blond hair were on his credit card.

Which reminded me—I needed gas soon. Panic prickled in my chest. My fingers tapped on the steering wheel.

I was too low on supplies and too close to the Canadian border. I needed to stock up before I crossed. I found a run-down Texaco at the next exit, but the only option I had beyond that was a sprawling Walmart two miles up. This was good, though. Nate knew I was a Target girl. If he was coming after me, he probably wouldn't look for me here. Still, I pulled into a parking space near the exit side. Close enough so I could get back to my truck fast if I needed to.

It was surprisingly busy inside for eight o'clock at night in upper bumfuck Washington State. Normal people everywhere buying normal-looking things. It wasn't hard to blend in with the crowd here, but even without the split lip and the black eye, I still would've stuck out like a sore, spray-tanned thumb.

I pulled my hood up and kept my head down as I tossed new clothes into my cart: practical leggings and a few long-sleeved T-shirts. Sweatshirt. Rain jacket. I grabbed the cheapest underwear I could find—comfortable cottons and a few plain, nude-colored bras. It was liberating to pass up the lace. Nate always wanted lace.

My mind kept wandering back to him too much today. Back to the sweet memories that went down like smooth whiskey instead of the ones that strangled my throat. He said he loved it rough, but too many nights had left me with purple prints around my neck for me to feel the same.

When I passed a mirror in an empty corner of the ladies' department, I forced myself to look at the black-and-blue map he'd left on my face. The gash on my cheek, angry red and puffy, would probably take the longest to heal. Hitting a dresser would do that.

I turned away and headed quickly to find the hair dye. Dozens of choices lay before me, but I had to think through what wouldn't turn out as orange as my ass. So I opted for my natural color—a dark brown, almost black, that I'd inherited from my mother.

Self-checkout was so slammed I thought about ditching my cart and bolting. I couldn't risk anyone seeing my face. I was already terrified of the trail I was leaving. Terrified the handful of bills I'd swiped from his wallet at three o'clock this morning wouldn't get me all the way to Alaska. I couldn't let him find me, but I also couldn't stand that I was still wearing clothes he'd bought for me. Every inch of my body felt like a transaction happening three states away. So I waited in line and ignored the concerned checkout attendant trying to catch my eye.

Fifteen anxiety-soaked minutes and $143.87 later, I was back on the road, debating with myself again as to whether or not I should find a rest stop to spend the night in or just keep driving until I couldn't anymore. I'd peeled out of Malibu sixteen hours ago, and technically hadn't slept in two days, but I refused to even consider the idea of sleep until I got to Canada. I'd stolen Nate's passport before I'd left, and chucked it and my pink iPhone into the Pacific Ocean on my way out of town.

By the time I got to the border, I knew I wouldn't make it much farther. I could feel how bloodshot my eyes were with every blink. The border services agent took one look at my passport and asked me to take off my hood. His expression went from suspicious to alarmed in half a second flat.

"Ma'am, can I ask if you're all right?" he said, handing back my passport.

"I'm fine. Thank you."

"Not in any kind of trouble, are you?"

"No, sir. Not at all." I smiled, and felt the cut on my lip crack open a little. "Is there a rest stop near here?"

"Yes, ma'am. One about a mile up from here, and another one about thirty minutes past that."

"Thank you."

He nodded. "You be safe out there, ma'am."

I pulled away from the booth, wondering if I should've kept Nate's passport with me. The Pacific was deep, but it wasn't that deep.

The water in the bathroom at the rest stop thirty minutes into Canada was warm, at least.

I scrubbed and scrubbed until my skin was raw, the baking-soda paste I'd mixed with lemon juice washing away the fake orange tan that stained my skin, causing the water to turn a resentful yellow.

My hair was another story. It'd sucked up the dark dye like water in the desert. I thought I could make it better by giving it a quick cut. I wanted a change. Instead, I got a chop job that looked like a fifth grader had done it. At least the color looked good.

My reflection almost scared me. I hadn't seen the woman looking back at me in years. A complete stranger. A doe scared of every headlight that pulled into the rest stop parking lot. Dark, wet hair. Blue-gray eyes full of fearful resolution. Yoga and the cute little Zumba classes at the country club had kept her thin, but not strong.

I could be strong, though. I had to be.

I slept in my backseat that night and dreamed I was in a motel instead. Through the watery, bruised void that was my dream, Nate kicked in the door and dragged me out by my freshly dyed hair.

• • •

It took two days to drive the coast of Canada. Two days of gas station junk food bought with Canadian cash that a nice man in a town called Quesnel had traded me for a couple of American hundred-dollar bills. I had no idea if he'd ripped me off, but I didn't care about the exchange rate, because I was here. In Alaska.

And I was fucking starving.

I'd had too much time to think on the drive up here. My mind had marinated in the things that had transpired to lead me here, and it was all my fault. God, I'd screwed up. I should've never talked to him. Should've never gotten in that deep. Should've never given up my life for him.

Should've never taken that long to get out.

I felt tears on my face again. My body wasn't going to forget that last beating for a long time. And I didn't want it to. The pain reminded me of that last horrific night. He'd chased me into the guest bathroom of our condo, and our maid, Yulanda, had found me on the floor hours later. I needed to remember what she'd said, the way she'd rushed me out of the house, so I could keep my foot on the gas.

*I don't want to find your body.*

"I know," I whispered to myself now, letting her words roll around in my head.

I mashed the gas pedal down to the floorboard.

Yulanda was how I escaped. Yulanda had known this day would come. Wise beyond her years, she cleaned me up that day and yanked me to her cousin's used car lot where we traded in my shiny silver Mercedes for the 4Runner. She helped me pack my bags in a hurry, then placed a key in my hand before I ran out the door. The key was to a cabin her brother owned out in the middle of the mountains. She said he only went up there during the summer, liked to go fishing for salmon. Luckily for me, it was the off-season. Fall had started, which meant I could be alone in the woods, where I could have a proper fucking meltdown and let my bruises heal before figuring out what I was going to do with myself.

Nate wouldn't suspect. He never got to know Yulanda. Never cared. And she wasn't about to say a thing.

Plus, this was Alaska. Not exactly the territory of Nate's perfect little bleached-out Barbie.

I tried to focus on something else. Like how my hands were sore from gripping the steering wheel for so long, or how my skin still itched from trying to scrub off my fake tan. I glanced over at the map spread out across the passenger seat. I'd picked it up in Quesnel, once I realized how fucking much of Canada there was before you could cross into Alaska, and was surprised by how much it'd comforted me over the last couple of days. I felt off the grid with the flimsy paper. Untraceable. Safe.

But it was too fucking quiet in this car, and the quiet wormed its way into my worst fears. It didn't help that I had been driving all day through the middle of nowhere. You'd think the picturesque scenery would quell my fears.

Luckily, I could see neon lights glowing up ahead. The word *Diner* flickered in a muted blue that had faded to something less abrasive than what I imagined it once was. Perfect.

I pulled into the cracked parking lot, eyeing the buckling wooden deck out front. The windows were fogged with god knows what, but at least the odd, canary yellow doorframe still had some life to it.

The inside was a lot more put together, at least. It smelled like bacon grease and lemon-scented Lysol. I felt every single look that landed on me when I walked in, and I focused on the two bobblehead hula dancers next to the register on the long, shiny counter to avoid the stares coming from the lone table of crossword-playing men in the corner. It was harder to ignore the whispers of the cook, though, or the woman at the counter who almost shattered my resolve with a single look.

*Ignore them. Just eat then get out of here.*

I picked a booth in the back corner close to the bright-red exit sign. The seat crackled when I sat down. I set my backpack next to me and reached for one of the flimsy plastic-cased menus. I hadn't eaten a real meal in days.

"Can I help you, hon?"

I tried not to jump.

Her name tag looked like it had soaked up some of the cigarette smoke that also had sucked the softness out of her voice. It read "Shirley," but that's as far as my eyes reached before guilt forced them back down to the menu, as if it was now of the utmost importance.

My splotchy fingers clutched at the worn menu, the patches of tan around paler skin showing me that I'd done a piss-poor job of taking the dye off.

"Hon?"

Shit, how long had she been standing there? I squirmed in my seat as her eyes trailed from the cut on my lip to the purple-and-blue bruise hugging the corner of my eye.

"What's good?" I asked. It was my turn to snap her out of her thoughts. I tried to hide the bitterness, but there was no hiding the bite in my voice.

I pulled my hood farther around my bruised cheek, hoping it looked like I was cold, but the ruse was up. Her brown eyes, decorated with tacky blue eye shadow, saw through my desperate facade. Sympathy poured from those eyes, but her lips remained silent with my secret.

It was so much easier before, but then again, before was something solemn women dared not acknowledge even among each other. Acknowledging it meant admitting there was a problem, and admitting it meant doing something, like leaving—which was easier said than done when Nate had the keys to the cage he'd built for me out of diamond earrings and tennis lessons. God, I hated tennis.

"Everything's good here. Breakfast, lunch, dinner."

"I don't—" I tried to steady my breathing. "I have no idea what to get."

She nodded, her eyes soft. "I can have 'em fry you up anything six ways to Sunday."

My splotchy fingers clutched at the worn plastic menu. My hands started to shake. All of a sudden, what to order was a decision I couldn't make. I had had to make too many decisions recently.

"It's okay if you don't know," she said with a shrug. "Blank slate, sweetie—means you've got plenty of options."

Fuck if I knew that. The only option I wanted was one where I could scream my head off in a cabin by myself.

"When you've got options, and none of them bad, the best thing to do is to pick one."

I wanted one of her cigarettes. I looked back at the menu. The first words that stood out were the ones at the bottom corner of the page. "Breakfast?"

"Always a good choice."

"Uh, I like pancakes." I mean, who didn't like pancakes?

"Eggs?" she asked.

"Can't hurt?"

"Sure can't." She wrote it down on her pad. "You get another side too."

My brows rose. This place should be called All Sides. "Right."

"So, choose one."

"Oh—um. Bacon?"

"You can't go wrong with it. To drink?"

I blinked. The sound of something sizzling in hot grease filled the air, diffusing the tension in the silence between us.

The vibration of a phone cut through the noise. My eyes looked up to see the crossword game briefly interrupted until the man ignored the call. I didn't know how he could ignore it because it sounded so loud, like my own phone vibrating on the Plexiglas, his name lighting up the screen with that picture of us I'd carefully picked out when we first started dating. It never changed over the years, unlike us.

The phone vibrated again. My fingers twitched for my own, but it was long gone at the bottom of the Pacific where it belonged. I'd stopped trusting myself with it, but even without it I wondered how many miles I'd make it before answering him.

Someone had switched the old box television in the corner to a football game. I listened to the cheering and the murmurs about how useless one team's defense was, but what I really heard was myself screaming when his fist met my face.

"Coffee and water please," I forced out.

They never tell you about this part.

In the movies and television it's always so easy; they're always so angry. I wish I could be that angry. Instead, it's claws I feel ripping my own heart apart because no one wants to admit that they still love the person who turned them black and blue. No one tells you that the anger doesn't come easily but the regret does. The self-doubt, self-deprecation, and self-loathing does. No one tells you what to do with the love you still have for them.

"Got it," she answered.

I hated being on my own, but right now it was all I wanted. I needed to pull it together. I couldn't have a

10

breakdown in a run-down diner in the middle of nowhere Alaska.

When she returned she set the coffee in front of me and lingered at the table, business cards looking back at me from under the sporadically foggy clear top. That damn phone rang again. It might as well have been him barking my name out. It took everything I had to keep a sob from slipping out. It would just be a few more hours, then I could lose it. No one wanted to see me like this, a blubbering mess of tears and shameful excuses, including myself.

"Are you all right?" She slid into the crackly booth seat across from me.

I couldn't remember the last time someone asked me that question and actually meant it, or expected an answer other than "Fine." No one really wanted to know the true answer anyway, they just wanted to be able to check the box off on their "I'm a good person" list before they headed down to Starbucks for something grande and nonfat.

The last time I told someone I wasn't fine, she just patted my hand in the ladies' room of that bougie country club Nate loved and told me, "Keep your chin up." It didn't matter that I had mentioned to her how Nate had gotten a little too heated and knocked me into the dresser, or that the bruise that I showed her hidden beneath my long skirt corroborated my story. It didn't faze her. In that moment I remember thinking that I should have just kept my mouth shut, that I was better off looking through the "Quotes" section on Pinterest for advice. At least the inspirational font and frilly art decor would have distracted from the hollowness of the words. At least the quotes wouldn't have gossiped or watched me like a pack of vultures waiting to rip apart the fresh corpse.

When I looked back at Shirley, I knew that I was far from that Malibu country club, and at this point, what the hell else did I have to lose? I was in the middle of Alaska, far from him and far from those people.

"No." It was so much harder to say than I remembered.

She nodded slowly, her own suspicions confirmed. "Do you want to talk about it?"

My head automatically started to shake even though inside I was screaming yes. Why couldn't I just say yes?

"Okay," she said, as if she was afraid her reply would further crack the already broken china before her. "How long since you left?"

"A little over a week," I lied. It sounded better than the truth, which was pitiful. A tiny part of my brain wondered if I would even make it a full week.

She nodded. "Where's your phone?"

"In the ocean," I admitted painfully. Although I wasn't going to admit that it didn't matter. I had a burner. Yulanda's number was preprogrammed, just for emergencies. There was another number I didn't dare program in, although it didn't matter. It was one I dangerously knew by heart.

"Good." She gave me a firm nod. "Leave it there. Belongs there and not in your hand," she added, although it felt like she meant more than the phone.

She stood and started to wipe her hands on her faded blue apron.

"Does it get better?" I asked, surprising myself.

Shirley paused for a moment, and when she spoke again, a softness had returned to her voice.

"You get better."

The cook hit the bell on the counter, summoning her away from my table.

My fingers slid through my short hair as the last few days' events danced around my head in a cruel ballet, caging me. I just wanted to be free. I wanted to feel like I could breathe again, but it felt like the weight of what I had done was suffocating me.

Shirley came back a few minutes later and dropped off a hot plate of pancakes, with crispy bacon on the side and scrambled eggs.

"Carbs help, wine helps, burning pictures of them helps, shooting at said pictures with a twelve-gauge also helps." She shrugged, her lips quirking into a small smile. "There's no right way to do this, but you will do this."

"Thank you."

"I do what I can," she said, and I believed it.

I took one bite and an embarrassing groan escaped me. The coffee chased down the carbs I practically shoveled into my mouth and eventually, Shirley was filling another cup for me and eyeing the flimsy paper map I pulled out of my backpack.

"Oh, sweetie . . ."

I couldn't meet her gaze. "I know, but I don't have a phone, and I needed a map."

"Where are ya headed?"

"A cabin—my friend's brother's," I replied. "It's quiet there."

"We need to get you a better map. Do you have a phone out there?"

I felt like I had been caught, but when her eyes met mine, there was no judgment. No disdain. Something else that looked like a fire, a spark, that seemed to move something in me. "I think there's a landline. And I don't. I picked up a burner phone once I crossed the border. Just in case of emergencies."

"I think Carl has a better map you can take." She nudged her chin toward the cook with a gray military buzz cut in the back. "You mind?" she asked, her chin indicating the stained sticky note with the address on it.

I peeled the note off and handed it to her. "No, that would be great. Thank you."

She winked at me with a hopeful smile and walked back to the counter. Carl whispered something to her that had her bellowing out a laugh. It didn't take long for me to finish my plate or for her to return to me. We traded plate for a worn map with a coffee stain on the far right edge of it.

I opened it up and quickly found the star drawn on an area next to my sticky note. My eyes wandered around the map—dozens of notes had been made about the area. North of the star, different-colored highlighters had outlined areas that looked like no-man's-land.

"'That's where you're headed," Shirley told me, her finger pointing to the star. A pink highlighter had been used to draw a path on the map from the diner to the star. Hopefully foolproof enough for me.

A smile tugged at my lips. My fingers moved past hers to the outlined areas north of the star. "What's that?"

"Private property," she answered right as the bells on the front door chimed.

Four large men walked in, a rigidness about them making me shift in my seat. It didn't help that Shirley's stance changed as she watched them, her arms crossed and her eyes trying to hide a flicker of fear. Their tight steps made it seem like they could snap at any second.

"I'm going to get you your check," she told me.

It was when she left to get my change that one of the men's molten golden eyes caught mine. They were so vivid, so bright. Like the sun roaring to life in Death Valley. There was something else there, too, but I was yanked away from staring when another's gaze found mine. He looked me over as he tied his greasy hair into a ponytail, his lips curled into a smirk. The other men around him started to quietly laugh.

Every hair on the back of my neck stood on end. Nate wasn't here to save me.

I hated myself for that thought.

Shirley walked back with my change and a to-go bag. Her eyes flickered to the table behind me, her lips thinning into a stiff line.

"What's this?" I asked her.

"For the road," she answered, clasping my hands over the bag. Her gaze came back to mine.

"You didn't have to."

"Don't worry about it, now you better get going. I wrote down our phone number here and put it in the bag for you, just in case. You need to watch out for washed-out roads. Happens this time of year. If you see one, don't go through it, turn around and come here. We'll figure something out."

I wanted to answer her, but if I did, I knew I would start

crying. She squeezed my hand before I stepped out of the booth, my gut telling my feet to walk faster.

"Hey, sweetheart!" a cold voice called as I reached for the metal handle of the door.

My body froze in place, my head turning even though my mind screamed to run.

Golden eyes bored into mine. A smile curled on chapped lips. The man tilted his head, nostrils flaring, then looked back at me. "Damn, baby, you smell good."

I threw the door open and sprinted to my car. My fingers fumbled with the keys as I looked over my shoulder at the diner window.

The men were still watching me—eyes locked on me.

My foot stomped on the gas, kicking up gravel behind me. There was something sinister behind their eyes, something that nagged at me even as I put miles between me and the diner. I half expected golden eyes to be looking right back at me every time I looked in the rearview mirror, and I half wanted to see Nate's hazel eyes smiling at me instead.

I hit the gas harder. The farther I was from him, the more difficult it would be for me to turn around. It was a thought that only brought his laughter to my imagination. I could see him now shaking his head at me, as if he had just caught me doing something silly.

There was only a black eye looking at me in the rearview mirror, and I couldn't run from that.

# CHAPTER TWO

My 4Runner, "Ted," and I drove until the diner was long out of view. I felt grateful for Shirley's map in the middle of this kingdom of trees. There was no way that any app would work out here—there had to be absolutely zero signal to work from. I eyed the pink line that Carl had drawn on the paper map. To my luck, which seemed to be running low these days, the map led me right to the road that fed off the main road—the one that would hopefully lead me directly to the cabin. Relief washed over me as I pulled onto the gravel path. A path of hope that quickly dwindled as the road led me to a fork.

"Shit," I hissed. I pulled over and looked at the map. There was no fork in the road on the map. "You have to be fucking kidding me."

I groaned, my mind trying to place where I was. I thought about what Shirley had said at the diner. I didn't think this was one of those situations where both options were good.

I shifted the car back into gear and looked at the map, then back at the fork. My mind churned and tried to piece together what made the most logical sense. Steering forward, and finding myself going left, down a windy road covered with trees and lush greenery, I couldn't shake off the eerie feeling from the diner. I checked the rearview mirror to find no one behind me, although it didn't settle the feeling brewing in my gut, just like this map felt like it wasn't getting me closer to Yulanda's brother's cabin. When I looked back at my map, it felt like I was reading a foreign language. There were no landmarks or mile markers to help me find my way. Just endless hills, trees, and unmarked roads that were all starting to look the same.

Hope started to slowly fade along with the sun as I drove and drove and found nothing. Exhaustion was eating at me again, my eyelids growing heavy. I had to at least try to squeeze in a few hours so I could keep going.

Of course this would happen. Of course I would get lost in the middle of the Alaskan wilderness right as the sun was setting. Of course I couldn't do something simple, like read a damn map.

"Nice work, Charlotte," I groaned to myself.

All I wanted was a nice bed, but all I found was more trees; and I didn't want to drive around on a crazy-ass goose chase in the dark. Finding this cabin would be easier when I wasn't sleep-deprived. I probably should have gone the other way at the fork, but at this point, I had no idea how to get myself back there.

I settled for a campsite with an overgrown dirt road leading into a wooded area where a meadow lapped at its borders. The temporary haven of grass and wildflowers swaying in the crisp breeze chased away the fear eating at the corners of my mind. For now, I had found a temporary oasis.

The sunlight was fading fast as dusk had comfortably settled in, but my feet followed the dirt road on their own. Curiosity flared in me as I examined deep tread marks in the dried mud that slowly disappeared into the grass. I bent down and eyed the grooves in the dirt. They were like small trenches that just vanished. In their place was fresh grass and wildflowers. Which meant someone had to have covered them up, but it didn't look like a great deal of dirt had been shifted around the area. If anything, the landscape looked almost untouched. Still wild.

"You're trespassing."

The deep voice was like a shot of espresso. I whipped around to find a man standing behind me. He was maybe in his midfifties with worn jeans and brown boots that were smashing out the last bits of a cigarette.

"You're on private property," he said, his hand flicking away a piece of scruffy silver-white hair that must have fallen out of his ponytail. I felt my head tilt as his silver eyes caught mine—eyes that, much like his hair, almost seemed to glow unnaturally.

"Private. Property," he repeated.

I shook my head with a blink, snapping myself out of his

gaze, and looked back at my car. I was close to it, not more than fifteen feet. If I had to, I could be fast enough to make it back to the driver's seat.

"I didn't see a sign. I thought this was a campsite."

He cocked his head, bright-silver eyes looking at me as if this whole conversation was a thorn in his foot. "Well, this is my property and you can't be here."

"I could be gone before the morning—"

"No can do, miss." He dug out another cigarette from the pack in his back pocket. "You can't stay here."

I nodded slowly. His new cigarette flared to life, smoke starting to twist from the end. "I was looking for my friend's cabin. Got lost looking for it—the map was hard to—I just need a place to sleep for tonight."

*Jesus Christ, get it together, Charlotte.*

I felt his gaze shift to my black eye. I knew he could see it. It may have been getting dark, but he wasn't that far away. It was like I could feel his gaze tracing the outline of it. My feet nervously toyed with a few rocks on the ground. "You're a long ways from cabins, girl. How the hell did you get out this far?"

"Trying to follow a map." I was still half shocked that I'd made it this far. "I turned wrong at the fork . . . I think?"

He nodded as something flickered in his eyes, but it passed too quickly for me to recognize it.

"There's a campsite about a mile from here. It will be on your right. In the morning, just go back down *this* road. At the fork, you take a right, not a left, and that will spit you out on the main county road that leads up to the vacation cabins."

I backtracked to my car. "Thanks," I answered. I would

go find Shirley in the morning. She could probably help me find the cabin during the daylight.

"Don't mention it," he replied while a cloud of smoke left his lips. "Keep an eye out!" he called after me. I looked over my shoulder. "It's getting dark. Wouldn't want any wild animals to get ya."

I didn't have to call Nate. I could hear him laughing in my head as Ted and I hauled ass out of there. His laughter was stifling until I pressed a finger to the button of the sunroof to open it. Fresh air poured in and quieted my racing mind, for now at least.

The campsite that the creepy old man had told me about was, in fact, exactly a mile away. It wasn't ideal. I wasn't a fan of being out on my own in the middle of the wilderness. But here, in the four walls of my car, I was far from Nate and in a place where I could easily escape if he showed up. Maybe it was the exhaustion or maybe it was the little bit of sanity I had left slipping, but right now this was my safe haven. He couldn't corner me here. He couldn't trap me in a room with only one door. I had four doors and my feet could easily reach the gas pedal.

Shirley's to-go package was tucked away safe in the passenger seat, and I was quick to lock all the doors before I pulled out my sleeping bag. It wasn't the sleek silver Mercedes that I had traded in for Ted, or the high-priced condo with a view overlooking the ocean that Nate loved, but it was a cozy den of my own.

My eyes started to drift as I watched the stars through the open sunroof. The air was cool, too cool for comfort, so I slid the sunroof cover shut before I snuggled down in my seat. The land of sleep called me away to the bliss of my mother humming to me while she stroked my hair. A bliss that was barely enjoyed before it was broken by a distant howl.

My eyes cracked open. Darkness clouded the car, seeping into it. I pulled the sleeping bag tighter around me while my sleepy eyes tried to blink awake.

Another howl sounded. Closer. Close enough that my eyes snapped wide-awake. Only the dark forest stared back at me, like open water. I could see the faint outline of branches swaying in the wind, but only silence was layered onto the blanket of darkness around me.

My heart picked up. Maybe I was being irrational? Dramatic?

*Thud.*

Something had hit the rear of the car. The car wobbled while I clutched the covers over my head. My hand slapped over my mouth as I peeked over the edge of my sleeping bag.

Blackness stared back at me like an animal licking its lips, daring me to step into its embrace.

"It's nothing," I murmured to myself.

*Thud.*

The car rocked hard, like a ship in an angry sea.

My teeth dug into my lip. A coppery taste filled my mouth while I sucked in a deep breath, bracing myself to move. My head whipped around in search of something, although I hoped that whatever that something was wouldn't show itself.

My eyes were clenched shut and wanted to stay that way, but my gut told me to move. Like a thief, I carefully slipped out of my cozy sleeping bag and reached for the keys. As I turned the ignition, there was another thud, this one closer to the driver's door, rocking the car again in another angry tide.

My breath caught in my throat as the engine wavered on me. The darkness around me seemed to grow thicker as my heart steadily picked up tempo in my chest. A cool sweat danced along the back of my neck while I continued to listen to the engine stutter.

"Come on, Ted!"

The engine turned over and I slammed my foot on the gas right as something slammed into the passenger's side door, rocking me right out of my seat. A scream ripped out of my mouth as I fought to find the gas pedal. Gravel flew around me.

Clenching the steering wheel, I slammed my foot on the gas, racing about ten feet into freedom. But in the darkness, I didn't see it coming. Something crashed into the front of the truck.

Metal groaned as glass shattered around me as the car started to topple over. I tried to claw my way back to the driver's seat, but a loud boom sent me ricocheting backward. My head hit the roof. Another scream tore from my lips as the truck started to slowly topple over onto its side.

There was a bang, crunching, what sounded like growl-ing—*growling?*—and the faint sound of a painful murmur. I think it was from me?

When I finally opened my eyes, I was met with silence. Pure, horrifying silence.

This kind of silence meant that I had to get out of here before it was too late. The creepy old man lived nearby—he had to have been close to have walked to where I was in the meadow. I made it over a thousand miles from one monster; I could make it another mile from whatever this was.

The silence was interrupted by glass cracking across the driver's side windows above me, and tiny shards trickled down around me like raindrops falling in a soft spring storm. I could see the moon peering through the spiderweb-shattered windshield, glowing bright and full in the clear night. Cold seeped into the car, sliding over my shoulders while glass continued to patter down beside me.

Suddenly, everything was too loud: the sound of glass hitting next to me, my breath as it came out of my mouth, my heart beating in thumps that I was sure could be heard for a mile, and my own screaming inside my head, which I knew would come out of my mouth if I opened it.

The metal easily dented as the thing on top of it strolled across it, drawing groans from the metal that preceded each new dent. The sound made me wince with every sickening assault on the strength of the haven I thought these four walls on wheels would provide me.

I had to escape.

I surveyed my options. Staying wasn't an option, but the windshield didn't look viable either. Kicking it out would be too loud. It was so black outside that I wasn't sure that even if I could run I would find my way to the road. The moon was out, yes, but the trees blocked it—almost as if they were determined to keep me in utter darkness.

But I had to move. In my mind, I could visualize the road. I could backtrack my steps to it. I just needed the cover of silence.

My brain chewed on the options. I needed a quiet escape—something that would not give away my location. Breaking a window open and running was a deadly trap. My eyes frantically searched the cab for options. The sunroof. I had closed the cover but left the sunroof glass open before I went to sleep. I could easily slide it open quietly and slip silently away. Well, I could only hope for such an outcome.

I clenched my eyes shut. I only had one chance at this. My toes wiggled in my shoes, legs ready to sprint the moment they hit the ground.

My fingers reached for the lid and paused. I looked around to make sure that I hadn't given myself away before reaching for the handle. Carefully, I slid the cover open. A cold breath from the great dark silence of the forest grazed my face. Cold yet inviting, like a siren calling me to my death. It felt like it would suck out my soul if I stared too long.

I didn't dare breathe. I pulled my shirt up to my mouth and bit down on it so I wouldn't be tempted to shriek. The darkness blew another soft breath into the interior. I quietly reached forward, pushing myself up as I started to crawl.

Soft dirt sank under my hands while I carefully slid out into the night. The minute my whole body was out of the car, I took off like I was running the Olympic one-hundred-yard dash. I dropped the shirt in my mouth and sucked in sweet breaths of air to keep my limbs moving.

But the darkness was a fog that was impossible to penetrate. The tiny fragments of light that made it through the thick trees only illuminated the forest around me, like shining a light into the deep of the ocean.

Limbs felt like angry nails trying to snare me as I pushed past them while I sucked in unsatisfying breaths of cool, thin night air. I was getting out of here. I was finding that old man. I had to keep telling myself that while my feet pounded against the forest floor.

My toe caught something. As I toppled down in darkness, my arms caught the impact with the ground, which knocked all the air out of my lungs. Something sharp pulsed through my shoulder and something warm and wet dripped down my knee. I tried to look but the moonlight barely lit what I had to assume was blood.

I took another breath; I could hear movement around me but didn't dare look behind me. I covered my mouth with my hand. A heavy crunch echoed through the forest, followed by another one.

Something was creeping closer.

There wasn't a road in sight. There was just darkness and what felt like a labyrinth of trees—until I spotted the moon's dim reflection on the main road.

Scrambling up, I darted for the road. Sweat beat down my neck while my fingers dug into my fists, which pumped into the scheming night.

I was only a few yards away, almost free, when something wrapped around my waist and yanked me to the ground. My hip took the brutal first hit before my arm was crushed underneath the weight on top of me. The taste of copper filled my mouth while stars blinked across my vision.

I reached forward to push myself up but brutal hands yanked me onto my back. Gold looked at me. Gold eyes with frizzy red veins around them. I blinked, hoping that when I opened my eyes the man on top of me would be gone, but instead I was greeted with a hideous gaze that I immediately recognized. It was the man from the diner. Except, now that he was closer, I realized his golden eyes were not sun-kissed; instead, they looked sick. Bloodshot. Like he had a bad case of pink eye.

I did the only thing I could think of as his mangy breath fanned my face. I kicked between his legs, nailing him right in the balls. The moment he doubled over was the moment I seized to run.

A low, guttural sound ripped out of the darkness to my right, and a large brown mass hurled itself at me again. I slammed down to the cold ground, knees scraping against gravel before I steadied myself on a patch of leaves.

Another growl pulsated through the shadows.

I looked up and found myself once again looking into golden eyes, but that was impossible. Completely impossible. Because the eyes were attached to a big-ass snarling wolf prowling toward me. An animal that licked its lips at its next meal. Me.

The snap of its teeth echoed through the forest. My own mouth snapped shut then opened in a scream. I had to pray that the old man, or someone, would hear me. But the wolf shook its head with a strange laugh, almost maniacal, as it stepped closer to me.

*Holy fuck.*

I pushed myself back until I was standing shakily again. I turned to bolt but stopped before I could take another step. Another ragged wolf, sandy brown with mud caked on its paws, was slinking forward. I turned again, but now the man with the golden eyes was back, walking my way like I was the lottery ticket he was here to claim.

"I always love a good chase."

A sharp breath tumbled out of my mouth. I searched for an exit, my brain trying to work out all the possibilities of how this could end. "Just let me go—I won't tell anyone! I swear!"

I turned again and my stomach turned over. The wolf was gone but in his place was another man from the diner.

"What the hell—"

*Crash.*

I was slammed into the dirt by the man with madness in his eyes, who took my shock as an opportunity to strike. I tried to claw my way out, scratching his arms, kicking, screaming, and beating him with all I had.

It didn't faze him. He just shook his head with a hearty laugh. This was a cute game to him, letting me fight back just before he backhanded me across the face. My ears rang with the jumbled sounds of growls around me. Tears streamed down my cheeks.

There was a soft clack of a belt buckle. Pants unzipping.

And then the man was on me again, tearing at my leggings, yanking them down.

I couldn't let this happen. I couldn't. I didn't come all this way to be raped and murdered in the forest.

Anger raged inside me. I clawed at his face. Bit at the forearm crushing my chest. He shifted his weight and forced my hands over my head with a bearlike paw, pinning me down with the full weight of his hips. Helpless.

He chuckled with a rotten smile, then slapped me again.

"I like it a little rough too," he said, bloodshot eyes drinking me in like a prize he knew he'd eventually win.

He grabbed my jaw with a rough hand, then slid it over my mouth to muffle my scream. Tears dripped into my ears as he lined himself up.

And then suddenly, he was gone, yanked backward into the darkness, his nails leaving slashes across my face and arms.

It took me a second to register that he really wasn't there anymore. I lurched to the side and pulled my leggings up with shaky hands. A bolt of pain shot across my ribs; white spots danced in my vision.

I could hear growling and grunting moving closer to me, but I couldn't tell from which direction. It felt like it was coming from all sides. My head whipped around, trying to find it in the dark. Then I saw it—a tall, dark blur tearing the golden man limb from limb, while another blur, grayish and black, fought off the two other wolves on its own.

I didn't wait around to see what happened next.

I scrambled to my feet and took off running, completely blind with terror, until a sharp pain and a harsh jerk timbered me to the ground.

The sandy-brown wolf had my leg in its mouth.

White-hot agony, wet and sticky, ripped through me as he clamped down harder, sinking his jaw into the meaty flesh above my knee. He thrashed his head wildly, jerking my entire body with it. I could feel every inch of his teeth shredding through muscle and bone.

I was still screaming when the beast released my leg. It stepped toward me, over me, my own blood spilling down its hairy chin and onto my chest. He licked his lips. Nuzzled at the side of my throat with rancid breath—

And then everything went cold. I felt nothing. Maybe I was losing more blood than I realized. I wrenched open my eyes to nothing but darkness again.

The beast was gone. I didn't know how. Maybe I was dead already. Thinking was becoming too taxing.

I rolled to my side, my leg useless as pain snaked through my veins. It was an animal of its own, like claws slowly spreading to each part of me. The Reaper coming to collect me.

I blinked hard, just in time to see a large grayish-black wolf dance around the one that had just bitten me. He growled and barreled into the sandy-brown wolf with a ferocity that made me want to vomit. The sandy-brown wolf didn't stand a chance, his neck bleeding out on the forest floor.

I looked down at my own bleeding leg. I could see bone. A stream of blood pumped out beside it in time with my slowing pulse, snaking across mangled flesh and onto the ground.

I blinked again and my vision swirled. Sleep was calling out to me again, but the black spots flickering in my sight told me this wasn't sleep. I wanted to hold on, but with every breath, my body felt lighter and my mind heavier.

It was impossible to resist the darkness's temptation. It was the whisper of a lover calling me to bed. Like the early days with Nate, when he would murmur sweet things in my ear that I could never hold back from.

My eyes drifted shut and I fell a little deeper.

Something was speaking to me. A robot-like voice in the darkness saying things I was too tired to comprehend. It made the peacefulness of this seem like a trap.

The voice spoke again. Curiosity and fear flared in me. I needed to open my eyes. Needed to run. To keep going. Pull myself up from the heaviness before it took me under.

The black spots had taken over most of my vision but vibrant silver eyes cut through the darkness to me.

Then there was nothing but the cold embrace of silence.

# CHAPTER THREE

I ran through the forest. Pitch-black and cold, the breeze in the night swayed through the trees like a bitter poltergeist taunting me. My feet stumbled over leaves and fallen limbs while low-hanging branches reached to snag me in their sharp embrace.

Thin, cold air did nothing to fill my lungs. I stopped and tried to find the light, the way to the road, but all I found was a pair of sick golden eyes staring at me. They neared until the glow revealed a face I knew too well.

Nate smiled at me, fangs peeking out of his lips. He cocked his head as his eyes greedily drank me in. "I told you that you couldn't run from me," he said coolly, before lunging at me.

My eyes opened as I gulped a breath of air. Pain greeted me like we were old friends, radiating through my body down to the place in my leg where I could feel my own heartbeat. I grabbed the sheets next to me, my toes fidgeting under the blankets.

"It was just a dream," I murmured to myself as my head rolled to the side. It was dim in the room, a small lamp providing the only source of light.

It looked like a cabin of some sort. Wood-paneled walls decorated with different trinkets. A photo of some ducks, a wooden bass with gold hooks for hanging coats, and a deer head mounted on the wall.

I tried not to panic. These people had saved me after all, whoever they were . . .

I tried to push myself up. Searing pain shot through my leg and started to slowly kick drum to life. The pulse in my thigh *thump-thump-thumped*, drawing tears to my eyes and causing me to collapse back on the bed.

*Deep breaths.*

My eyes slowly drifted down the plaid comforter to my leg. Fingers slowly peeled back the blanket to find a large bloodstained bandage wrapped around it. Memories poured back to me: that night. The wolves. The creature. The bite.

My heart raced as the images of my attack poured into my brain. Wolves. Big-ass wolves. I had never seen anything like them. I tried to push away those images. Push away the images of the wolf tearing into my leg, or of the golden-eyed devil who had tried to sate his needs with my body.

Tears tried to push their way out. A sob yanked through me. It was like I could hear Nate next to me, shushing me and telling me he was sorry but he couldn't help it when I made silly mistakes. I covered my mouth and pushed the pain down. I wouldn't cry. Now was not the time. I needed to get up and figure out where the hell I was, and who had saved me.

The sound of murmuring snapped my gaze to the green door across the room. I pulled the covers up while my heart danced in my chest.

Voices outside grew louder while the air around me felt like it was also holding its breath.

"She's just going to be a burden and a royal pain in my ass," a man groaned from behind the door. His voice gravelly, and ice-cold.

"You don't want this on you!" another man pleaded, his voice so smooth it almost sounded like a song.

"I've had enough of this!" the ragged voice growled, causing the green door to shiver.

My eyes went wide as I watched it vibrate. "What the fu—"

Light pooled into the room as the door was thrown open and the lights were turned on abruptly. I had to shield my eyes with my arm so they could adjust to the harshness. I tried to make out what was happening as loud footsteps thundered toward me.

My eyes opened to meet the end of a double-barreled shotgun.

I screamed and grabbed a pillow to shield me. I tried to squirm away but the pain radiating through my injured leg only turned me into a flopping seal on the bed.

It was the man. The gray-haired goon who had told me

to get off his property. He cocked the shotgun as his frosty, silver eyes narrowed at the sight of me. Silver eyes that I couldn't forget. Silver eyes that looked like the ones I'd seen before it all went dark.

He was the one who saved me?

"Levi, stop!" the man behind him barked.

Levi looked back at the man, then at me, his blazing silver eyes finding mine.

"She won't make it, Derek!" he spat back.

"Wha—stop—*please!*" My words tripped over themselves, struggling for survival as they left my lips. "Please don't. Please don't do this!"

"I'd be doing you a favor," he replied with a disturbing gentleness.

Would he? Part of me wondered if my life was better off nonexistent. Then a better part of me stomped it out. I hadn't made it this far only to die.

"Please don't." My fingers gripped the pillow I was holding in front of me like a shield. "Just let me go. I won't say anything!"

"Levi—Levi, *stop*. You don't want her blood on your hands," the man behind him said. Levi scoffed, and the dark-haired man stepped closer, determination in his deep-brown eyes. He looked at me sympathetically, then back at Levi, who was nothing but an unforgiving mountain. "Levi, it's the law. You know the law."

"You think I give a shit about that law?"

"You should! You want the council down here doing an investigation? Or human police sniffing around? Have fun explaining all of that to your brother!" The dark-haired man snarled as he pushed his fingers through his locks. They were as close to black as you could get. "It's not your decision!" he hissed. "It's hers!"

"You know she won't survive the turn, Derek. Look at her!" he said, breaking eye contact with me to look directly at Derek. "She's already a black-and-blue skeleton as it is."

I winced because it was true. My body felt like someone had steamrolled it and then fed it to the pigs.

"I don't know that and neither do you!" Derek snapped. "She could make it. You don't know the future. You don't get to decide for her!"

"Make what?!" I desperately asked.

They ignored me.

"The success rate is low!" Levi yelled.

"You can't just kill an innocent person!" Derek screamed back.

Levi tossed a hand in the air. "You lost your damn mind? It doesn't work like that, she—"

"I'm sitting right fucking here!" I roared, traitorous tears streaming down my cheeks. "I'm sitting right here, *goddammit*." Gulping, I tried to muster whatever courage was left in me. Which was very little once I took another look at the gun. "Now, are you going to tell me what the hell is going on or are you going to shoot me? Seems like a lot of trouble to save me if you're just going to put a bullet in me."

Levi opened his mouth but Derek stepped slightly in front of him, partially blocking Levi from me. He cast me an apologetic glance, then faced Levi again. "What is there to lose? Time? Compared to the lifetimes we will live?"

Who the hell were these people?!

Levi whipped his head back to Derek for a pregnant moment, then lowered his gun. A low growl reverberated out of him. "This is your responsibility."

There was no way a man could growl like that. I must have hit my head too hard. Or lost too much blood.

"It is yours too!" Derek hissed back, his lips rising enough to show fangs.

Fangs.

*Fangs* were hanging from his gums. Chills ran over my skin.

"She will need you. You know the law, Levi!" Derek snipped. "Don't make me call Lander!"

Levi growled back and started to speak, but my strangled scream beat him to it. I clamped my hands over my mouth. Every instinct in my gut told me to run.

Derek's fangs instantly retracted into his gums. He walked carefully toward me with his hands up. "I'm sorry. Really . . ."

I shook my head, scooting away from him.

Levi leaned lazily against the door to watch. I started to shake.

Derek moved to sit on the edge of the bed. His soft eyes made him seem safe, but the fangs in his mouth said otherwise. "I'm sorry, I didn't mean—we didn't mean to scare you."

"Who *the fuck* are you people?!"

"My name is Derek. That lovely asshole behind me is Levi. We, um, found you the other night."

"*Saved your ass* the other night," Levi corrected.

"What?"

"You remember what happened to you?" Derek asked. I nodded slowly. Like I could forget. "You were bitten. Not just by a dog. But by a . . ."

He paused, turning to eye Levi behind him.

"By a what?" My voice was shrill. "Jesus, just say it!"

"By a *werewolf,*" Levi snapped.

I laughed. I couldn't help it. The pair of them looked at me like I had lost it; I'd lost a lot of blood during the attack, so maybe I was losing it?

There was no way they were serious.

"A what now?" I said, wiping the tears away. Another nervous laugh did a piss-poor job of hiding my panic. "No, but really, what was it?"

"You were really bitten by a werewolf," Derek said gently.

Levi huffed and rolled his eyes.

This couldn't be real. Werewolves weren't real. They were only subjects of strange fantasies and terrifying dreams.

I shook my head slowly. "You can't be—those are just fairy tales." My mind reeled with questions I couldn't believe I was even considering.

Derek pinched his brow. "All right, fine," he said.

He stood up, turning into a blur of color that zipped around the room. He paused at the wall, looking over his shoulder before taking a step up the wall. He waltzed up the wall and onto the ceiling like he was taking a stroll on the beach. He paused when he was directly above me, a smirk on his lips.

He jumped, tucking his feet into a somersault, and landed gracefully next to me on the bed. "Still feel like laughing?" he asked.

My mouth dropped open. Oh, he was real all right. I clutched the pillow closer.

"Listen, we're not going to hurt you," Derek said.

I held the pillow tighter in front of me. "Your fangs—"

"I won't hurt you, I swear."

"But he—"

"Levi will not hurt you either."

"He has a gun."

"No one is going to kill you," Derek firmly stated. "Levi, put the gun away."

Levi's low growl made me shiver again.

"Stop, Levi!" Derek hissed, his eyes going black.

Levi grumbled out a string of curses as he set the shotgun down and leaned it against the wall. He walked over to a rocking chair with a blue, star-patterned quilt lying over it and took a seat.

Derek took a deep breath. His warm brown eyes were back and the fangs were gone. "Listen, I swear we will not hurt you, so let's just calm down," he said with a soft smile. "Deep breaths. I'm sure the pillow would appreciate that."

"A werewolf?"

"Yes."

My fingers clutched the blanket. I looked back at Levi, who was watching me curiously. "Is that what you are, then?"

"Levi, why don't you show her?" Derek asked.

"Show me what?" I had to get out of this place. These people were certifiable. There was no denying that.

"What you'll turn into if you survive," Levi muttered as he stood and started to take his clothes off. "Which you won't. Humans rarely do. And I would say your odds are shit, since you got bit by a bunch of rogue wolves."

Derek rolled his eyes and moved in front of me, blocking my view of Levi, who was standing half nude in the center of the room.

There was cracking and breaking as his body began to quickly contort in sickening directions. I felt vomit rise in my mouth. I didn't want to look, but I couldn't help it. I leaned to the side and looked around Derek's body to see something that should not be real. Hair was sprouting through Levi's skin, teeth peeked out from his lips, and his head contorted into a muzzle. More cracks sounded as his body shifted and fur rolled over his skin. My mouth dropped.

He had changed into a large black wolf. A black wolf with bits of gray dusting his back. He was huge, more like a horse in the room. He looked back at Derek and me with an expression that seemed annoyed.

He stepped to us, his muscles rippling beneath the fur.

"What the *fuck*?"

A rumble came from his chest. My mouth clenched shut.

"*Levi*," Derek warned.

The wolf turned to the vampire, whose fangs had started to peek out of his lips defensively, and snorted. He cocked his head, silver eyes almost amused with me before they vexed over into something else.

"Levi," Derek snarled.

Levi huffed and reluctantly turned away, walking on four legs out of the room. There was more cracking that sounded again in the cabin followed by a series of curses. I heard another door open and slam shut. Derek looked down the hall.

"Where's he going?" I asked, because I wanted to make sure I stayed far, far away from him.

"On a run," Derek said simply, like it actually was.

"Am I going to die?" My voice cracked. I felt like the walls might start to crumble at any second.

Derek sat back down on the bed. "On the third full moon from the day you were bitten, you will shift."

"Into what Levi is?"

He nodded. "Yes, into what Levi is."

My hand flew over my mouth to hide the sobs. This couldn't be happening. I was trying to start over. I was going to start a new life. How did all of that get flushed down the drain so fast?

Derek tugged at his hair, watching me carefully. "What did you say your name was?"

Should I tell them my real name? Do I give that part of me away? "Renee."

He narrowed his eyes and cocked his head. "Your real name."

Apparently, using my mother's name was not going to work. I guess it didn't matter.

"Charlotte."

He smiled gently again and sighed. "It's going to be all right," he said. "I think you just need some sleep, and then maybe a stiff drink? Yeah? There's a lot you need to know. I know this is probably overwhelming."

"Is he going to kill me?"

"No," Derek said firmly. "I promise." He stood up and headed for door. "I'll let you rest. We'll talk when you wake up."

"Why are you doing this?"

"Well, I'd rather you not die. Don't you agree?"

I wasn't sure how to answer. All I knew was that I'd seen what I'd only ever read about and seen on television just unfold in front of me.

Derek left me alone to lose it in solitude. If they were right, there was no escaping now. My body was a time bomb. I could run a thousand miles away and still not escape it.

I lay back on my pillow and wished Nate was here. For a moment it felt like his nose was touching mine. The thought itself broke me. I hated that it broke me. I hated that I still craved that feeling of butterflies in my stomach that he gave me.

I closed my eyes and tried to think of something happier, but all I could hear was Nate laughing at me. I could see him perfectly, looking suave in his Ray-Bans and with his chambray shirtsleeves rolled up to his forearms. The sunshine made his hair look almost gold.

He looked over at me and pushed his glasses onto his head. *What have you done, Charlotte?* He chuckled, delighted by his own joke. His laughs felt like sandpaper; his fingers, fillet knives carving up my skin. His smile twisted, opening wide with sharp teeth descending past his lips and out of his mouth. Fangs.

*What have you done, Charlotte?* he asked again, his warped voice haunting me and his eyes filled with a hunger that was nowhere close to love.

He walked toward me with blood dripping down his chin, golden skin slowly fading into sandy-brown fur. He moved behind me and wrapped his arms around me, a position I knew too well with him.

His teeth raked across my neck, over goose bumps and throbbing veins. I could feel his fangs pressing into my skin before there was a scream—*mine*.

I bolted upright in bed, hands flying over my mouth to stop the sound. Violent sobs broke through my fingers.

I somehow stumbled to the bathroom. I turned the knob on the old, rusted sink, splashed water on my face, and looked in the mirror, then wished I hadn't.

It wasn't the bruises. It was my eyes. They were a raging blue storm glowing like the neon sign at Shirley's diner.

"No," I snapped, my chest aching.

The door flew open. Derek looked around frantically, then down at me. "Hey, it's okay. You're safe. Okay? No one's coming for you." He reached for me but I twisted away until my back hit the bathroom wall. "Okay. It's okay."

The tears took over. "My eyes." I panted.

He nodded, looking at me carefully. "It's normal."

"How do you know?"

"I've seen many werewolves shift, and a few humans. Come," he added, "let's get you to bed. We'll talk in the morning."

I shook my head at him. He sighed and sat down opposite me, leaning against the cabinet. I felt tears start to run down my cheeks as sobs ripped through me.

I couldn't remember getting back into bed or falling asleep. He must have waited and then carried me back.

• • •

I woke up to something cold on my leg. I winced slightly as a prickly feeling took over.

Derek snapped his eyes to mine, his fingers covered in the same white cream smeared over my mangled flesh. "Sorry, I know it stings. I thought you were out cold. Can I?"

"Sure," I answered, while my groggy mind started to slowly churn to life.

Carefully, he dabbed more cream on with featherlight touches. "There's a bottle of ibuprofen on the nightstand. You'll want to take some."

I reached over and unscrewed the top, then shook out four pills. Derek handed me some water, and I gulped it down with them, praying they would kick in soon.

He took my glass and set it on the nightstand. "So . . ." He bit his lip and reached for some gauze. It was woven, soft from the looks of it, but still felt like sandpaper going over my leg. I clenched my mouth shut and tried to be a good sport, because I knew he was probably trying to make this painless for me. "How are you feeling?" he asked.

"How am I supposed to feel?"

He shrugged. "Most humans would be more hysterical, I would think?"

I answered his shrug with a shrug of my own. How *was* I supposed to feel? Grateful that I had lived? Fearful that I could die? A limbo between the two? Should we add a conga line with a bad DJ as well?

"I don't know," I admitted.

"How did you come to this part of the woods, sleeping in your car, all on your own?" he asked.

"I guess you could say another monster was chasing me."

He nodded but said nothing in return, and I was grateful. I wasn't ready to talk about my life, especially with two people I knew nothing about. "Are you hungry? You were out for a few days—"

"A few days?!"

He nodded with a long sigh. "Your body is trying to adjust to the bite. It's natural for bitten wolves." He put tape over the bandages. "I think you need some coffee and some breakfast."

"As long as I'm not on the menu." A playful suggestion to hide my inner fear.

He laughed. "You're not my type. You're already starting to smell like your beast, and for me, that smell will never be appealing."

"I smell like a dog?"

He let out a heartier laugh. "Don't refer to them as dogs. They hate that. But yes, you're starting to change already."

I smelled my own hair. It was grungy but I certainly did not think that I smelled like a dog. Derek just rolled his dark eyes and stood up. He pulled some of the bedspread back for me. "You want to try walking?"

"Is that okay?"

"It'd be good for you to move. You don't have to go far. Just around the cabin."

I blew out a breath. "Why not?"

Carefully, he helped me out of bed. I felt like a monkey falling out of the barrel all the way down the hall and into the cozy kitchen. The entire lodge felt sturdy and warm.

I only made it as far as the counter before Derek opted for carrying me to the table. I sat down with a groan while he zipped to the kitchen. It was decorated with forest green cabinets over cedar countertops, with a few appliances: an old Mr. Coffee that had seen better days, a toaster that looked like it probably burned toast more than it toasted it, and a small blender with the letters worn off its buttons.

Derek walked over to the stained coffeepot. He picked up the empty kettle and groaned. "Dammit, Levi."

Levi was nowhere to be found, but the sound of his name made the hairs on the back of my neck rise. I had no desire to see his mangy wolf ass or his shotgun again.

The coffee maker gurgled to life, giving the kitchen a much-needed human touch that suspended the fantasy for just a moment.

"I went back for your things," Derek called over his shoulder.

I hadn't realized I was wearing my own shirt and soft cotton shorts.

"You dressed me?" My throat went dry at the thought, all the scars and bruises on me screaming to life.

"Believe me when I say that there is nothing about *that*"—he waved a spatula around in a small circle at me—"that interests me. No offense. And your clothes were no good, completely soiled. I couldn't let you lie around in those. How do you like your eggs?"

~~Nate loved them sunny-side up. We always had our eggs~~ sunny-side up.

"Scrambled," I said. "Or in a basket."

"How does in a basket with some bacon on the side sound?"

"Why are you doing all of this?"

"Well." He cracked two eggs into a bowl. "The law says that if you take in a bitten human, you are responsible for that human, so we are responsible for you. That, and, well, I've been around many years and seen my share of humans shift. It would be a shame to let you die. It's not right. I know we don't know each other, but I can't sit back and let someone innocent die."

"Many years?"

"It's rude to ask someone their age, you know," he teased as the smell of coffee wrapped around me, making my mouth water. "Cream or sugar?"

"Both."

Nate always had to have his coffee black. No tenderness, just black.

Derek blurred around the kitchen like he was the Flash before he appeared in front of me with my coffee. I didn't realize I was holding on to my seat for dear life until he set the mug on the table. "Sorry. Vampire speed. I forget."

I stared at him.

"Drink up," he said happily. "If you weren't having a bit of a fit, I would be much more worried."

I picked the mug up by the handle with trembling hands. "I have a lot of questions and I would like the answers . . . please." I needed to get some details worked out. He was right—I had no idea who they were, and while they were playing nice now, that did not mean they would later.

"I was human once, and while it was a long time ago, I still remember the shock. Eat, please, and ask me whatever you want."

"Anything?"

"Nothing is off-limits except for some of the vacation stories." He paused. "Specifically Vegas," he added with a shrug. "My husband would probably not love that. He can be a little stiff at times."

My cheeks reddened. "Where's he?" I asked as I took a sip of coffee and tried to think of anything else besides the elephant with fangs in the middle of the room, but it was all my mind could register.

"He's traveling for work. He's a professor and wildlife researcher. He'll be back in a few weeks," he explained, before returning with a plate in hand. He set it in front of me: perfectly scrambled eggs, cheese sleeping inside a thick piece of toast, with crispy, caramelized bacon accenting the side of the plate. Although bacon in and of itself was never an accent piece.

I started to cut into the meal, the eggs soft like butter. "How did you guys even find me? You said that wolves bit me, but Levi said they were rogue wolves? That it made my odds worse?"

Derek walked back over to the coffeepot. "Right now, we're on pack land. Meaning that there's a wolf pack that owns and guards this land—think of it like its own small town. Anyway, we were alerted by someone on patrol about activity the night you were attacked. Levi found you first—"

"But he pointed me to another campground and left?"

Derek topped up his coffee cup. "I don't know, all I know is when he came back, he was irritated. He wanted to go back and check to see if you were still there. When we got there, well, you know the rest." He took a long sip of coffee, eyeing me curiously. "How, if you don't mind me asking, did you even get out here?"

"I was looking for my friend's cabin. I was going to stay there while—" I paused and looked at my plate. My fingers involuntarily touched my face where my black eye was fading.

"Whoever did that deserves to be put in the ground."

I licked my lips, not daring to meet his gaze. "I am apparently horrible with a map and I took a wrong turn. There was this fork in the road and I, well I . . . I was just so tired," I explained, my voice cracking. My eyes fell as the tears threatened to spill. I hadn't allowed myself to properly cry for days and it was also catching up with me. Taking a deep breath, I looked back at Derek. "I hadn't slept for days, I just drove and drove and drove. I seem to have the best luck."

He gave me a sympathetic smile, not disagreeing, which I found refreshingly disturbing. Even if I did have shit luck, at least they weren't Nate.

He walked back to the table and took a seat by me. "They can't find you out here. This place, the pack land, is protected by magic. They can't hurt you."

That's where he was wrong. Maybe Nate couldn't lay a hand on me, but he could still hurt me.

I didn't answer because I wasn't ready to open that door for a stranger.

"The rogue wolves?"

Derek nodded. "Some wolves get sick. Usually it's when something tragic happens—think of it like someone splitting their soul in two. Their mind goes mad, their body deteriorates along with it. Usually they try to go off and die in peace."

"The ones that attacked me did not seem crazy." If anything, they were calculating. Incredibly coherent.

"I know," he agreed, taking another sip of coffee. I opened my mouth to push, but instead Derek said, "So, your shift."

I dropped the rogue topic but tucked it away for later. "How does it work?"

"On the third full moon from your bite, you will shift. On every full moon between now and then, you will take a step closer, if you will. The moon will draw the beast out, but you have to keep her at bay. You're not ready, and if she comes out too early, it will kill you."

"The moon? Like, the full moon?" I asked.

"Wolves are bound to the moon. We all are."

I shoved more food into my mouth, relishing the buttery taste of the toast combined with the creaminess of the eggs.

"I can make more of that," he said, eyeing me cautiously.

I wanted to say no. I was used to saying no. Nate had only liked my curves up to a certain point.

I wiped my mouth, cheeks flooded with embarrassment. "Uh—I don't want you to—"

"It's no trouble, Charlotte. If you're hungry, then you should eat."

"Okay," I replied reluctantly. "Thank you."

He took another sip of coffee and zipped to the kitchen. I hadn't realized how vintage it was, how everything in this cabin seemed like a piece of history. All the furniture looked handmade, and showed its age from years of wear. On an end table there were a few framed photos of two men that looked like they had been taken in the early 1900s. The stove that Derek was cooking on was old. Gas. Creamy white, like something out of a '50s-inspired movie.

I shook my head. I had dozens of questions, but there was one that was burning in my mind.

"So is it true? Do most humans die?"

"They do," he admitted, more easily than I would've liked him to. "Humans are not made for the shift. It's not easy. A werewolf, well, a born werewolf, has a DNA strand that helps them to be what they are. They are born with a biology able to handle the shift. They may look human from time to time, but their DNA is quite different," he explained as he put a piece of toast in the skillet.

"How does it happen?"

"It's long and painful, I'm afraid. Even for natural-born Weres. When Levi first shifted, I think it took him a little over four hours from start to finish. With the few humans I've seen, I remember it took much longer and it was much more brutal. It's not easy," he added.

"So, the other shifts, then, you shift a little bit?"

"That's right." He nodded and mixed cheese into the glass measuring cup of eggs. "Your body basically takes a step, becomes more Were and less human."

The sounds of Levi's bones cracking during the shift echoed through my mind.

"But you've done this?" I asked.

"Only a few times. Really, I've just watched. Levi did—"

"So, you're saying . . ."

"He is what you will become. He's done this many times with both natural born and humans alike."

"He wants to kill me. He held a shotgun up to me. How can you be so sure he won't?"

He poured the eggs into the middle of the toast. The skillet crackled in delight. "He is arguably mildly homicidal toward everyone, even me. But he won't kill you. Besides, it's the law and he knows it."

"Right. The law. What's that about?"

Derek nodded while he pushed the toast around. "The law states that if you find a human who is bitten, then you're responsible for them," he said, pointing his spatula at me. "But it's up to the human to choose what they want.

"You have two choices: the first is you can die. Listen, there's nothing wrong or dishonorable in that. Plenty of people have chosen that route. We would, besides making it completely painless, take care of any affairs. If you want your family to think a bear ate you, we will make it so."

"And the other option?" I asked. The topic of my own death was not something I wanted to dwell on.

"We help you. If you choose to live, then we will do everything we can to make sure that you have the best chance at surviving."

"And you'll do it? Like, for real? I don't understand why you would do that when you don't know me."

"Levi and I will," he corrected. "Besides the fact that I would rather not see someone innocent die, the law could make a mess of things. If a human dies in your care in our world, or on your land, it could cause a lot of trouble. An investigation from our council, not to mention potentially more humans sniffing around." He shook his head. "It's in the pack's and Levi's interest to keep you alive. It's less of a burden to them."

I sank back into my chair. The only thing Levi would probably help me with was getting up close and personal with a shotgun. I doubted he cared about this damn law anyhow.

"Levi has done this many times," Derek said. "He's going to be your best chance."

I was toast if he was my only hope. "And the pack?"

"They know you're here, but I told them to give you space until you decided what you wanted."

"I don't want more people," I found myself saying. I wanted peace and quiet. I wanted to have a proper breakdown. I didn't want any more questions about my bruises or my scars. I didn't want any more sympathetic gazes or judgmental eyes. I just wanted to breathe again.

"Lucky for you, Levi hates pretty much everyone as well."

"I don't want to be a leech. I don't even know you. I have some money, I could pay you for the trouble?"

"Per the law, you're our responsibility. You owe us nothing," he said with a sigh. "Besides, what kind of people would we be if we made you pay us for something like this?" he asked with a small laugh, although in my mind I could think of plenty who would demand payment. "But winter will be here soon enough. If you make it, then you'll be bunking with us.

"So once your leg is better, we'll need you to pull your own weight. There's a lot to do, and it would be nice to have an extra hand. It will be good for you, help you build your strength."

"I can do that," I said. "How long until this first full moon?"

Derek brought over the new plate and set it in front of me. "A week."

# CHAPTER
# FOUR

My eyes glowed again that night. I found myself staring in
the mirror, watching the blue glow radiate around me. I had
been hot all night. It had woken me up in a hug of sheets
sticking to my dewy skin. A symptom that was "normal,"
according to Derek. Werewolves' body temperatures ran
warmer than humans.

The next morning, the smell of coffee pulled me stumbling into the kitchen. Pancake batter was sitting in a bowl
on the counter and bacon was crackling in a pan, but no one
was tending the kitchen.

A shout caught my ears. I turned my head toward the
front window that the dining table sat in front of.

Derek was outside standing across from Levi, who had his back turned to the house. I stepped closer to the window and peeked around the curtain. Carefully, I unlatched the glass frame and cracked it open enough to listen.

"You cannot just avoid this responsibility!" Derek stated. "You can't lock it away like you did yourself. This affects all of us! Not just you!"

"You don't think I don't know that?!" Levi growled back. "You think I want the council up my ass?"

"It's not just your ass!" another voice snapped. I craned my head to look but only saw Derek, Levi, and the stone column. The same column that matched the others that surrounded the house. "If you don't want to deal with her, turn her over to us," the voice stated.

Levi was looking at the forest, beyond the column. As was Derek. I turned my head more to see who it was but couldn't get a decent angle.

"She doesn't want to. She's not ready," Derek calmly explained. "Look, she was beat up—I think running from someone. It's going to be a lot for her to be around people, and she's already in a delicate state. She needs some time."

"She doesn't have that," Levi snapped. "Why the fuck do you care anyhow?"

Derek hissed. "Because I remember what it's like to have your choice taken away. Because I think that innocents like her deserve a chance. At one point you thought the same. Remember?"

Levi crossed his arms, his back tensing so tightly I thought it would rip his shirt.

"Why do you care?" Derek asked. He cocked his head, body shifting until he'd squared off with Levi. "You could have dragged her off to the pack already."

"Could have."

"You haven't."

"Seems like you would have thrown a fit."

"Like that ever bothered you before." Levi's teeth showed a heinous smile that forced the breath in my throat to catch. He licked his lips while Derek shook his head. "Admit it. You care. I was there with you when we rescued her. You carried her home. You."

Levi looked up at the sky then back at Derek. "She was about to bleed out. I was taking her to the closest place so we could help her." He shook his head, spitting on the ground next to him. "I may be a piece of shit, but I ain't about to let a woman get raped on my land, or leave her to die."

Derek sighed. His eyes were hard, resolve firm.

"Enough," the voice said. "Are you going to bring it up, or am I?" Derek sighed, his gaze slightly softening as he eyed Levi expectantly. "The rogues."

A growl vibrated off Levi that was so cold it felt as if the columns shook. I found myself stepping back, grabbing the ledge of the windowsill as my heart raced.

"They weren't normal," Derek said. "She told me they didn't seem crazy. Levi—"

"We should have kept one alive," Levi said, so calmly that it sent a chill down my spine.

"Are you sure it was rogues?" the voice asked.

"Their eyes," Levi snarled, another growl vibrating off him, causing the limbs around the trees to shake.

"If that's the only symptom how do we know it's not something else?" the voice asked.

"For fuck's sake!" Levi barked. "I know a rogue when I goddamned see one! You would do well to remember that they don't always seem out of it, or have you gotten lazy over these last few years?"

"Don't lecture me!" The voice shot like a bullet right to the gut. "I was there that day. I remember the rogues. You weren't the only one who witnessed it."

"I wasn't, was I?" Levi spat next to him.

"Why are you so against helping her?" Derek sighed tiredly. "What's it going to hurt?"

"There's no use committing to something living in the land of maybes," Levi answered, stepping toward the other side of the lawn.

Derek shook his head. "Levi, you bastard—you're the only one in this pack who has helped a human before."

"She was bit by a rogue," Levi countered. "She can't go with the pack."

"We could contain her?" the voice offered.

Levi looked down at his feet with a bitter laugh. "No, you couldn't." He looked up, silver eyes blazing into the forest. "And we both know you couldn't pull the trigger and put a bullet in her even if she begged you." He paused, nostrils flaring as the wind breezed through the yard. "I may not give a shit about her but I'm not about to let some wild rogue pup loose on my pack," he finished, then turned and stalked across the yard.

"*Your* pack?!" the voice barked.

I cocked my head, holding my breath as Levi stilled. He looked over his shoulder and muttered something that made Derek cringe, as if the thought pained him.

He disappeared into the forest, into darkness, as Derek stayed rooted in his place. I released my breath and tried to quietly step away from the window, but my foot caught on a chair.

It slammed into the table with a groan. My head snapped up to find Derek staring at me through the window.

"Shit," I whispered to myself.

# CHAPTER FIVE

I was frozen in place when Derek walked back inside the house. I wasn't sure if I should try to make a run from him or confront him, but in the midst of trying to decide, I found something in me holding my feet in place. Something telling me to straighten my spine.

Derek held my gaze for a long moment, before that something in me that felt like a tiny fire pushed me to speak. "He lied to me for many years. For a while I lied to myself to make swallowing his lies easier. I think it's time you tell me what's really going on."

Derek looked at his feet with a nod. "Have you eaten?"

"I'm not hungry."

"Let's get a coffee to go. I want to show you something."

He poured two cups into travel mugs then helped me outside. My toes touched the soft grass of the lawn as sunlight grazed my cheeks.

He waved me forward, toward a greenhouse that was off to the side of the house. I took a sip of my coffee and followed with feet that were ready to bolt if I needed to.

"Who were you talking to? Before?"

Derek opened a panel to the greenhouse. "Lander. Levi's younger brother. He's currently in charge of the pack."

I stepped inside to a paradise that felt like it was still in the full swing of summer, not the end of it. Three long columns of lush plants made up this haven. Fresh air rushed in and rustled the dainty wind chimes hanging near a set of navy wingback chairs on an oriental rug, a small bookcase and a record player nearby.

"Is he going to come for me?"

"Is that what you want?"

"Is he going to come for me?"

Derek shook his head. "They could, but considering how injured you are, he agreed it would be best to let you rest here. I figured . . . look, I don't know the whole story, but from what you told me, I figured you'd want some privacy." He paused before studying me carefully. "And if you go rogue when you turn, well, it will be easier to contain you out here. Try to help you."

He eyes were kind, and pleading. I nodded to him. I didn't want a bunch of people asking questions that even I wasn't ready to ask myself.

"What exactly is going to happen to me?"

"Let's start with the basics." Derek stepped forward,

gesturing to the chairs in the back. "Every full moon, you'll take a step toward becoming a wolf. The last moon, you'll shift completely," he explained before stopping in front of the two ornate blue wingback chairs.

I took a seat in one and crossed my legs. Derek sat in its twin, then took a long sip of his coffee. "Each shift, you'll notice physical changes. I can't tell you how much. It varies for everyone. But I can tell you that for humans, it's rare for them to make it to the end. It's very strenuous, and takes a toll on the body that usually kills them."

"How does it start?" I found myself whispering.

He leaned back in his seat. "A fever. It's always a fever. You're going to feel like you're burning up. Usually, for both humans and natural-born wolves, we try to keep ice on them or sit them in an ice bath.

"Bones will break, Charlotte. You're going to have your limbs try to rearrange themselves to that of the wolf that is being born inside of you. I've seen humans die in awful shapes because they did not have either the physical or mental stamina to keep going. You have to more than want it. You have to believe you can do it with every fiber of your being and work with that inner wolf to help yourself make it."

I cocked my head, watching him closely. He was holding back. I could sense it. This longing in him.

"Tell me."

A long breath rolled out of his lips. He wiped a hand over his tired face. "How much did you hear this morning?"

"Enough."

"Lander is concerned because you were bitten by a rogue wolf." My heart sped up as dread seeped into my gut.

"Normally when humans shift, it's because their wolf mate has done it, a friend—one case I saw was a man who turned because he paid another wolf to bite him. That was a long time ago. Never has it been from a rogue wolf. Never."

"Are you saying I'm going to turn into one of them? A rogue wolf?"

Derek shrugged. "Personally, I don't think so. Lander is always more cautious; he thinks there may be a good chance. Levi isn't sure.

"People in our world say that when she created the werewolf, the Moon Goddess stripped a man of half his soul so she could put that of a wolf into his body. The man, of course, was unstable. Losing half of himself made him mad. The Moon Goddess recognized this flaw in her design and gifted the man with a mate. His other half was the complement to his soul, and would prevent the madness and fulfill him every day, just as he would fulfill her.

"The madness, the craze, is what we call 'rogue' in our world. It occurs when a wolf either loses something so essential that it breaks their soul—like a mate, a child, a pack—or if a wolf never finds their mate, their other half. You can't exist with half a soul."

My chest seized. I had just escaped one man with his iron fist around my soul; I was not about to give that up to just anyone.

"I don't—I didn't even want this! I wanted to—fuck! I wanted to start over. I want my life! I wanted away from my husband and now you're saying that I'm going to lose my fucking mind if I don't settle down with some asshole I don't even know?!"

Derek held his hands up. "Not exactly. Listen, normally after you shift, you have a period of growth where you bond with your wolf. Typically, wolves join packs—the pack bonds help the wolf grow and prevent the madness.

"But eventually," he said cautiously, "your wolf will crave its mate, and push you to look for them."

I chugged down some of my coffee as my hands shook. Anger filled me. Why was it that I could never seem to seize the reins of my own life?

"One thing at a time, okay?" he offered. "It doesn't happen like that right away. For Levi, it was a while before his wolf pushed him to find his mate. A really long time, all right?"

I eyed him. "Levi has a mate?"

Derek's eyes widened slightly. He cursed under his breath. "Had." He sipped his coffee. "Don't repeat that. Please?"

I swallowed and nodded. "Shit."

"Because you were bitten by rogue wolves. Normally, we wouldn't have to think about it until much later, but—"

"There's a chance I may go mad when I shift," I said, finishing the sentence for him. I sat my coffee down and stood.

I paced back and forth. This was utter bullshit. Angry tears formed in my eyes.

I paused. "And what do you think?" I asked, hardly daring to look at him.

"I think that nothing is ever set in stone. I think that you're stronger than you look. And I think that if you fight hard enough, you have a bloody good chance."

I wiped the tears away and bit my lip. I could hear my

mother's voice in the back of my head. "Life is what you make it," she used to say.

"And this council?"

"Probably best if they don't know we have a human here who was bitten by a rogue," Derek offered. "We don't need another investigation," he muttered under his breath.

"Another one?"

Derek groaned. "Your hearing must be getting better. Damn wolves. It was a long time ago, and it's Levi's business."

Meaning he would say no more about it. I started to pace again. "And why doesn't he want anything to do with me?"

"Because he's being a pain in the ass," Derek grumbled, taking another sip of coffee. "But he is the only one in this pack who has helped humans shift. I could ask Lander, but Lander has never helped a human before. That, and we agreed that it's safer out here in case, well, you know . . ."

"Levi's an asshole," he offered, scooting forward in his chair. "He's crude. Stubborn. Obstinate. But the man has helped humans. I've talked to him, but I think it would help if you did as well."

"Fuck me," I groaned to myself.

"He's not the boogeyman," Derek offered. "Talk to him."

My feet froze. My heart picked up. Derek stood and stepped toward me. He put a hand on my shoulder. "Do you want to live?"

The words wouldn't come out of my mouth but I managed a shaky nod of my head.

"Then do it."

• • •

That night I was hot again. When I woke, my hair was sticking to my face and my shirt clung to my skin. Vibrations rolled off my heaving chest. They reverberated angrily while this strange noise clawed from my throat. The bed shook under me, like a quiver of fear.

I jolted up with a gasp. I clutched my neck before moving my hand over my mouth. A sickening chill rolled down my back.

Levi was sitting in the corner chair in my room. There was a bottle of Jack Daniel's on the end table next to him and a revolver in his hand. His eyes glowed bright, like two moons staring at me through the darkness.

"What are you doing here?" I demanded.

He didn't say a word. He simply cocked his head as if he was half expecting me to jump out of my bed like a spider monkey.

"Are you going to kill me?"

"Do you want me to?" his gravelly voice replied.

I found myself at a loss of words. I knew he would kill me if I said yes. I knew I should say no, but something made me hesitate.

"No," I answered firmly.

He leaned back in his chair, eyes watching me carefully. "The answer is no."

"I know about the rogues," I found myself saying. He stilled in his seat. "And I know about the law."

His amused laughter cut me off. He took a sip of whiskey. "You think I give a shit about the laws?"

"But Derek—"

"Didn't explain the law properly."

My heart plummeted. He took another sip then wiped his mouth with the back of his hand. "The law says that we are both free agents right now. We are not bound to you until after the first full moon. If a human makes it through their first full, then you're stuck with them. Until then, it goes both ways. You can choose to die or the werewolf party can choose to turn you over to the pack, who will have to handle your ass. And that's your werewolf lesson for the day."

"But your brother agreed that it was best that I stayed out here," I countered.

He cocked his head, his fingers teasing the cylinder of the revolver.

I paused and let out a long breath. "Look, I need you. If Derek is right, you're the only one who can help me."

Levi rolled his eyes. "Why should I? Plenty have worked harder than your melodramatic ass. Moping around here like you're in some movie and feeling bad for yourself. Plenty of people have busted their asses trying and died."

"Well, excuse me if I've been trying—"

"Jesus Christ, girl." He rolled his eyes then took another swig from the bottle. "Life is hard. Get over it. Excuses aren't going to help you now."

"You piece of—"

"Shit?" He nodded with a dark chuckle. "I am a piece of shit, but I'm not wrong."

"I'm not dead yet, and I'm not going to die."

"You sure about that?" he said with a smirk. But it wasn't really a question.

Anger grew deep in my belly. I wanted to scream. Or spit. But I couldn't overreact. It was only painful when I did that.

"I mean"—he half laughed—"do you even want to live?"

"What kind of a question is—"

"An easy one. Answer it."

It was an easy question. It should have been easy to answer, but it wasn't. The words were hung up in my teeth. "Yes." It sounded awkward coming out of my mouth.

"Why?"

"Because . . ." Something bubbled in me. A small fire sparking to life. "Because—it's my life! It's my goddamned life and I want it back! I want it back, and I want to make my own choices again! And you don't get to take that away from me, you fucking asshole!"

He watched me for a moment, then took another drink. I wasn't actually sure if my rant had done anything but humor him for a moment before he would let the revolver end me. All I could do was hold my breath and stare at the gun.

I didn't want to die. I wasn't sure of much anymore, but I was sure of that. I hadn't made it this far to have it end so quickly.

"How about this? You make it through your first full moon, and I'll help your sorry ass."

"You're serious?"

"As a heart attack."

I couldn't let him scare me. It was the only way to save my life, and I wasn't going to let him bully me out of it. "Deal."

"Now," he said. "First order of business, who is going to look for you?"

"No one."

"Bullshit." He let out a long huff then leaned forward in the chair. "Husband isn't going to come after you?"

"He wasn't my husband. He may try," I admitted. "He won't find me. He has no idea."

"No idea?"

I shook my head. "No idea at all. He—he would never picture me as someone who would do this."

"This?"

"Get lost in the wilderness. I think he'll figure I would stay closer to home. But I don't know. He could."

"He has no idea where you were going?"

I shook my head. "No. No idea."

Levi nodded, eyes watching the bottle for a long moment before he said, "We'll play that one by ear. He will probably look for you, but whether he makes it all the way up here . . ." He paused and took another swig. "We'll see. What about family?"

I shook my head. "No." I had an uncle but I hadn't spoken to him in years. He hated Nate. I chose Nate over him. Just like I chose Nate over everything that used to be mine.

"But?"

I leaned against the headboard. "My friend. She's why I'm here. She was our maid. Her brother has a cabin out here that I was trying to find. She gave me the key and told me to run, hide out until I figured everything out."

"People cannot know about us."

"I understand—"

"No." His jaw clenched. "They cannot know. Ever. You call her tomorrow and cover your ass."

I bit my lip and nodded.

"So you've helped humans?"

"Three. To be exact," he answered, eyes watching me carefully.

I nodded and found myself looking at the moon outside. "How did that go? How—did they make it?"

"Plenty of humans have tried, and many don't make it. Usually one of the earlier moon-shifts gets them." Levi took another drink from the bottle. "Of the ones I helped, two did. One didn't. They all had been bitten by their mates."

I turned back and caught his gaze, which seemed to have softened slightly. He sighed and leaned back in his chair. "The first time, I reached out to Derek's sire, the vampire who made him, and asked for help. No packs around here had anything like that happen before. But I had a young wolf who went off to the mainland and met a girl, and well, next thing you know I've got a frantic kid and his mate on my doorstep."

He leaned an elbow on the armrest of the chair. "Derek's sire, Leo, had given me some advice, but it wasn't helpful. There wasn't any magic we could use, no potion, herb, modern medicine, or anything to make the shift bearable."

"What about painkillers?" I asked.

"Well, you would think it would be a good idea, but a few ibuprofen won't do much when your fingers are breaking one by one. Anything heavier makes your mind loopy, and you need your mind to be thinking clearly," he added.

My eyes flickered down to my own fingers. The splotches of fake tanner were almost gone, but they still clung to my hands. I curled them into the sheets while my heart started to flutter in my chest.

Levi took another sip from the bottle then offered it to me. I shook my head. He shrugged and took one more drink then set the bottle on the end table next to the gun.

"The first time—the first time is hell for everyone. Normal wolves, natural-born wolves, are built for this. Our DNA is hardwired for this. It's long and painful, but for the most part as long as you're healthy, you do just fine. I've seen some wolves die from it, but it's pretty rare. Usually they're too weak—sick.

"I never heard screams like that in my life. I won't ever forget them. I ordered the pack to stay away, because I wasn't really sure what was going to happen and, just in case something bad happened, I figured they'd want their privacy.

"And damn, it was such a long night. Normal wolves take between four to six hours on average. This took ten. And I thought she was dead a few times. I was convinced. But she pushed through. We just kept helping her as much as we could. Kept giving her water, icing her down—her mate held her the whole time."

"What happened to her?"

"They stayed here for a while then moved mainland. They both wanted to travel. I haven't heard from them in a while."

"And the other two?"

"Same story as the first. One was from another pack— Talia's. They're south of us, but Talia had no idea what to do, so I went down and left Lander here. This time it was a male. Thought he wouldn't make it, either, but he was a stubborn man. Really stubborn," he said with almost a smile on his lips. "Made it. Took around eight hours. I think part of him was irritated at the thought of missing the football game the next day. I think at one point he said, *Any way we can wrap this up faster?*" Levi added with a breathy laugh.

I wanted to laugh with him, but instead, I held back. He looked back at me as his eyes started to glow a little brighter. "He's moved onto the mainland with his mate too. I can see if we can get in touch."

"And the last one?" I found myself asking.

He let out a long breath. "She was a spitfire. She seemed so strong. I remember telling Lander I thought she'd be okay." He paused and shook his head. "She had handled everything full up until then so well. Like a cakewalk."

He reached for the bottle and took a long sip. "She didn't even make it four hours. She died in a position that rendered her unrecognizable. It came so fast—the wolf did—and she just—I kept telling her to go slow. There wasn't a reason to rush, we had all night. But that wolf came fast and hard and she . . ." He paused again to look at me. "We cremated her and told her family on the mainland she was in a car accident so no one would ask why they were getting ashes back instead of a body."

My throat felt like it was going to collapse. I swallowed back the tears as my fingers gripped the blankets under me. "And her mate?"

"Lost his fucking mind," Levi said quietly. "We tried—" He shook his head and leaned back in his seat, looking at the moon. "Threw himself off a cliff in the middle of the night."

My hand went over my mouth. I blinked back the tears as something boiled in me. I wiped my tears away, unable to look back at him.

"Each moon, you take a step. This beast in you is going to try to come closer. Your body is going to change and stage itself to be ready for the final shift. But like I said, plenty of humans around the world never make it that far. The ones I helped were fucking lucky."

"But if I make it through this first moon, you'll help me?" He cocked a brow with a snort. "That's our deal, right?"

"They all had good reasons to fight. You understand that, right?"

Something felt like it was going to vibrate out of my chest. I felt my own jaw aching to snap at him, the foreign feeling causing the breath in my throat to catch.

Levi tilted his head. I blinked, sighing heavily, before looking back at him. "Their reason was a good reason," I acknowledged. "And no, I don't have a mate—frankly, I don't want another fucking asshole attached to me. I had one of those long enough." I shook my head as anger pulsed through me. "I want my life. My life. Me. Isn't that enough?"

"You tell me," he answered, as he reached for the bottle.

I sat back quietly while he stood up slowly then tucked the revolver into the back of his pants. "Deal's a deal," he answered before walking to the door. "It's not so fun, is it?"

"What?"

"Finding out the monsters in the fairy tales are real," he said, lingering for a moment at the doorframe for my answer.

I closed my mouth. Our monsters were very different. Because for me, the moment he left me back in the darkness, the monster I ran from would be chasing me in my dreams.

# CHAPTER SIX

The morning sunlight picked up the silver in Levi's hair in a way that almost made it look as if it was glowing. I had seen people pay ungodly amounts for that shade of silver, and it was growing in a mess on top of his head. It figured he could've cared less—like Levi himself, even his hair was cool without any effort.

Levi watched me closely while the line on the other end of the phone rang. I wished he would leave me to this humiliation on my own.

I clutched my coffee with one hand and struggled to hold my burner phone with the other as my hands grew balmy. Derek had biscuits in the oven that should have made my mouth water, but my nerves had chased my appetite away. If

Levi hadn't been here, then I would have thrown up.

"Hello?"

My breath caught. "Uh—hey, Yulanda."

"Charlotte?"

"It's—uh—it's me. Sorry it's been a few days. I just—I made it."

Lie number one came out easier than it should have. My stomach churned.

"Oh, sweetheart," she murmured. I could hear kids in the background before a door slammed. Silence replaced the happy laughter of children. "You're okay?"

My heart was pounding. My tongue was starting to feel heavier in my mouth. "I'm okay."

"And you found the cabin? Did you make it to a store to stock up? My brother has a lot of things canned, but you'll need fresh groceries."

"I found it. I was going to go to the store today. I had a lot left over from some things I picked up along the way."

I paused. I could imagine her now. Her eyes softening while her brow furrowed. She always had this look of understanding when she was trying to put the pieces of me that Nate had torn apart back together.

"Charlotte," she said. "Charlotte, please tell me you're not going back."

"I'm not," I replied. And that wasn't a lie. "I'm not going back to him. Ever."

The moment the words left my mouth was the moment I knew I could never take them back.

She released a breath. "Promise me?"

Tears pooled in the corners of my eyes. It wasn't anyone's

fault but mine. I should have left a long time ago. "I promise," I choked out. "I'm sorry. I put you through—"

"Never mind that. You never apologize. Never. Do you understand me? This is not your fault." She paused. "Do I wish you would have left earlier? Yes. Do I wish I would have said something earlier? Yes. Do I wish I could go back in time and drag you out of that house? Absolutely.

"But that's the past. Past is the past. You need to let go of it and look to your future. You have so much time ahead of you. Don't let him have any more years of your life."

I blinked hard as the first tear fell. A bottle of emotions had been capped for too long. Anger, bitterness, self-loathing, and even rage bubbled inside me. "I don't know why I couldn't just leave," I found myself saying, my own voice breaking. "I can't get him out of my head. Why is this so hard?"

*Why is this so fucking hard for me?*

"Because you loved him, baby girl. There's no shame in love. The shame is on him for abusing you and your feelings."

"But you're right," I admitted. "I should have left sooner. I was so stupid."

"Enough of that," she stated. "Enough. You only need to worry about yourself."

I nodded. "Has he tried to look for me?"

She sighed. "He won't find you. He has no idea about my brother."

"Please tell me you don't work for him anymore."

"Like you, I wish I would have left a long time ago. But I couldn't have left you alone with him."

I sucked in a painful breath and wiped my eyes. "I'm sorry, Yulanda."

"Stop with that. Just worry about yourself."

"If he comes looking?"

"If he does, he's going to snoop around us first. I can let you know if I hear of anything."

"Please do," I replied with a sniffle.

"I'll do what I can to throw him off. Promise me you will call if you need anything? I mean it, Charlotte."

"I promise. Thank you." Tears rolled down my cheeks. "Thank you so much, Yulanda."

"Be safe, Charlotte," she told me.

"You too," I answered, before hanging up.

My body shook as ugly sobs came out of my mouth.

"Charlotte?" Derek asked, lingering at the door while my body slowly began to break all over again. Eventually, I found myself clinging to him while I cried in the ugliest way. I could very well be dead soon. The thought of Nate coming after me seemed so tiny in comparison to this ugly truth.

"It's all right," Derek said. He was petting my hair almost like my mother used to. It always calmed me down when I was little and the storms outside were the monsters I couldn't hide under the covers from. But now, it did anything but that. Because when I opened my eyes, I saw silver ones staring back at me. Fear hummed through me but there was something else starting to break through the fog. Something else smoldering like the embers of a fire. I wasn't sure what it was, but ever since I was bitten, it was making itself more and more known.

Levi held my gaze for a moment, something flickering in his silver eyes, but I couldn't place it, because it was gone as soon as it came. He didn't ignore me after that, but he wasn't exactly trying to make friendship bracelets with me either. Rather, it felt like he was stalking me the way a vulture stalks a dying animal. Just close enough to smell death.

I knew my days were numbered—I had three left, to be exact.

Within those three, my body seemed mostly healed from that night the rogues attacked me. The fake tan still held on to the corners of my body, but every shower I took washed more of it down the drain. The only thing I couldn't run from was my scars. The jagged pink lines would always be a reminder.

I also had started to put on weight, and I wasn't sure how I felt about it. Derek claimed that I needed the meat on my bones, but I just felt like a calf being fattened for slaughter. In the back of my mind, I could hear Nate commenting on how chubby I was letting myself get.

I just wanted him out of my head, but the closer I got to the full moon, the more vicious he became in my dreams. His hands would turn to claws and his mouth into a muzzle that I could hear growling at me until I realized that it was my chest vibrating when I eventually did wake up.

The day of the full moon Derek tried hard to keep my mind off things, but I still felt like a soda being slowly shaken up. Anxiety ate away at me, while the lunch I ate eventually ended up in the toilet.

"So, when does this thing start?" I asked as I put a fork down on the table. I had tried to push the inevitable out of my brain, but now I was looking straight down the barrel at my fate. There was no more putting it off.

Derek had made a giant dinner of cheesy lasagna for me, although my churning stomach wasn't thrilled at the sight. I still ate some to be polite. It would be a shame to let all that cheese go to waste.

"Go on, Levi, tell her."

The hair on the back of my neck rose. Levi was pouring himself a glass of wine, bright-silver eyes looking right at me. "Once the moon is out, it can start anytime. Sometimes right after for some, and sometimes much later into the night. It's different for everyone."

"How long does this first time take?"

"Depends," he answered. "The other humans it was on and off all night. Some ended early in the morning, before the sun came up, and some it wasn't until daybreak that it ended."

I licked my lips and looked at my fingers. The thought of each of them breaking one by one made all the food in my stomach feel like bricks.

"So, the beast comes closer this time?"

Levi nodded. "You're going to feel like she's trying to rip out of your skin. Some things may break, some may not."

He pushed the cork back into the bottle.

"And?" I asked.

His broad shoulders shrugged. "Probably best if you don't let her rip out of your skin."

He walked outside with his glass, the door slamming and springing Derek to life. He zipped around in the kitchen then over to me, stopping right as he uncorked a bottle with fancy cream tissue paper wrapped around it.

"We don't tell Levi when we unwrap bottles. Got it?"

"Why are you doing this?"

"You keep thinking that way, then he's right—she's going

to rip you apart. But I don't think that's really what you want, is it?" It wasn't. I nodded, even if the words wouldn't come out of my mouth, because I had no desire for that kind of death. "If you can't fight for what you want, then why would anyone else help you?"

He left me with a glass of wine and my meal, which I ended up inhaling. If there was one redeeming thing, it was that this had to be one of the best meals I'd ever had. Even with all the fancy five-star restaurants Nate always wanted to try, nothing beat a home-cooked meal from someone who actually gave a shit.

After dinner I cleaned up the kitchen while Derek ventured outside. When he returned, he had a dead snow-white rabbit in hand. He set it on a stump outside used as an end table, next to a rocking chair. His eyes glistened in the dusk as they caught mine. "Come out here!" he called through the screen door.

It was a soft dusk out, the kind that held the magic of night and promise of day all in the same breath. Silence crept over the yard. The breeze through the trees was quiet—almost as if it was being careful to not disturb something.

I licked my lips as my nerves sizzled to life. Nothing crazy had happened yet. I wondered if the two of them had been blowing smoke up my ass. But I knew better. The minute I looked at the moon, I knew there was something about it. Goose bumps broke out over my arms at the sight of it—a sight that drew me in like a siren.

"I need some blood." His voice broke me out of my trance. I blinked and looked over at him. He had a pocketknife out and a bowl next to the rabbit. "Small cut should do it," he said, pointing to my hand.

"Uh—why?"

"Tradition for wolves in their shifting phase. You make a sacrifice to the moon so she will show you favor. You give her the blood of something pure, along with a sacrifice of your own."

I returned my gaze to her in the sky. It felt too quiet now, like the forest was holding its breath. Ripping my gaze away, I nodded at Derek. I would take whatever help I could get at this point.

He made a small cut in the center of my hand, drawing a hiss from my lips, and quickly moved the bowl under my palm. "Sorry, I don't need much," he said, letting blood pool in the bottom. "That should be good. Better go wrap that up."

"Is there anything else?"

"A few more things," he replied, slicing the rabbit's neck over the bowl, where its crimson blood swirled with my own.

My stomach churned at the sight. I walked back into the kitchen as my heart started to flutter in anticipation. Mechanically, my hands reached for the sink and rinsed the blood off. It swirled down the drain, dark stains on shiny silver; the next thing I knew, I was puking into the sink.

"Fuck me," I groaned, wiping my mouth off.

I reached for a glass and washed my mouth out, then spit into the sink. I had to get a grip. But all I could do was wait. I hated the wait.

I found myself sitting on the porch and watching Derek. He picked some moonflowers that grew in large pots and dipped them into the blood mixture. He had me hang them in the windows of my room, giving me something to distract myself, but I could feel my stomach eager to churn again.

I paused and wiped some sweat off my forehead after I hung up the last flower. I was hot. I wiped my forehead again and stared at the sweat on my fingers, my heart picking up in my chest as realization came to me.

I thought I had just been working up a sweat, but I was close to panting. I shouldn't be like this from this amount of work. This felt like I had been sprinting around the house with a thick coat on.

"Shit," I murmured, my eyes still stuck on the glistening beads of sweat on my fingers. I could feel another one slowly rolling down my cheek as I tugged at the collar of my shirt.

Something cut through the air, making a light whistling sound. "You're going to want to strip down."

I froze. My eyes snapped up to meet Derek's. "What?"

"You're getting hot but you're going to get warmer. You won't be comfortable. I promise, you'll thank me."

"I don't—" I wasn't about to let two strangers see me half naked. I was more self-conscious even than being around Nate, and he had seen every ugly inch of me.

"Something loose then? Shorts? Big shirt? I can bring one of mine?"

"Okay." I gulped with a nod. Sweat rolled down my back between my shoulder blades.

He zipped out of the room while I took my shoes off. I had barely pulled my socks off when he set a gray shirt and some shorts on the bed next to me. "You're going to be fine," he told me.

He stepped out and let me change into the things he'd brought me. But even in his clothing that hung loosely on me, I was burning up. It still felt like the material was hugging me in the wrong places, sticking to and grasping areas that I didn't even know could feel this swampy.

"Can I?"

"Yeah!"

Derek stepped back into the room and went straight to the windows, opening all the blinds.

"What are you doing?"

"So her eye is on you. Hiding from her now would be bad luck."

I tugged at the collar of the shirt again. "Right." I wiped some sweat off my brow then sat back down on the bed.

Derek whizzed out of the room only to return with the bowl, and motioned for me to tie my hair up. "Hold still." He dipped his finger into the blood then traced a line on the outside of half my face—from the edge of my brow all the way to the tip of my chin.

"What's that for?"

"Moon's favor," he said. "I'll get you some water."

"What now?"

"Wait," he said, forcing a bleak smile. "I'll be back."

I found myself leaning against the windowsill. I could feel the blood on my face running with the drops of perspiration. I pressed my cheek to the cold glass, but it didn't help. Everything felt too tight. Too hot. Steam was literally rising off my body.

I kept moving my cheek to try to find a cool spot on the window. My fingers rose to the glass while I blew out a long breath. I felt like I couldn't get any fresh air—I wanted to get out of this hot skin that felt like a permanent sweat suit.

Derek tried putting baggies of ice on me, but those melted quicker than he could refill them. The cold wash-cloths were no better. They ended up clinging to me like my clothes.

"How much longer?" I gurgled through the water I was chugging. It felt like I had crawled through the desert. My mouth was like sandpaper, and no amount of water was sating me.

Derek reached next to him where he had coolers lined up with ice, water, and towels. He grabbed another water from the bottom, quickly uncapped it, and lifted it to my lips. "She's getting closer—"

A whimper of relief came from my lips. I tilted my heavy head to meet the bottle. Water spilled into my mouth and all over my front as I chugged it down in messy desperation.

I pulled away with a cough. "She?" I croaked.

"The moon," Derek answered, his eyes looking to the sky through my window. "I'll be back. I need to get the extra bag of ice in the kitchen."

I closed my eyes. My body felt so heavy—every heart-beat felt like a kick drum inside me, the beats demanding that I listen to it, and only it, while also shaking me down to the core.

The sound of footsteps nearing the room tempered my racing heart. "Did you get more ice?" I asked.

"You've made it this long. I'm surprised. Fever usually kills humans off."

My eyes shot open. I stopped listening to the drum inside

me. Something about his presence in the room yanked my attention to him.

Levi pulled a chair up next to my bed and took a seat, watching me with amusement before he looked outside. He closed his eyes, as if taking a deep breath, then opened them to reveal glowing silver eyes. His pupils pulsed to life like there was something else watching me behind him. "Like Derek said, we can't escape her."

My head rolled to the window. She was high and heavy in the sky, light reaching into the night like hands extended to combat the darkness. I found myself moving closer, the glow from her rays so calming—I wanted to go outside and let them comb over me. Hug me. It felt like they were the only thing that would keep me safe. But then her light pulsed, and when it did, something inside me ignited.

A sharp cry tore out of my mouth. It felt like that rogue wolf was biting my leg again. The scar felt like someone had poured gas on it and lit it on fire. The pain rushed up the veins in my legs in a rampage, coming through the rest of me with hot malice that rendered a silent scream from me.

It moved all the way down to my calves while also pummeling right through my stomach. I felt my back arch unceremoniously. My fingers clawed at the bed while my mind spun in circles. I tried to listen to the beat of my heart again, but as the pain moved to a new part of me, I was forced to listen to it and only it. I tried to take tiny breaths, breathe through it, but it was angry, lashing out at me as if it was screaming at me to pay attention.

"Charlotte!"

I knew it was Derek shaking me, but his face looked

like a blur through the tears and black spots taking over my vision. The cold water he gave me a sip of brought me closer to reality, but the heat of my body only made focusing on the present a losing battle.

"It's early, Levi," Derek said, his voice sounding slower than I remembered it.

"The moon wants what she wants. We can't stop her," Levi replied, his voice cutting through the heat wave around me and coming in almost too clear for comfort. "Go, Derek," he ordered, as another wave of pain rolled up my leg and right to my stomach.

"Levi—"

"There's nothing you can do now." The pain was picking at my gums. My canines were almost itching before a stabbing feeling took over. "She has to do it on her own." He paused for a moment, his eyes softening as he looked at Derek. "You won't want to see it."

Derek stepped back, looking down at the ground. Conflicted, he looked up me with a sad smile. "I'll see you at breakfast," he told me before he stepped out of the room.

*He doesn't want to say good-bye*, I thought.

My back was arching away from the needles crawling up my spine as something scratched at my brain. My head rolled toward the window. The feeling was too great for me to fight. I opened my eyes to look at the moon and immediately regretted it, because the minute I saw her full figure glowing in the night sky was the minute I felt something roar to life in my mind. I sucked in a breath, the presence so loud and so clearly *there*. I looked back at the moon and felt this thing move in me. My eyes trailed down to my legs where ripples curled over my skin as something pushed closer to the surface.

"What the fuck?!"

Levi's eyes were glowing brighter in the dim light of the room. He snapped his gaze over to mine. "Do not let her out."

"Her?" I groaned as the scratching started. It felt like it was scratching at my skin from the inside, trying to get out. I cried out as needlelike claws felt like they were raking against the inside skin of my arm; I looked over to see actual claw marks start to appear.

Levi grabbed a cold towel and wiped the blood off. "She. Your wolf. She's here now. She wants out—you're not ready. You let her out and that's it. Both of you die."

Another moan rolled out of my mouth as a wave of heat and pain tided over me. "How?" I begged. "She's not even real. How?"

Levi chuckled darkly. "Oh, she's real all right. She's as real as it fucking gets right now. If you can feel her, then you can grab her—then you can stop her. And by the looks of it, it seems like you can feel her."

I bit my lip so hard that blood pooled in my mouth. I wanted so badly to look at the moon but knew better. I was terrified of what would happen if I did. I was terrified I wasn't strong enough to stop her if I did.

Closing my eyes, I tried to "find" her. Tried to "feel" her. And he wasn't wrong. It was like I could feel her pacing back and forth in my mind. She was anxious, angry, and absolutely over being held back. She wanted out, wanted to run free.

With my mind, I reached out to her. Carefully, I approached until I could gently nudge her with my brain. I felt her pause her pacing as curiosity surrounded her. I held my breath, hoping she would calm down, but that was a wasted hope.

Another wave rolled over my legs. My scar started to rip open, blood rolling over the new skin. She charged forward, ready to run right out.

But I was done being a fucking doormat that people could bulldoze over. I grabbed whatever it was and yanked it back. Another cry came out of my mouth as the knifelike claws raked along my ribs.

"Bitch," I hissed. I could feel her snapping out of my mind. She slammed her jaw shut, the sound of her teeth sending chills over my skin.

"She wants to come out," Levi said before he leaned forward. "You either are going to let her win or keep her where she belongs."

"How?" I squealed. Needles felt like they were trying to pierce my gums. She was so angry—an anger I wasn't sure I could beat.

"That's up to you," he replied. A challenge.

Another wave of pain pulsed through me. In the back of my mind, I could hear Nate laughing at me, shaking his head at my insolence before his eyes turned angry. A familiar fear flared in me.

She paused her raking claws at my skin to pay attention to the memory. It was then that I felt the shift of her anger away from me toward him. She wanted to rip his throat out. She wanted to jump out of my skin so she could claw his eyes out. I paused as the memories of Nate kept playing. It was as if I could feel her paw at them for more—like I could feel her hunger to *know me*.

I held my breath as an idea flared. What did I have to lose at this point? I closed my eyes and let the memories flow—all of them. I let her see the things I never wanted anyone to see—let her know about the true monster that had been chasing me. If she, this beast in me, was going to be part of me, then she deserved to know about the demons we had to dance with.

But the memories only enraged her. She wanted to jump out of my skin, but this time it felt like she was hungering for Nate's blood and not mine.

I yanked her back again, already growing tired of this deadly game of tug-of-war.

I rolled my head to see Levi looking straight at me. My nail beds felt like they were being stabbed with steak knives, but somehow, I held on. I hadn't made it this far so this thing could kill me, and I would be damned if I was going to let someone like Levi see my last breath.

I could feel another pulse of pain coming for me, and in that moment, it felt like I was slipping. In that moment, I was in my old backyard picking flowers with my mother while she drew in her favorite sketchbook. Wind was blowing through my hair. It smelled like fresh detergent and wildflowers. My mom had all the sheets drying on a line outside.

I could hear a whining behind me but I didn't turn around because I could see my mother. She looked around from one of the sheets, her mouth frowning at the sight of me. "What are you doing here, Charlotte?"

My eyes found Levi's. Besides the light from the moon, his eyes were like the light of a lighthouse pulling me through the fog.

A stabbing feeling twisted in my leg while tendrils of torment tried to rip at my skin, like Nate had ripped at my clothes my last night at home. I had told him to stop, begged him to wait until the morning when he wasn't drunk, but he hadn't cared. He hadn't been able to find the clasp to my bra that night—I still had the red marks all over my back from his drunken confusion.

She was clawing at that memory. I hadn't wanted him that night, but at the time it was hard to think that I deserved better.

A sharp pain in my fingers snapped me back to reality. I could hear myself crying out for my mother while the coppery taste of blood filled my mouth. It felt like either Nate was going to rip me apart in my memories or this thing in me was going to rip through my skin so she could sink her teeth into him. But she, this beast in me, paused for a moment before I felt her yanking at me, like she wanted me to join her in the fight.

Swirls of silver looked at me. My hand reached for them because they felt like hope, but something hit me then, like his fist had. It took all the air from me until there was nothing but the ringing in my ears while my lungs burned for oxygen.

There was a blackness calling to me. This time, I didn't want to follow it. There was nothing peaceful about it this time. I wanted to scream for help but I couldn't hear a sound come out of my mouth.

Levi opened his mouth, but a wave of pain hit me again. His silver eyes were looking at me and his mouth was moving, but the blackness was clawing me down. I wanted to hold on. I had to hold on. This time, I couldn't give in.

"I don't—I want to—" My voice sounded nothing like me. "How much—longer?"

"Until she's gone." His eyes looked like the moon. Glowed like it. In that moment I half wondered if they were truly that silver or if I was delusional.

"I hate her," I gasped.

In that moment I did. In that moment I hated whoever could condemn anyone to this much pain. This hell was worse than whatever Satan's worst sinners must be suffering deep in the circles of damnation.

Levi nodded then leaned his head on his hands, which were folded together as if in prayer. "I do too."

# CHAPTER SEVEN

The two bullets on my nightstand had a strange mosquito-like hum coming from them. I slowly reached for them, and the bullets singed my finger even though I barely grazed them.

A small growl vibrated through me. I stuck my finger in my mouth then pulled it out to look at the burnt skin on the tip.

*What the hell was that?*

I blinked and felt something move, like another presence in my mind. It was faint, almost like a ghost hovering on the edges of what felt like my sanity.

I froze and focused inward, but every time I got closer it darted away, as if we were playing a game of keep-away. I looked around the bedroom, emptiness around me until I felt a tingle in my mind.

"Charlotte?" There was a light knocking on the other side of the door. Derek cracked it open enough for me to see relief flood his face.

I looked at my hands then back around the room. Everything looked the same but nothing felt the same. Because I felt different. I couldn't put a name to why; I only had the feeling that felt like trying to hold on to a dream after you've awakened.

The feeling of Derek carefully hugging me felt too good to be the former. "I'm so glad you're okay."

"Why did you leave?"

"Levi was right, you needed to do it on your own," he replied with a sleepy smile.

I sat up a little more in bed, wincing from the ache that was making itself known. It felt like I had been chewed up then taken through a meat grinder. "I passed out. I thought . . ."

He shook his head. A warm smile tugged on his lips. "You were in and out of it most of the night. Levi said he thought you weren't going to make it a few times, but it looks like you did."

"Levi—"

"He sat with you. He said he had to see it for himself or he wouldn't believe it."

"Right." My mouth was so dry that I almost choked on my own spit. I looked around again to double-check that I wasn't in fact dead.

"The bullets, they burn?"

He nodded. "Silver. It can kill a werewolf, vampire too. Some legends are, in fact, true."

"Fantastic." I guess I was going to have to pawn my jewelry after all.

Derek laughed and stood. He held a hand out for me. "Come on. I made a killer breakfast, per usual."

Dazed, I nodded. "Sounds good."

I tried to get out of bed on my own but almost ate the side of the end table. My whole body felt like Jell-O that someone had taken Thor's hammer to. Derek caught me then proceeded to help me walk into the kitchen, where the smell of cinnamon and coffee became lures for my legs to move.

"I made cinnamon rolls," he told me with a proud smile. He paused so I could grab the side of the kitchen counter, then zipped over to the oven.

I found myself smiling at the sheer miracle of the situation until I saw Levi sitting at the kitchen table. He was reading a worn hardback copy of *The Count of Monte Cristo* and drinking a cup of coffee, like it was Sunday morning. Was it Sunday?

Somehow, my feet carried me over to the table to sit across from him, my mouth trying to hide the groan from the pain in my legs as I sank into the seat. Levi glanced at me over the top of his book. "I see you didn't die."

"You would know, wouldn't you?" I said. Derek coughed to cover a laugh. He zipped to me with a cup of coffee. "Thank you."

He winked while Levi rolled his eyes. I took a long sip of coffee and leaned back in my seat. My mind was still trying to comprehend everything that had just happened, that would eventually happen.

"You should have some orange juice. It's good for you."

"*The Count of Monte Cristo.*"

"It's a classic," he answered simply.

I leaned forward and found myself reaching for the pitcher of orange juice. "So, I take it you're going to help me now?"

"A deal is a deal, Charlie girl."

I opened my mouth to respond when Derek set a plate down in front of me. Three giant gooey cinnamon rolls, scrambled eggs, and three hearty slices of bacon. "Oh my god." Derek laughed his way into the kitchen while I snatched up my fork.

"Eat up. We have a lot to do today," Levi said.

"We?"

"You want my help or not?"

I said nothing, just nodded. He put his book down and took a long sip of coffee. "You will do as I tell you, understand?"

"Yes," I replied, with a firm nod, this thing in me creeping forward to investigate him further.

"You feel her, don't you?" he asked, and the thing inside me shifted at his words, like she was trying to prove to me as well that she was truly there.

My words caught in the back of my throat. "Her," I said more to myself, as realization fully set in that she was in fact real. In that moment, I felt the ghost sizzle to life in my mind.

*She* was there. So present and so alive. A moment both exhilarating and utterly terrifying. A moment that escaped as quickly as it had come, then *she* faded away like fairy dust on the wind.

Levi leaned back in his seat, holding my gaze as if the confirmation of his belief had spit right in his coffee. He got up, hissing a string of curses under his breath, and walked over to the coffeepot to pour another cup.

I took a long sip of coffee while my fingers massaged my temples.

"Let's talk."

My eyes snapped up at him as he walked back to the table. "Okay?"

He took a seat across from me and leaned back in his chair and crossed his arms over his chest. "To survive, you need two things: a strong mind and a strong body. Obviously, you're short on both of those."

"Thanks a lot," I grumbled.

He shrugged. "Is what it is, but we're going to have to build up your strength and get some meat on your bones. We'll start easy then work you up until your body at least has a fighting chance."

"And my mind?"

He smirked. "Start easy and work your way up. It's not just about wanting to live. And it's not just about believing that you can."

"Then what's it about?" I huffed.

Levi took another sip of coffee. "Accepting that you can die."

My breath caught in my throat. Levi took one last sip of coffee then stood up from the table. "Come outside when you're finished," is all he said before he left.

After breakfast, I dressed in some yoga pants, old sneakers, and a worn gray sweatshirt from college that I refused to give up. If it was cooler outside, I couldn't tell. My skin still felt feverish, but Derek told me it was normal. Apparently, my body was still adjusting. My temperature would start to run about the same temperature as a werewolf's did, which was higher than a human's.

When I made it outside, Levi was out there already, smoking a cigarette by the pile of logs stacked off to the side of the house that he seemed to have some kind of distain for. He looked at it with a sour expression, as if the whole thing was completely rotten. I looked at him then back to the woodpile, mostly to see if I could figure out why it was so displeasing to him, but I found myself at a loss.

"So this is . . . ?"

"What you'll be doing today," he replied. He walked over to a green plastic chair that faced an old stump with a worn axe leaning against it and sat down. Slowly, he propped one foot up on the small red cooler in front of the chair.

"Which is?" I asked as I looked around.

"Chopping wood." He took a drag of his cigarette and flicked some ash off to the side. "What does it look like?"

There was a pile of split logs lining the house that reached almost to the roof, and an equally as intimidating pile of wood that had not been chopped opposite it. I felt unease run through me as I shifted on my feet. "I—I've never done this before. I don't even know how."

"Fair enough," he answered, almost too calmly for comfort.

He casually stood up and strode over to the pile of

unchopped logs. Picking up a round piece, he walked back to the stump and placed it end up. "You set it like this on the stump. You want a piece that's about this size. Anything smaller you can stack in the chopped pile, anything bigger you double-cut, got it?"

I nodded again. I didn't see how the hell this was supposed to help me, but I didn't want to fall from his good graces, so I kept my mouth shut.

He looked back at the stump and picked up the axe next to it, then swung it around and sliced the log like it was butter.

It didn't look so bad.

"Aim for the middle, and it will split." He laid the axe against the stump then settled back into his chair.

"So that's it? I'm splitting logs all day?"

"Exactly."

"Really?"

"Really."

"And this is going to help, how?"

"Remember that part where you agreed to do what I told you?"

"Remember that part where you also said you would explain what's happening to me?"

Levi arched a brow before leaning back in his seat. "We have to start you off easy."

"This is easy?"

"Yeah." He laughed. "This is easy."

"Easy." I snorted.

"You've got thirty days," he said. "Thirty days until the next full moon. You think last night was bad? You better think again. You will need any strength we can build to help your ass."

"And what if I do go rogue? What if I go nuts?"

He looked at his cigarette then sighed, looking back at me with a firm gaze. "My brother likes to worry his damn ass off. Useless worrying about something that's so uncertain."

"But it could happen?"

He shrugged. "It could. You dying next month could happen too." I bit my tongue and looked at the ground. "Today, you worry about chopping those damn logs. You take each day on its own and worry about what's in your control. You'll drive yourself nuts asking about what-ifs."

"What will happen to me if I go crazy?"

"That scenario is only possible if you make it to the last moon, and you've got to make it through this next one first. Focus on that—now stop wasting time. Get chopping."

I bit my tongue and reluctantly strode over to the pile and looked for a log that seemed doable, although the piece I chose was heavier than it looked.

As instructed, I set it end up, then reached for the axe, stumbling because I underestimated how heavy it was. Levi was watching me with a cocked brow. I tried to ignore him and focus on the log in front of me.

Gripping the axe in my hands, I tried to model exactly what he had done. I tried to aim right for the middle, but when I swung the axe over my head, it was too heavy and I was too clumsy. I didn't even dent the log. I knocked it down.

Levi almost fell out of his chair laughing. I looked over at him, seething from the embarrassment running through me. He stood and picked the red cooler up by the handle. "You keep at that. I'll be back." He walked around to the front of the cabin.

I rolled my eyes and put the log back on top of the stump. I gripped the axe hard and tried to center myself. Because you were always supposed to center yourself. Right? But after another swing, it didn't matter if I had centered myself or not. The axe barely sank two inches into the log.

This went on for what felt like an hour. Me trying. The log getting knocked over. My arms burning with the effort. I watched log after log roll off the main stump with barely any scratches made on them. Each time I would turn around to ensure that Levi had not witnessed my failure; each time I would look at an empty forest and wonder if the trees were secretly laughing at me.

I went back to my log, determined to make something happen. But when I swung the heavy axe, all that happened was another failed attempt.

"I see you haven't made much progress," Levi said as he walked back to his chair. He set the cooler down next to him, watching me with devious delight.

I shot him a scowl but held my tongue. Again, I put the stump on the log, and readied myself to swing the axe. I swung the axe once more, but all I got was a whole log looking back at me.

"You afraid of that log, girl?" he asked as he dug around in the cooler and pulled out a can of beer.

"No," I growled. "It's just a log," I added as he popped the can open. It wasn't even ten in the morning and he was already gulping down beer like it was ten minutes until happy hour was over.

"You sure about that, Charlie girl?" he asked as he wiped beads of beer from the corner of his mouth.

He took another long drink then chucked the can away and dug out another. I bit my lip and looked back at my penance.

"It's just a stupid log," I grumbled to myself as I placed it back on the stump. Again, I swung the axe. At first, I thought I'd split the log, because the axe vibrated so hard it felt like my wrists were going to snap from the reverberations. But when I opened my eyes, I saw that the log was still standing upright, with my axe halfway through it.

"What the hell?"

"Just a log. Ain't nothing to it."

I ignored him. It was probably best not to let him get under my skin. My emotions always backfired on me, which was the last thing I needed right now. Instead, I took a deep breath and tried to visualize the shot. I always heard Nate bragging to his golfing buddies that visualizing things turned his game around. He always swore by it.

Something scratched at the back of my mind, slowly opening the heavy door that I had locked. The low chuckling in the background cracked the door open. I bit my lip and swung the axe again, only to completely miss the log.

Something kicked the door open a little more. My pulse picked up while my skin prickled.

"This is better than a damn movie." Levi snickered, only stoking the fire that was growing in me.

This thing in me was scratching at the door now. It was

almost open enough for *her* to escape. I knew I should hold *her* back. I knew I should try to hold back.

He leaned forward on his knees. "Go get another. Start again."

I marched back to the pile and found another log the right size and set it back on the stump. Levi took another long sip of beer while I gripped the axe in my hands, which were already starting to blister.

"All right, let's see if you can make more than a dent. Although I won't complain if you don't. This is by far the most entertaining thing I've seen in a while."

I felt a growl rumble out of my chest. A low growl that drew a gasp out of me at the same time.

Levi's brows raised. "You angry about something, Charlie girl?"

"Is that normal?"

Levi chuckled. "Nothing about you is normal."

"Excuse me?" I was trying to focus. I needed to shut him out so I could focus.

"You heard me." He laughed.

"What—" I paused and leaned back to look at him. "What the hell are you even talking about?"

"Getting a little pissed off isn't rocket science. You did it last night, now do it again."

"Pissed off?" The moment I said the words was the moment I felt the beast in me take a step out of the door, as if the words in and of themselves were an invitation.

"Mmm," he hummed into his can of beer.

"Who says I'm not pissed off?"

He almost choked on his drink from laughing. Levi

wiped his mouth off, while this thing in me stepped closer. It was like she was licking her lips, laughing in her own twisted madness. "Your man beat you black-and-blue, and you're not even the slightest big angry? I mean, hell, do you even know what it feels like anymore?"

"Of course, I—"

"Bullshit!" He laughed again before he took a long drink. His words echoed through my mind, striking down the lies that were marching forward to take their normal stance on the front lines of my fucked-up mind. Lies I let Nate lay while I cemented them down, because apparently it was all my fault too. "Stop avoiding it and just let it out," Levi said simply.

He dug a cigarette pack out of his back pocket and watched me like he already knew what was coming. I resisted the need to chuck the old beer can at him because I could feel it coming too. I could feel this thing starting to tear down the lies and open the door for truth to flood in.

Nate wasn't here. I didn't need to calm down anymore. I needed to let myself feel again. There wasn't a need to walk on eggshells. I could get angry as hell and there was not a damn thing Nate could do about it.

My hands moved on their own. I felt the axe swing fluidly around me with a fury that I instantly needed more of. I needed to prove to myself that it was real. The pent-up emotions poured out of me while I poured myself into my swing.

There was a loud *thud* with two more smaller *thuds* following it.

The log split.

That fucking thing actually split.

I stood there shocked for a second, and stared at the two pieces that had previously been one, lying on either side of the stump.

"Go on, get a little pissed off, Charlie girl. I think this is gonna be real good for you."

I wasn't sure if Levi was absolutely off his rocker or a complete genius. But all I knew was that I wasn't ready to let go of whatever this feeling was.

I chopped out of anger, out of frustration, out of this new drive from the beast in me. My mind wandered far from here while I fell into a hypnotic daze where the dreams I once had of Nate and I being married and raising a family were gone—shredded. Everything was fucking shredded. The aspirations I had that he would be the man I fell in love with, along with every "I love you," were torn into pieces. Pieces I chopped away at in my mad craze.

Each piece of wood was like a memory I was killing— each piece reminding me that I was just as guilty because I stayed. I should have left when I caught him with her. I should have left the first time he got too physical with me. I should have stopped telling myself that his last name behind my first name would have made things better.

The guilt was just as powerful as the anger. It wrecked me. It washed over me and had me hacking and hacking until I was just hacking at the stump in a whirlwind of tears.

Someone yanked me away then yanked the axe out of my hand. Levi was gone but Derek was holding me while I cried angry tears against his chest. My hands were shaking, itching to chop again, but I had chopped almost the whole pile. If I kept on going there would be nothing left before the sun even began to set. I guess it didn't matter. It already felt like there was nothing left for me to tear apart anyway.

# CHAPTER EIGHT

Through the kitchen window, I could see Levi outside. He was standing near one of the strange rock columns that lined the perimeter of the house, pacing back and forth like he was walking on some arbitrary line. He had been at this for about fifteen minutes. Walking, talking, or even downright yelling at the forest like he was having some kind of an argument with it.

I took another sip of coffee then picked up the last piece of bacon and took a bite. Derek had made a pan of home-made cinnamon monkey bread for breakfast. With my luck, all the good food he was always cooking would make me too fat to shift. I took another bite of bacon right as Levi stopped his pacing and marched back to the house. Over my shoulder I could see Derek turn back to the dishes he had been washing in the sink, a sloppy attempt at hiding his staring at the same strange sight that I was watching.

He wiped his hands on a red-and-white polka-dot dish towel then crossed off another day on the calendar hanging on the fridge. The second full moon would be here soon, and already the anxiety was eating away at me. I had no desire to experience pain like I had last month again, but it wasn't like I had much of a choice.

The door swung open and hit the wall with a bang that demanded attention. Levi strolled through the door. Without a word, he walked straight to one of the forest green cabinets and pulled out a mug then filled it full of steaming coffee. He took a long sip, without a flinch, and looked at me. He took another sip, his brows furrowing as if the sight of me was souring his morning.

"Go get dressed. You're running today."

Derek didn't say anything. He continued to wash the dishes. Levi picked up the paper and walked back outside with his mug, leaving me to a screaming silence.

When I walked out to meet Levi, he was leaning against a tree smoking a cigarette. His hair was tied back in a low ponytail and he wore jeans that had holes in them from wear.

"Start running." His eyes looked over to one of the stone columns as smoke danced out of his lips.

My gaze followed his. "Is everything okay?" It was just a column. The forest was quiet around it, or at least it seemed calm enough.

"Of course," he replied. "Now get moving."

"Where?"

"Doesn't matter." He took another drag. "You won't be able to make it off the land. I'll know where you are."

"How?" I reached down to adjust the tongue of my tennis shoe.

His eyes were already glowing and his pupils were pulsating like there was more than just him looking at me. He took another drag, his silver eyes glowing brighter with each breath he took. I paused as the thing in me stepped forward. Something behind his eyes moved, and that was all I needed to bolt.

My feet pumped against the ground to the beat of my heart as adrenaline drove every single one of my steps. The need to soar on its wings and push harder became insatiable. A high started to hum through me, an electricity that tickled through my veins while I ran with the wind, hints of the coming winter blowing swiftly through the trees, orchestrating a dance of falling leaves to the forest floor.

My lungs started to burn, but in a way I had come to love. The Pilates class I had committed myself to before was more of a social gathering than a way to strengthen my body. I was more worried about fitting in with the herd of brand-clothed females than I was about the class. With all the exercise Levi had been putting me through, I found myself welcoming the soreness every morning. Because with the aches came the achievements, both small and large. Like now—I knew that I could push harder. Go further. Run longer. I could do more, and believed in my ability to do so, which was more than I could say for myself before everything started.

I slowed as I turned a corner to catch my breath and take

note of the scenery around me. It was quiet, but not in a way that invited eeriness. It was serene, a gentle lullaby sounding through the forest as the crisp wind shook the tree limbs.

*Snap.*

The forest went silent. All of it. Even the wind felt like it was holding its breath in a moment when my heart was all I could hear.

*Snap.* I skidded to a halt.

I sucked in a breath. The hair on my neck rose as the forest quieted around me. If I'd learned anything since I'd been here, it was that a silent forest was never a good thing. I felt the beast in the back of my mind perk up, as if she was flipping her own ear forward to listen.

Another *snap* was all it took for my feet to pick up again.

*Where the hell was Levi?!*

I wove through trees and my eyes searched for the way back to the house—to safety. I didn't think that I could run this hard, this fast, but my body was a constant source of surprises these days. This thing in me pressed at my mind, almost as if she wanted me to turn around and confront the danger. I had no desire to do that. I was already fighting hard enough to stay alive. The last thing I needed to do was walk stupidly into my own demise.

I paused to catch my breath before picking up the pace again, hanging a sharp right toward a familiar path home. My legs pushed hard against the ground as the way back started to resonate with my memory, but I couldn't help the feeling of something breathing down my neck, catching up to me.

There was crunching behind me.

I ran faster as the sound only grew louder and louder.

My heart raced and fingers of fear felt like they were wrapping around my ankles, trying to yank me backward.

My body pushed harder as the need to flee grew feverous inside me. I found myself leaping on impulse. But right when my feet left the ground something slammed into me like a freight train. My body jolted sideways, skidding across the fading green grass until I smacked right into a tree. Groaning, I pulled myself upright as low growling silenced the forest once again.

In the back of my mind, I could hear Nate laughing. An image of him leaning forward on our balcony with its overpriced view, the soft colors of dusk caressing his skin like I used to, flashed through my mind. He looked over at me and chuckled. "Really, Charlotte?"

Groaning, I looked up to find myself alone in a clearing. A quiet clearing.

"Levi?" My voice shook, and the feeling that something wasn't quite right set in.

"Levi?" I called again as I stood back up.

A snapping caused my head to whip around to the sight of a black wolf standing at the edge of the forest. Silver eyes stared right at me. "Levi," I breathed, stepping closer.

The wolf cocked its head at me. A tingling buzzed in my brain. *She* surged to life, sizzling to the front of my brain. I stumbled from the forcefulness of her presence.

Blinking, I peered closer at the wolf, spotting a tip of white on one of its ears.

This wasn't Levi. Levi was all black. There was no white on his ears. I remembered that much from the sight of him shifting in the bedroom for the first time.

Whoever this was, I realized that he had me where he wanted me—cornered. I knew what happened in situations like this. I had no desire to feel another man's hands on me or to look at more bruises. Which was laughable. Wolves like this had teeth. I needn't worry about bruises because there wouldn't be anything left of me.

"Who the fuck are you?" I hissed, my feet planted in the ground as *she* grew more vibrant in my mind. "Well?!" I shouted. My voice was angry but my hands were shaking—fingers trembling—giving me away.

"Lander?!" I turned around to see Levi stomping toward me, his eyes glowing like angry fireflies.

He stepped around me as the other wolf stepped back into the woods. Levi paused in front of me and looked over his shoulder. "Did he say anything to you?"

I cocked my head. "No."

"Did you say anything?"

I shook my head. "No."

"Was he alone?"

My brows furrowed. "Is something wrong?"

Levi rubbed a hand over his face, his brow furrowing. "Charlie, was he alone?"

"I think so," I answered.

Levi sighed, his brow relaxing, which only fanned the flames of my curiosity.

I opened my mouth to probe Levi for information, but a crunching snapped my gaze forward. Levi stepped in front of me, but peering around him, I could see a man who looked like a younger version of Levi walk out of the brush.

Lander wiped his hands on his gray sweatpants then

pushed one through his white-blond hair, silver eyes trained directly on me. "So," he said, looking back at Levi. "Are you going to tell her?"

Levi crossed his arms over his chest. I took another side step to get a better look. "Charlie, this is my pain in the ass brother, Lander."

Lander rolled his eyes. I took a step forward. "Tell me what?" I asked Lander.

Lander shook his head at Levi, laughing under his breath. "Levi." He paused then looked up at me. The glow of his silver eyes softened before he smiled tiredly at me. "That you're moon-blooded."

I felt my brows rise before I found myself looking directly at Levi. He shook his head and smiled dangerously at Lander. "Has anyone ever told you that you're an exhausting asshole?"

"Levi?" I pushed. "What is he talking about?"

Levi's eyes cut to me. "It's not important."

"Bullshit," Lander hissed.

"We don't even know if she's going to make it through the next moon."

"And what about the trackers that have picked up her scent? The pack knows."

"Of course, they fucking know!" Levi grumbled.

"Why shouldn't they know?" I asked.

Both of them went silent, exchanging glances in a silent conversation that left me back in the dark.

I turned to Levi. "You promised. You can be a dick about it, but you fucking promised. What the fuck is happening to me?!"

He looked away from Lander then back at me. "Shit," he hissed. "All right, but back at the house. We don't know who's listening." I turned with wide eyes to look at Levi. He shrugged. "People are nosy. The pack can be even worse."

He stepped back then walked to the other end of the tree line. I turned to look at Lander, my mind running in circles as the secrets seemed to start dancing around me. Lander stepped next to me, offering me an easy smile.

"Come on," he said. "Levi's right. The pack is nosy."

"You're the one he's been talking to?"

Lander nodded as we began to walk toward Levi. "Someone has to check on him."

"Why leave him out here?"

Lander breathed a laugh. "He makes his own choices."

I narrowed my gaze then trotted after Levi, feeling the need to stay close. He looked over his shoulder at Lander and rolled his eyes.

"So, are you—"

"Wait until we get into the house."

I snapped my mouth shut, stomping next to him until we approached the cabin. Derek started to wave until he looked over the three of us. He nodded to himself then zipped inside.

I stormed past Levi and ran up the steps to find Derek opening a bottle of wine.

"It's not even noon."

Derek shrugged. "You're going to need this."

Levi walked in after me, grabbing a coffee cup. He poured it full of coffee left over from the morning then added in some whiskey. Lander closed the door behind him, eyeing Levi's mug.

"I'll take one."

"The fuck you will," Levi grumbled.

"What do you want, Lander?" Derek asked.

Lander huffed and took a seat at the bar. He looked at me then at Derek and Levi. "To talk about her—"

"My name is Charlotte."

Lander looked over at me, eyes latching onto mine. I felt *her* surge forward again. Dance like she was ready to ignite. Lander's eyes widened. He looked back at Levi, jaw clenching. "She's fucking moon-blooded and she has no idea. The pack—"

"That's your job to handle," Levi snapped.

"And your job is to take care of her," Lander shot back. "She has no idea what she is—what the hell are you thinking?! Do you even know what—"

"Enough!" I found myself saying. "I am right here and you will tell me what the hell is going on. Now."

Levi took a long drink from his mug. "Shit," he hissed. "Fuck—fine. Lander, this is your fucking fault."

Lander leaned back in his seat. "Derek, can I get something to drink?"

Derek sighed, nodded tiredly at him. He started to zip around while I took a seat at the edge of the bar.

"They say—well, our kind say—that some wolves are born with the blood of the moon in them," Levi began. "The moon is who created us, according to wolves. Usually, it's generational. Moon-blood is usually a trait passed down from the original wolves to their children. However, every now and then there's a new wolf that's moon-blooded that doesn't have a direct tie to the original families."

"But someone usually figures out a tie," Lander pointed out.

Levi shrugged. "Not all the time."

Derek slid Lander a glass of whiskey on the rocks. He took a sip then nodded reluctantly. "Not all the time," he repeated in agreement.

"What does it mean?" I asked.

"Usually moon-blood wolves are stronger. Think of it like the stronger pups in the litter."

"And," Lander added, "you can always smell the moon-blood on them. Before and after they shift. Usually, you start to smell it after their first moon."

I nodded as my fingers started to tap on the counter. "So, I smell like this? Like moon-blood?"

Lander chuckled. "Oh yeah," he said. "Pack trackers on patrol picked up your scent, hence why I am here," he finished, narrowing his gaze at Levi.

"But I can't smell either of you, or whatever it's supposed to smell like," I said.

Lander nodded. "You won't for a while. Maybe after the next moon when you shift a little more. You've got more traits now, but remember, it doesn't all come at once."

Levi shook his head at Lander. "I told you to keep the trackers away."

"With the rogue issue, you think that I could sell that kind of shit to anyone?"

"What rogue issue?" I asked.

Both men stilled, looking at each other and conversing silently in that telepathic form that was starting to grow annoying.

The hair on the back of my neck started to rise while something burned in my chest, vibrating its way to my fingertips. Levi whipped his gaze to me, the glow of my own eyes dancing around his silver irises. "I have a right to know. Are they coming after me? Coming to finish the job? Waiting for me to fucking lose it like them? And what—why did you not tell me I'm this fucking moon-blood thing?!"

"Because what's important is that you focus on surviving, and anything else seems like a distraction."

"Bullshit," I hissed.

"They won't come for you," Lander answered. "But how they attacked—it's highly unusual. They are never that organized. I would have doubted it, but the whole area smells like them, like rotting death—it's highly unusual and has the pack and our neighbors on alert. Usually, we know of rogues in the area, monitor them. They don't normally pop up."

I shook my head, which felt like it was starting to spin. Lander sighed before looking at me with an apologetic smile. "There's one more thing."

"Of course there is," Levi grumbled.

"The diner called. Shirley said a man was looking for her."

"You know Shirley?" I asked.

"Yeah, we know Shirley," Levi answered.

Lander licked his lips and cautiously looked back at Levi. "Someone from California was asking about a blond woman out here. Had a picture he was showing the staff. Shirley kicked him out and said they haven't seen anyone. She wasn't sure if that satisfied him enough to get him to look elsewhere."

My heart froze in my chest. My feet moved on their own until I was in the greenhouse, sitting next to the lush bushes of basil that still thought it was a nice summer day out. A summer day that I tried to let my mind melt away to, but that didn't stop the racing thoughts from spinning round and round my head.

Derek came in later to check on me but gave me my space. He didn't prod, which was a good thing. I felt like a time bomb ready to burst with the least bit of incentive. I eventually came in once the dark set in. Lander had left and Levi had long since gone to bed, but I only found my way into a restless sleep.

The next morning Levi woke me up early to run again. This time he had a created a path for me to follow closely, marked with white *X*s on the trees.

Frustration fueled each step I took, but "I told you so" and "Of course he would follow you" felt like bricks weighing me down. My lungs burned after only two laps; my mind raced even more.

"This isn't a leisurely jog."

Whipping around, I caught sight of Levi leaning against a tree. I shook my head. "I needed a break."

"Break's over, now move it."

I rolled my eyes and started to run again. I hated how easily Nate's man had found me. How easy it was for them to come so close to me. They wouldn't be polite about dragging me home, and Nate would certainly not be polite when I arrived.

The whole thing put everything at risk—everyone. All

the people who lived as part of this "pack" I hadn't even met—people who were probably better off before I'd crashed right into their world. I had to fix it. I had to figure out how to get Nate and his guy off my trail.

Looking up, I spotted Levi a few yards ahead of me in a pair of gray sweats. He shook his head. "Pick it up!" he called back.

I ignored him. I needed to think and put the pieces of things together. However, my lack of obedience didn't please him. He put his hands on his hips, a move similar to one Nate used to do when he was displeased. "You ran like a lightning bolt the night those rogues were after you, now move!"

My feet skidded to a stop. I turned on my heel as something fired inside my chest. "Rogues that you don't want to talk about," I said. "Or tell me anything about."

"It's not for you to worry about," he answered.

"Bullshit!" I hissed. "The rogues, the P.I. Nate sent? Why can't you give me some answers!"

"You probably already know more about that P.I. than we do," he pointed out. "Seems like it's not your first time."

My throat clenched because he was right. It wasn't my first time. I had run once before. More like attempted to run. An attempt that was very short-lived.

"Why the hell do you hate me so fucking much?" I found myself asking. I bit my lip as his eyes went wide, feeling the anger move me to step forward. "Look, I am really sorry I crashed into your life. Believe me, this is not what I wanted, but you owe me answers. You owe me the truth. This moon-blood thing? You can't hide that from me."

Levi chuckled under his breath. "You are a giant pain in my ass and now a pain to the pack. Do you even realize the threat you pose to everyone? You could go rogue. That means you're a danger to yourself and everyone around you, which we'd have to contain. And now I've got some controlling-ass human sending his puppets up here snooping around, threatening to expose us. And on top of that, I have to deal with you—moping around here feeling sorry for yourself with barely any fight to survive. So excuse me if I don't want to be best friends."

"Fuck you."

Tears pooled at the corner of my eyes. I didn't want to cry in front of him. I didn't want to give him that.

"You want answers, so do I. Like who the hell is this guy you're running from?"

"It's none of your business!" I hissed.

"I pulled three rogues off your ass. I think it is."

This wasn't his business. I hadn't agreed to him being my therapist.

I swallowed my trepidation and stepped toward the low sound of rumbling.

"He did a real number on your face. Haven't seen a woman beat up like that in a long time."

A rumble ripped through my chest with vibrations that shook all the way to my fingers. I felt *her* stand up in the back of my mind. Aware. Alert. Ready.

"You don't get to do this. You don't know a damn thing about me," I shouted, my eyes catching sight of leaves slowly settling next to a tree. He had been there. I was sure of it.

"Not fun when someone who doesn't know you starts to

poke and prod you for questions they don't deserve answers to, is it?"

Tears ran down my cheeks. I quickly wiped them away. I couldn't let him see his victory. I couldn't let him know how much I was breaking inside. How I hated myself. How I hated the pathetic excuse of a woman I had let myself become.

But something came over me. This thing in me, it felt like it was dragging something forward. It felt like pure outrage mixed with a little insanity, but the feeling of it slowly starting to weave through me made me think that it was my redemption.

Because he was wrong. He knew nothing about me. I may have run before, but I was done running now. I may have run into Nate's arms to escape the sorrow of losing my mother, but I wasn't running back to him or that life. I knew I had to talk about it. I knew I needed answers. And if Levi wanted to know exactly what that monster did to me, I'd be more than happy to tell him.

"You're right!" I tossed my hands up then looked around for him. I found myself stepping forward. "You're so right, Levi. What do you want? An award for being an on-point asshole?"

He said nothing but I could imagine the angry look on his face. I didn't care. I was taking his advice after all. Getting a little angry. A little mad. A little pissed off.

"You're so right!" I turned and caught sight of bushes shaking. "What? Do you want a fucking award?"

His eyes were glowing, almost all black, the silver lining barely visible. He lit a cigarette he had dug out of the pocket of his sweats, the forest growing quieter while he lit up, the smoke doing little to hide the rage behind his eyes.

"You want to know about this?" I lifted my shirt up and showed him a scar that was on my hip bone. "We got into a fight. I tried to turn away and instead I found myself falling into the corner of the coffee table. He told me I was just clumsy. I told myself for years that he was right." I laughed bitterly. "That I was just some clumsy bitch, but you knew that already, didn't you?"

He said nothing, just cocked his head and watched. "And what about these?" I turned and pulled my collar down so he could see the two blotchy scars right above my shoulder blade. "Because he was just trying to hug me, he totally didn't realize that the lit end of his cigarette was there. God he was just so stupid, wasn't he? Horrible accident."

"If you want me to feel sorry for you, then believe me, I won't."

"You want to know what happened that night?" I was prowling toward him now, doing what the new nature in me dictated. "He came home drunk and high, and pissed off. That wasn't unusual. He wanted to have sex and I said no because I was furious about finding pictures on his computer of him and his intern.

"He said he would make it up to me, but I wasn't having it. Him sloppily thrusting himself into me wasn't going to fix that. He called me an ungrateful bitch. I didn't understand how he could do this to me, he was supposed to love me! Be with me!

"I didn't even believe he'd hit me at first until he did it again." I paused while the breeze picked up again. "Then he was on me. I just lay there and prayed that it would be over, that he would be done with me. That it would just be over—"

"Charlotte—"

"He wasn't done. I don't know how I got away, but somehow I locked myself in the guest bathroom. I put a towel over the mirror so I couldn't look at myself."

I looked back at Levi, catching his eyes changing into something else. Becoming more human, less beast, as the breeze broke the silence around us. "You want to know about Nathaniel Lane? He is the type of asshole who would make you look like a puppy. He's got too much time and too much money and has family connections to the police and politicians. He won't stop looking for me, and I am really fucking sorry that in some way you have to deal with him. Because he is the devil."

This thing in me was coming closer, watching Levi while he took a drag of his cigarette. "You can be a piece of shit for as long as you want, but I'm not going to play these games with you. You agreed to help me, and helping me means telling me the truth. I'm not that delicate. I won't break. If you can learn anything from Nate, it's that I won't break," I snarled, my chest vibrating.

There was nothing left to say. I was done with his bullshit. I'd run from a man who had used me as a punching bag; I wasn't about to become someone else's.

My feet started to backtrack. I didn't want to show fear, but I wasn't staying—not with him in the middle of the forest where I could easily disappear. And I was *not* about to turn my back on him.

Levi didn't move. He watched me before I turned and

walked back through the silence of the forest that felt like it was quiet in reverence. I hated it. I hated the blank slate the quiet left for my own brain to run free in. Because all that was left in the silence were my own thoughts. And I hated the sound of those more than anything.

# CHAPTER
# NINE

I had lain in bed with no success at sleep for what felt like hours. Like sand slowly dropping in an hourglass.

The light tapping on the door made me sit up in bed. "Hello?"

The door cracked open. Levi looked at me, a bottle of gin in one hand and two empty coffee mugs in the other. "Sleep?"

"Not really." My heartbeat picked up.

He nodded more to himself than to me. "Come on, then."

There wasn't anything as murderous about him now as there had been before, but that didn't calm my pounding heart as I followed him outside.

Light mist was falling out of the night sky. Levi took a seat on the top step, where the roof still protected us from the drizzle. He opened up the bottle and poured the clear liquid into a mug then slid it over to me, before pouring himself some. "Mind if I smoke?"

I shrugged in response. I doubted me saying no would stop him. He pulled out a pack and fished a cigarette out. I took a long sip of gin as he lit his cig.

"I didn't think you were a gin person."

His tired eyes found mine. "I'm not very good at this," he admitted, before adding "I can be a real piece of shit. I have a tendency to think that less is more—sometimes you end up hurting people when all you're trying to do is protect them. I can be a grade A asshole too." He took a sip from his mug while flicking some ash off the end of the cigarette into the rosebushes. "What he did, your ex, it's more than shameful. You did the right thing, and he won't find you here."

"It feels like he already has."

"This place is protected by magic," Levi said. "It's like an illusion around the land that most humans cannot see through."

I thought back to the clearing I had parked at the night I was attacked. To the trail I had followed in the dirt. "The tracks—"

"Magical border." Levi spoke up. "Those tracks kept going, you just couldn't see them. He won't find you. The people at The Hole are friends of ours. They won't say anything."

"The Hole?"

"It's a small general store next to a gas station—safe for

our kind and humans. We've known the owners for a long time."

I nodded my head. "But what do we do? What if he files a missing persons? What about the man he sent up here?"

"If he was going to file one, he probably already would have," Levi pointed out.

I bit my lip then slowly agreed. Nate may have had friends who were cops, but explaining to them why I ran away was a story he didn't want anyone to know.

"Regardless," Levi said, "Lander is going to have someone follow him to see what he knows, then Derek will take care of it. He'll compel him with a new story to take back to Nate. Case closed."

I blinked. "Compel?"

"Vampires." He looked up at me, his eyes tired. "They can compel humans. Command them to do things or forget things."

"What?" I sucked in a breath.

Levi chuckled before he took a drag. "It's one of many reasons it's good to have a vampire around. Regardless, the pack can protect itself from outsiders."

"But the pack? What if I turn rogue? What if Nate does come after me and someone gets hurt?"

"The pack can handle itself. Nate, well, I wouldn't mind if he paid a visit. Feel like I'd have a fun time with him."

My brows rose high as a darkness crept across his brow. The kind that could only be attributed to the monster within. "And me. What if I lose it?"

Levi sighed. "We've all lost it a little at one point or another. Sometimes you can't stop it. You find your way back.

Find something that's worth finding your way back for."

He turned to look at me and it was then that I saw it. My sight had only slightly improved since the last moon, but in the darkness I could spot the faint red lines that slowly danced around the silver of his irises. They were so tiny, only a few of them, that from far away they would be impossible to see. But they were still there. Still holding on. Still quietly present. To the normal person, if they looked close enough, if may have looked like he had allergies or was getting over pink eye. But the sick feeling in my gut knew better.

My breath caught in my throat. Levi took another sip of his drink, then I took a large one of mine.

"Is that what you did?" I found myself asking. "Is that why you're out here?"

Levi snorted a quiet laugh. He nodded at me in amusement then took another drink. "Let's play a game, Charlie girl."

"What kind of a game?" Derek's room wasn't far. If I screamed, he would hear me.

"You say two things that are true, one that is not, and the other person has to guess which is the lie. If you guess wrong, you drink. Although you don't really have to be wrong to drink."

I'd played this game in college more times than I wanted to admit. The fact that Levi, a werewolf out in the middle of nowhere, knew a frat boy's favorite drinking game both surprised me and did not surprise me at all. "I've played this before."

"Then you're going first." His lips turned into a smirk as he sipped his gin.

I rolled my eyes and took a drink myself. "Fine," I said

with a huff. "Okay, I am an only child, I grew up in Colorado, and my mother has seven sisters."

"Your mother did not have seven sisters."

"What? How would you know that?"

"You're a bad liar." Eyes meeting mine made me believe him. Eyes that felt like they were always able to see my inner truth regardless of how hard I tried to hide it.

"Your turn."

He scratched his jaw, the cigarette dwindling slowly between his fingers. "I am over a hundred years old, werewolves can never have chocolate, and I love vodka."

There was no way this man was a vodka guy. Gin? Yes, but gin was also a sad man's drink, and there was nothing cheerful about either Levi or me tonight. No, Levi wasn't some Real Housewife trying to keep things "skinny." As for him being old, well, if Derek was as old as she suspected, then Levi's age could be probable.

Inwardly I just hoped the chocolate was a lie. "Vodka?"

"I actually don't mind it from time to time," he contended, his eyes almost dancing in laughter at my disbelief.

I took a sip from my mug. "So, what was the lie?"

"We can have chocolate," he remarked, his lip twitching into what I thought could be a smile.

"So how old are you then?"

He rolled his eyes. "I stopped counting a few years ago. I think I'm like a hundred and fifteen, give or take."

"Wha-what?" I shook my head. "And Lander?"

"Well, he's younger but not by much. He's maybe in his nineties at this point." He sighed into his mug. "It's your turn, Charlie girl."

"Fine. But I mean how?"

"We age slowly. Vampires don't age at all. I think Derek is pushing five hundred."

"No way."

"Yes way." He mimicked me with another eye-roll. "Welcome to the world of supernaturals. It's your turn."

Jesus Christ, he was old. I took a sip of my gin and tried to focus on what I was going to say. "Okay, uh, my father was a huge Broncos fan, I transcribed old notes for a law firm before all of this, I hated living in Malibu."

He watched me closely like he would watch a book unfold for him. He took another drag then a sip of his drink. "Broncos." Reluctantly, I nodded. He was too good at this for comfort. "What team?"

"I don't know." I shrugged. "He died when I was young. Cancer. I remember football being on from time to time, I don't really remember what team he liked. I don't really remember much about him."

He let out a long breath and looked back into the night. "I'm sorry."

"It is what it is."

He nodded as this strange awkwardness set in. "I've always lived in this house, I hate peanut butter, and I hate these goddamned rosebushes."

"The rosebushes." They were just bushes. It seemed a little arbitrary to hate them.

"Drink up," he said with dark amusement lacing his voice.

"Why?" I coughed after swallowing the liquor wrong.

For a moment he said nothing—he just puffed on his

cigarette before he looked back at me. "Like you, I hate reminders. You're not the only one running."

"What's the lie?"

"The house. I grew up in the pack with Lander. At the pack house. My father moved us away after a while, he wanted more peace and quiet as the pack grew."

"There's a lot of them, then?"

He nodded. "We're one of the larger ones in the area."

"One more?"

"All right, Charlie girl."

"My mother hated him—" I paused and tried not to think of Nate. It was painful to think that half of undergrad was wasted with him, and the other years I could have been chasing my own dreams were wasted away too. "My uncle hated him, but a part of me still loves him."

Levi watched me carefully as the mist picked up, giving me cold kisses on my face. "Your mother."

"She never met him," I responded. He eyed me with a question that I knew I would have to answer as well. "She died before I went to college. Car accident."

He let out a long breath through his nose and eyed my cup. "Want some more?"

"If I do, I'll just be more depressing."

"Gin does that," he noted.

I took a sip from my mug and nudged my chin toward him. "Your turn."

"A vampire's bite won't totally kill a Were, once you go rogue you can't come back from it, and there's never been, to my knowledge, a human who was moon-blooded."

I bit my lip and leaned back against the railing. The

other two seemed logical, but just from what I knew of the supernatural, it would seem legit that a vampire's bite was potentially more lethal. "A vampire's bite?"

Levi shook his head with a smile. "Drink."

I rolled my eyes and took a sip.

"It depends on how much you get in your system. Think of it like a poisonous snakebite. Sometimes you live if not that much gets into your bloodstream, and sometimes you're not that lucky."

"So most humans—"

"Lander is looking into it. See if something he finds can help you. We've never heard of it." He shook his head with a laugh. "You're a lucky little shit, you know that? Most humans die their first full. Even the strong ones. Here you are, fucking moon-blood too."

"But I may go rogue." I paused then looked back at him. "The lie."

"Find something to hold on to. That wolf in you, she's trapped. It's like shaking a closed Coke bottle—the moon demands that she come out. Even after you shift, you can't go too long without letting her out, otherwise you'll start to go a little mad. That's the case for all wolves. But you need to learn to work with her. You're going to be with her for the rest of your life. Fighting with her is only going to make your life miserable, but if you do go rogue, then it's going to make coming out of it impossible."

I looked back at his eyes, back at the faint red that I could now spot. "How—"

He took a long sip of gin then stood up. "Better get some

sleep. It's going to rain tomorrow and you're swimming before the weather turns."

"And Lander? The pack? These people who can smell me?"

Levi picked the bottle up. "Lander will handle that."

"I don't want anyone hurt because of me."

"You start to worry about other people, you're going to forget to worry about yourself, and hurt someone in the process because you're too damn stubborn to see how your actions affect people around you," he murmured.

He paused and looked at the sky. I stood slowly, biting my tongue because that statement didn't feel like it was meant for me.

"You cannot keep me in the dark anymore."

He nodded. "I know."

# CHAPTER
# TEN

The water was steadily rolling along, lapping gently at the bank where a rowboat was tied to a hook nailed into a tree stump. It looked pleasant enough. Like a photo that you might find on a postcard at any gas station. But it felt anything but pleasant. Tree limbs were stretching out over the sand like hands desperately reaching for water while jagged boulders peeked their faces out of the water. The water may have been lapping quietly, but under it I heard a hunger.

Levi untied the boat and set his cooler inside. He pulled out two oars and started to row us upstream, trailing cigarette smoke behind us. Water slowly licked at the sides of the boat, a few waves splashing my arms.

"Where does this stream go?"

He paused his rowing. "See those mountains in the distance?" I turned to look at where his hand was pointing behind me. Tall snowcapped mountains were in the far distance, although it was normally hard to see them with all the rain and cloud cover. Today, we got a rare view, although the clouds behind Levi threatened to steal that from us.

"Yeah," I answered with a nod.

"The water from this stream comes from what flows off those mountains. There's another river that runs up there too—between it and the mountains we always have a steady current."

"Where does it go? This stream?"

Levi took a long drag. Cigarette smoke swirled behind him as if it was trying to match the current of the waves. "It goes to the ocean. This stream eventually will connect to a river farther south that will dump into a small bay." I looked back at the mountains—ragged steeples jutting into the sky that made me wonder if anyone had ever dared to try to reach the top. I am sure someone had—I'd seen enough of those crazy wilderness shows. But these mountains felt wild, like they still held dominance out here. Not mankind.

"The stream is usually filled up in the summer when the snow starts to melt and runs off those mountains," he added. "But we get overflow from the river north and any flow of water from a storm on the mountains—right now it's getting fed by all the rain running off the slopes from the storms we've been having."

"Anyone ever go up there?"

"Wolves do."

My brows rose. I turned back to look at Levi. His eyes grew hard. He took another drag before his silver eyes sliced past me to the mountain range. "They keep to themselves. Not a bunch of characters that you'd want to run into."

"Why not?"

"Because they'd make me look like a puppy," he half snarled before picking the paddles back up, ending my line of questioning as he rowed us upstream where the current started to grow more violent, almost as if it was angry at our intrusion.

Waves crashed bitterly into the boat, jolting us from one side to the next. I ended up trapping the cooler between my legs so it wouldn't fall out. Levi didn't falter. He kept on rowing, oars cutting into the water like it was butter. Levi eventually slowed his rowing and opened the cooler. He pulled out a bottle of beer.

"You swim, Charlie girl?" he asked as he popped open the bottle with the fish-tail opener screwed to the side of the boat.

I looked at the water then back at him. "Yes."

Levi nodded, almost in relief at the answer. An answer I knew was a mistake. His hands were around my waist and tossing me into the water before I knew what was happening.

Hundreds of cold fingers crawled over my body as the cold undercurrents sucker punched the breath out of me. Immediately, I scrambled for the surface. My hands fought through the cold until I bolted through the surface with a painful gasp. I clasped the side of the boat wearing a new coat of painful goose bumps.

"Are you insane?!"

His boot pushed me off the edge. A thick twisted brown rope was thrown at me. "Start pulling."

"I thought you weren't supposed to kill me!" I called while I frantically grabbed for the rope. "I thought—you're supposed to be helping!"

"I am." He took a sip of his beer and leaned back in his seat like he was living in Margaritaville. "The faster you move, the faster we get where we're going."

I blinked hard as my legs struggled to tread water. "Seriously?"

"Yep."

"Did you do this before? With the others that shifted?"

"Did it before, did it myself. Just start swimming, Charlie."

He didn't even open his eyes. He just took another sip of his beer while the sun rolled over his skin.

The shore was close enough that I could make it, and a strange masochistic part of me wanted to take on the challenge. Prove that I wasn't useless. That I had a fighting chance.

I had grown stronger. Running and chopping wood every morning with Levi had started to tone my body. It was strange. The last time I looked like this, Nate had pinched my hip with a disapproving gaze. Derek just looked at me with approval. It was a strange limbo but I couldn't deny the feeling of being strong again, being able to run again, and run farther than I thought I could each day.

But even as my strong arms and stronger legs propelled me forward with the rope tied around me, the current that I swam against continued to fight against me. Cold water shattered over my face, knocking the breath out of me, while the twisting waves made kicking a nearly impossible task.

And it was cold. It was as cold as the inner circle of hell. No matter how much I moved, the freezing water made every muscle and limb in my body feel stiff—like concrete.

A wave rolled me under the surface. I opened my eyes in the dark water, but it was just a soulless gaze looking back at me. In my mind I could hear Nate laughing at me. He was looking at me from the edge of his father's fancy sailboat, with his not-so-boat shoes on and a bright-teal shirt that made his skin glow. "The water's so nice, baby, isn't it?" his voice whispered in the depths of my brain.

Something snapped at the memory, clawed at it even as I tried to claw my way to the surface. My hands found the edge of the boat. I coughed out some water, trying to regain my breath, when something shoved me back into the current.

"You can rest when we get where we're going." Levi's voice was harsh like the stream. He sat back in his seat, finishing off his beer with a long sip. He dug out another one, popping it open with a smirk.

"Which is?!" I called as I swam forward.

"To never-never land, Charlie girl!" he answered, tossing a half-eaten apple at me.

Something in me pushed forward. It felt like maybe it could be the beast, but it could also be this new vein of anger that had continued to dwell in me since the first day at the woodpile. I started to swim again into the current of fists beating me over and over, praying that we would reach a shallow area where I could walk.

Lucky for me, my feet soon found the bottom of the stream. I rejoiced inwardly, mistakenly thinking that walking in shoulder-deep water would be easier. The skin on my waist was chafing raw from the rope rubbing it. I took the rope off, thinking it would be easier to pull the boat with my hands, but the bottom floor was treacherous.

This stream wasn't just made of water. Rocks, branches, and other objects hit my legs. My feet ached from stepping on sharp stones that I had no real way of seeing. Eventually, I gave up walking and retied the rope around my waist so I could swim again. It was deep enough and my feet couldn't handle another second walking over the jagged rocks.

However, the minute I started to paddle, a wave knocked into me and forced me under. I was tossed and turned in the cold arms of an angry lover, something too familiar and too terrifying. Something hard and jagged hit my arm. Something else was pawing at my mind, wanting to come closer, and that was more dangerous than this current.

The coldness around me was starting to freeze my brain; coherent thoughts were suspended in the airless frozen domain of darkness where I tumbled. My hands frantically searched for the surface while my legs kicked with all their might to free me.

When I grabbed hold of the boat, I spat up so much water that I could have filled up four of Levi's empty beer bottles. My lungs were burning. My eyes blinked the water out of them. My legs were floating behind me. My mind, tired of the fight.

"Either you're going to let this stream take you, or not. It's your choice."

I coughed more water. "You're not supposed to kill me."

Anger was brewing in me. How stupid was I? How idiotic was he? The anger coiled in me, licking its lips while I looked back at the water.

Dark and turning like it was curling its finger at me to come forward. Beckoning me to try again so it could chew me up in the current that made up its jaws. I wasn't sure if that or the beast starting to anger in my mind was more terrifying at the moment. It was hard to think straight when I was sure that I couldn't feel my toes anymore.

"If you keep looking at it like that, then it's going to eat you up and spit you out two miles downstream."

"What?" I coughed out. My lungs were still burning, still desperate to fill with air.

He was right in front when I looked up. Silver eyes looking at me, the pupils in them growing slightly wider, as if the animal in him wanted to take a closer look. "Either you're going to swim or not."

"I've been swimming."

"No, you haven't."

I opened my mouth then closed it. His words sank deep within me. Words that opened the door for something that had been clawing at me. "If you can't trust yourself or her, then you might as well let it take you."

"She—" I paused and took another deep breath. "Will rip my skin off."

"Only because she wants to come out. She's going to be half of you, you want to be afraid of half of yourself all the time?" I didn't answer because I already knew the answer.

Levi leaned back. His calloused hands pushed me back into the water. "Get going."

"You're an asshole."

"I know." He got back in his seat and picked up the cigarette he had laid in an ashtray, then eyed me expectantly.

I looked back at the rushing water. All I could hear was the rushing sound of Nate's whispers slicing at me. I closed my eyes, forcing those away while something else stepped out.

My arms went to work as this thing, this beast in me, crawled carefully forward. It was like she knew how I felt about her—how she terrified me—so she was cautious, yet steadily with me. She wanted to come out, but for now, it felt like this would satisfy her. Helping me—helping us—would be enough.

She was humming through me now. This feeling, this fire in me was distracting me from the cold and putting me in a zone where it was just the sound of my hands cutting through water over and over and over again. A few times a wave would get me and knock me under, but each time I would fight my way back to the surface. I was so tired of drowning. Of letting the current take me without a fight. Of saying yes, all the time, or nodding when I wanted to tear all my hair out.

Another splash hit my face. The hum was buzzing through me; fire was slowly burning through my toes to my fingertips while I found my own current against the raging one charging toward me. I didn't even feel Levi yanking the rope until he finally yanked me back to the boat.

He pulled me back in, then put his oars back in the water. "The rocks are slick here."

"Here?"

He nudged his chin toward a shore where green grass was littered with fall leaves. I leaned my head back while the sun raked over my skin.

"Come on."

I jumped out and helped him pull the boat onto the sandy shore where smooth boulders covered by soft moss made the water look less dangerous than it was. Levi grabbed the cooler while I grabbed a blanket from the bottom of the boat, grateful to Derek, who probably put it there.

"What's this place?" I asked as we walked toward a big oak tree with what had to be hundreds of initials carved into the trunk. I pulled the blanket around me and reached out to trace the deep grooves carved into it.

"Are you going to come over here and eat?"

Levi set the cooler down in a grassy area.

"This tree?" I walked toward him, the beast in me wanting me to turn back to the tree, but my stomach was more in control of my movements now.

"It's important to the pack here."

"How?"

"When there's a new leader, they swear to the moon to protect the pack. Seal it in blood on that tree. It's a blood oath," he answered casually, while opening the cooler that thankfully had more than beer in it. He pulled out tubs of food, some bags of chips, and bottled waters that made my mouth water upon sight.

"A blood oath." I paused. "What's that mean?"

"It means you don't ever—ever—want to break it. Breaking a blood oath breaks off a piece of your soul."

Note to self. I looked back at the tree one more time. A chill ran down my spine at the sight of all the bloody handprints.

Shaking my head, I took a turkey sandwich and tore into it, almost tearing into my hand with each bite. Levi took another sip of his beer then opened up a small container of chicken salad.

"How does this work? The pack?" I asked through a mouthful of chips.

"First off, don't talk with your mouth full. We may be wolves, but we do have manners." He took a bite of his chicken salad, careful to swallow before talking again. "We've worked hard to stay secret. Over the years, it's been harder, but we're very self-sufficient." He watched me carefully for a moment.

"If I survive, I'll get to meet more of them?"

Levi shrugged. "Do you want to?"

I looked up at him, finding a small smile tugging on his lips. I bit back a laugh and leaned back. "It's not that I hate people, unlike some of us," I teased, narrowing my gaze at him.

He snorted a laugh and took another drag of his cigarette. "Just worry about what's in front of you."

I nodded although it was hard to keep my mind from sprinting a mile ahead of where I was.

"I never thought I would make it this long," I admitted.

"What do you mean?"

I shrugged. "I never thought I could be away from him.

I never really could get a plan together. I always got scared. Even when it was bad, even when he—" I paused and let my fingers pull the collar of my shirt over to show the little silver scars in the shapes of dots over my collarbone. "Cigarette—it was an accident, like everything else."

I felt *her* move inside me, almost quieting. Giving me space while making herself, her support, known.

"What changed?"

"He almost killed me," I answered quietly. Hot tears burned in the corners of my eyes. "I want to hate him. I want to be normal. I want to meet other people and not worry they're going to see my scars and ask questions. I hate the fucking questions."

He pulled out another cigarette. "People praise scars in our world. It's a sign that you've protected something, someone, or yourself. Usually, the wolves with more scars are the ones that are more respected." He paused, lighting up the cigarette before taking a long puff. "You don't want to answer someone's question, then don't. Your business and not theirs."

"That easy?" I laughed as a tear slid down my cheek.

He shrugged. "No, but it works."

I wiped my eyes and pointed back at the tree. "How do you all live out here? How has the government not caught on?"

I took another bite of my sandwich while Levi took a drink from his beer.

"Weres are all over the world. As are vampires and witches—"

"Witches?"

He rolled his eyes. "For the most part, in North America, our kind is usually in the north. We don't do well in the heat, but there are wolves in South America, Australia, and Africa that have adapted."

"Everyone survives a little differently. Up here, at least in our region, we are pretty self-sustaining. Most packs have their own doctors, farms, livestock, infrastructure—our region gets along well, so we can easily trade with each other. We live off the grid, though some packs live closer to cities or have cities in their borders. But most of the time the concrete jungle and our kind don't mix well.

"However, we do need things like money and vehicles to function. Other modern things. The pack, or at least this one, owns a few businesses. The revenue enables us to provide for pack members. Lots of wolves work too—usually it's jobs where it's easy to hide who they are."

"But if you own a business, then arguably you're not totally off the grid?"

"It gets convoluted," he admitted. "The less humans know, the better."

"Have they ever stumbled on the pack before?"

"Mhmm." He took another drag of his cigarette. "It's one reason that peace between vampires and wolves is important. If a human stumbles onto a pack, it's usually pretty easy to get a vampire to come up and wipe their memory of us."

I leaned back and tugged at my wet hair, a million questions racing through my mind. "How—how did you even get here?"

"That tree." He nudged his chin at the tree with all the initials carved into it. "Legend says the moon called the first of this pack to this land. It says that they walked to this tree where they could feel her calling them. And according to the legend, it was on this tree that they swore to her an oath to protect the land and the ones who lived on it."

"The moon?"

"We're called to her, all of us," he said, his voice dropping lower, almost bitter. I arched a brow at him. "Moon Goddess is kind of a big deal among our people."

"And you?" His eyes looked like they'd turned a lighter shade of silver, while the pupils of his eyes went a hair wider. He snapped out of his trance before taking an agitated puff of his cigarette.

"You felt her that night, you tell me."

There was something scratching at me to push more, but he was evasive, and I had a feeling that he would only be more evasive within this conversation. I made a mental note to prod Derek for more answers.

While this Moon Goddess sounded like some kind of crazy cooked-up nonsense the naturopath at the overpriced health food store was always going on about, I couldn't deny what had happened to me. I couldn't deny how I felt that first full moon. A shiver ran down my spine at the thought.

"I don't know why I'm telling you all of this," Levi said, snapping me out of my thoughts. "Chances are you're going to die anyhow."

"Do you really believe that?"

He scratched his jaw and shrugged. "Wouldn't be the first time I saw it happen, doubt it will be the last." He looked back at me, quiet for a moment before he looked back at the stream. "I guess we'll see."

# CHAPTER ELEVEN

When we got back the rain was starting to pick up. Levi pulled a black tarp over the boat while I ran to the house to tie another one down over the firewood.

Derek was tending to the fire when I stumbled inside. "There you are." He zipped to me and shook his head. "Get those off and I'll toss them in the dryer for you. You can have a bath in my bathroom if you want?"

"I'll shower off. Really, I'm fine."

He put a hand to my forehead, then nodded. "Weres always run a little higher than humans. Still, it doesn't mean you can't freeze," he added. "How do you feel about pizza?"

"How do you feel about true love?"

He snickered while I pulled my hair out of its ponytail.

"I knew we were meant to be. Just don't tell Elliot," he teased.

"He's here?" I asked, anxiety swelling in me.

Derek shook his head, walking back to the kitchen. "In a week or so. I'll get you some extra towels."

I gave him a mock salute then scurried to my bathroom. When I closed the door, I pressed the back of my hand to my forehead; I didn't think I felt warmer, but then again I wasn't freezing, which I realized was crazy considering what I had been doing.

After I showered, I threw on some leggings and a sweatshirt. The rain was picking up outside, tapping on the window like it wanted me to sneak out. I found myself staring into the mess while I ran a comb through my hair. There were a few hidden blond streaks in it that I must have missed when I'd dyed it in a rush. I tried to tuck them away, but with my new short cut, there was no longer a long curtain for them to hide behind.

Lightning flashed across the sky. The window of my room looked out into the storm that was whipping the forest into a tornado. Silver eyes cut right through the rain and beamed at me through the glass. I shook my head but they were still there, behind the thick brush where I couldn't see who they belonged to.

My hand froze. I felt cold as the eyes held my gaze, trying to creep into the deepest parts of my soul. A part that had me wondering if the eyes I saw were really hazel instead of silver.

Another flash of lightning, another blink, and they were gone. I rushed to the window. The sound of Nate laughing echoed in the back of my mind. I shook my head, trying to banish his sour memory. What was Levi even doing out there?!

"Holy hell!" Levi's voice grumbled.

My feet carried me to the bedroom door. I flung it open, and there was Levi, soaking wet in his clothes. He couldn't have been out there by my window and fully clothed. If he shifted, then he would have been butt-ass naked.

Levi cocked his head at me. "Can I help you?"

I looked back to my window, the rain pounding harder at the glass. A cold finger ran up my spine. There was nothing in the bushes but darkness, but I was sure of what I'd seen.

Was it the rogues? Had they come back for me? Were they stalking me?

"Charlotte?" My head whipped around to Levi. I looked back again at the dark window that was playing games with my mind. "Where?"

His voice was low and quiet. I turned and he was a few feet from me, taking another step toward my bedroom. I swallowed the fear creeping up and pointed outside.

He nodded then turned back to the kitchen. "Get some socks on. It's cold."

"Levi? What—what was outside?"

His eyes were glowing when he looked back to me, blacker than silver. "Just get some socks on."

Derek was chopping some basil in the kitchen, once again trying to avoid the elephant in the room. I looked back to my room then at him. "What was that?"

"Nothing for you to worry about," Derek replied. He put the knife down then walked to the cabinet and pulled out a stemless wineglass.

149

"It was watching me *in my* bedroom, Derek." He paused, eyes meeting mine. "Was it the rogues? Do you think they came back?"

"There's no rogues to come back. We tore them to shreds."

"What if they have friends?"

"You saw their eyes?" he asked. I nodded. "Any redness? Looks like pink eye or someone who's been scratching their eyes incessantly."

I shook my head. "Silver."

"Rogues always have redness in their eyes, it's one way to spot them," he explained. "Levi will find out. Why don't you help me with the pizzas? No use fretting over what we don't know."

I wanted to push the topic further. This thing in me wanted to push harder, but I knew I would have to wait for a better moment to climb over the wall that Derek was building. I took the glass from him then took a long sip, the wine calming my nerves as lightning flickered across the sky again. I looked back at my room—to the window—but there was nothing. In the back of my mind I could see him shaking his head at me and my "wild imagination."

I yanked those thoughts back, letting this thing in my brain tear at them while I chopped cherry tomatoes with Derek. The thunder cracked again while this small fire built in me. She ripped at the memory of Nate, ripped at the memory of the eyes watching us.

Levi walked back into the kitchen wearing dry clothes and his normal scowl. He opened the cabinet where the wine-glasses were and pulled one out. He grumbled to himself, letting out a string of curses, before he walked back to his room.

When he returned, he put socks on the counter in front of me. "You don't need to walk around barefoot when it's this cold outside," he told me.

"Who was it?" I asked.

Levi paused, looking at me then Derek. Derek's eyes widened and he hissed. Levi ran a hand through his hair. "My fucking nephew." He looked back at my feet. "Get some damn socks on."

I slid onto a barstool and shoved the socks on while *she* crept forward. I could feel her frustration. Her need to protect. Her irritation with so many half-truths—I'd heard enough of those for a lifetime.

Levi opened another wine bottle.

"This isn't nothing. He was watching me. In. My. Room. Has he been watching me? What does he want?!"

My chest felt like it was going to start vibrating.

Levi paused his pour and looked over his shoulder at me, his pupils dilating when his eyes met mine. He grabbed his glass and turned to face me, and the reflection in it of my own eyes glowing made my heart skip a beat.

"The moon-blood. He smelled it and got nosy."

I bit my lip with a nod. "So is the rest of this pack going to be nosy?" The last thing I wanted was to be secretly watched as I stumbled through this whole fucking thing.

He shook his head. "No. Lander has something from the local witches to throw them off your scent."

I cocked my head. "He went to witches about me?"

Levi sighed. "He wanted to see if anything could help if you—"

"Went rogue," I finished.

Derek tapped the counter. "Look, regardless, Charlotte deserves her privacy. Liam needs to mind his own business."

"I don't think he'll come around here for a while," Levi answered darkly.

The beast in me calmed at his tone, although my mind was racing, which was only going to lead to anxiety-fueled dreams.

That night in my dream Nate kept telling me that he would keep me safe. He told me this as he slowly started to strangle me—sweet words with sinister hands that squeezed the air out of my lungs.

When I woke up, daylight was breaking through the clouds. I peeked through the blinds, and could have sworn I saw the bushes move.

• • •

The next morning Levi had me running on a path that he had marked earlier that morning with white spray paint on trees. It wasn't a big loop, but it was enough that eventually the jogging started to ease my mind. I felt her come closer while I pushed along the winding path, this desire to truly run coursing through me.

My feet picked up, racing along while this new energy sizzled through my veins. I came along a turn, curling around a tree with a white $X$ on it. Unfortunately, I hit the turn too fast. My feet lost traction and I found myself falling face-first into a pile of leaves.

"Shit," I groaned.

Slowly pushing myself up, I spat out the foliage that had found its way into my mouth and sat up. Wiping the dirt off my face, I let out a long breath as a prickling crawled over my neck.

I felt her race forward so fast it almost knocked me over. Carefully, I stood up and looked around. Only lonely trees and bushes looked back at me, but the feeling of someone's eyes crawling over me grew. My head turned toward the path I was supposed to follow, but I felt her almost snap at the thought. Like she was trying to yank me away from a trap.

A sharp breath escaped my lips. I turned the way I had come, but the sight of that path left a sour feeling in my gut.

So I did what seemed reasonable. I bolted off the path and into forest.

Branches and bushes slapped my skin as an all-too-familiar feeling of terror swept over me. The beast in me pushed me to run harder. I was close to the creek, and if I could find it, I could jump in and swim home. I had swum it enough to know how to get back.

My head turned just in time to catch the shape of a black wolf with blazing silver eyes racing neck and neck with me.

"Fuck!" I hissed.

I tried to turn but realized that I needed Levi or Derek. I wasn't going to outrun this thing on my own.

I slowed enough to suck in a breath so I could scream, when something grabbed my leg, yanking me down to the ground.

The cold ground felt as hard as concrete. It scraped my skin as I skidded across the dirt until the base of a tree stopped me. Panic danced over my spine. Looking around, I couldn't see anyone, until some bushes rustling nearby caught my attention.

Standing, I readied myself to scream, praying that I wasn't too far away for someone to hear me. Although screaming had never really saved me in the past.

"Please don't!" The plea came, causing my throat to catch.

A young man stood before me. He had both hands up, a nervous look on his boyish face. Silver eyes like Levi's and Lander's looked back at me. A mop of white-blond hair sat on top of his head. He was tall, at least as tall as Levi but built just like Lander—lean, toned, and at the moment, completely shirtless.

"Please don't scream. I swear I'm not going to hurt you. Please?"

I cocked my head. I had trusted a good-looking man before when he begged me not to panic, not to be scared, and that had only led to more pain. Even now, the familiar feeling of my shaking hands reminded me that those days were not all that far behind me.

"What do you want?" I asked. The courage I had built up over the weeks that I had been here cracked easily as fear tumbled through me.

"I just—" He paused. His hands slowly fell to his sides. "I wanted to see if you were real. Dad . . . I could smell you on him. I guess I was just curious?" he added with a shrug, tossing in a smile that showed off his dimples.

My brows rose. A familiar feeling of sweat was building on the back of my neck. I swallowed back the panic and tried to stay calm as the beast in me paced. Her irritation started to seep into me, chasing my fear away with a new feeling of agitation. "You were watching me in my room."

"Yeah . . ."

"That's fucking weird," I snapped. An angry breath rolled out of my nose as my fingers curled into my palm.

He bit his lip, nodding. "It is. I'm sorry." His fingers scratched his hair. "Honestly, I thought Levi had finally lost it and was making it up."

I felt the beast inside me move, like *she* was snapping her teeth at him, as if she wanted to show him how real we both were. "Do I look made-up to you?"

He let out a nervous laugh and shook his head. "No, I think you're really real and really pissed. Fair. I am—look, I'm really sorry. Really fucking sorry."

Nate rarely said sorry. Usually everything was always my fault. I crossed my arms over my chest.

"So, what do you want?"

He shrugged. "Well, I mean, if you make it, you'll be pack. It might be good to know someone other than my crazy uncle and my dad."

"And Derek."

He nodded. "And Derek."

The beast in me pushed closer. I could feel *her* curiosity as *she* looked him over. I felt heat rush to my cheeks and swatted it away.

"Look, I'm really sorry. Honestly, I wasn't sure if you were real or if any of the rumors were true and . . . I wasn't trying to be nosy. But, I mean, look, I can take a hike—I'm sorry," he rambled, stepping back toward the brush.

"Wait," I found myself saying, stepping toward him. He paused, cocking his head at me. "What rumors?"

He walked to a nearby tree and leaned against it. "Just things floating around the pack. They love to talk."

I rolled my eyes. "Awesome. And what are they saying?"

"Honestly, you shouldn't worry about it. They just like to speculate."

"I would like to know," I pushed, rooting myself in place.

He sighed and looked at the ground. "The first is that you're a baby rogue that Levi is trying to save. Some people think when you turn you'll lose it—be a danger to the pack. There are whispers about you being moon-blood—which honestly is why I snooped. It's like, unbelievable."

"It's all pretty wild," I murmured.

His eyes snapped to mine. They grew wide, like he finally understood a mistake. "I'm sorry. I forgot . . . this must really fucking suck."

A laugh escaped my lips. I nodded. "Yeah, this is all not what I had in mind."

He gave me a small smile. "People like to talk. They'll get past it. Honestly, the rogues on our land were the biggest issue."

"I'm sure they were," I replied. "I would rather not run into any again."

His smile fell. "I'm sorry. We haven't heard of any more sightings, if it makes you feel better."

"It doesn't, but that's good," I admitted. I sighed and looked over my shoulder. "I should get back. You should go before Levi comes looking for me."

"Shit, you're right," he agreed.

He pushed off the tree and slowly walked toward me, his hand extended. "I'm Liam."

He paused in front of me, his eyes watching my hand meet his.

"I'm Charlotte," I answered, shaking his hand. "You're Lander's youngest son?"

He rolled his eyes. "No, that would be my brother. I'm the oldest. Wise and well aged at twenty-one years if I do say so myself."

A laugh danced out of my lips. "Enjoy your youth while you can."

His smiled, dimples showing. "Let me know if you need anything," he told me as he stepped away.

"How would I do that?" I asked.

He tossed his hands up. "I don't know. Put a candle in your window or something?"

"Is this an excuse to watch me in my room again?"

He rolled his eyes in a way that, for a moment, made him look like Levi must have in his younger years. "You're never going to let that go."

I arched a brow. "Nope."

"Well, wild one, you can't leave something where your two mother hens will find it."

I narrowed my gaze, only to find his playfully narrowing at mine. "Fine," I grumbled. "I'm keeping my blinds shut."

"Fine," he teased back. "What is your S.O.S. object going to be?"

I shrugged. "Who knows? We'll see what I dig up."

He nodded, pausing in front of the brush. "So, can we hang out again?"

"Tomorrow is the next full—" I shrugged. "Let's see if I make it first."

He nodded, a grim look on his face. "I hope you do."

"I hope I do too," I answered, stepping back toward the path.

He was gone in a flash. I heard the snapping of twigs and crunching of leaves echoing as he blazed through the forest.

The breath I felt like I was holding escaped my lungs. I leaned back against a tree, looking at the spot where the boy with blazing silver eyes had smiled at me and for a moment had made everything feel like it was going to be slightly better.

But I knew better than to trust sweet smiles and pretty eyes. That had only got me a black eye of my own.

When I made it back to the house, Levi was gone but Derek was in the house working on bread rolls. He paused to smile at me. "How was the run?"

"Fine, not too muddy," I answered.

"You were out for a while," Derek said.

I nodded. "It felt good to run."

Derek smiled as the lights started to flicker. The hair on my arms stood upright as the lights went off entirely. Derek groaned. "I'll get some candles. Levi will have to see about the generator. The house," he said as we walked to the cellar, "is solar powered. Panels on the roof. But every now and then we have a shortage. Go on and change clothes. I'll start a fire."

Derek tossed me a flashlight that I took to my room. Before even changing my clothes I closed the blinds tight, double-checking them to make sure no cracks could allow my new friend to spy on me. I found myself laughing at the notion while my cheeks heated, a feeling I hadn't felt in so long.

Immediately, I banished the feeling. I didn't need that right now. I didn't need another man to control me and leave his mark on me like the last one had.

After I changed, I came out and Derek whisked me to the kitchen to help him finish the rolls. "Is it frothy?" I asked as I eyed the yeast in the water. Derek said it had to be frothy, although I wasn't sure if this muted brown was what we were going for. It was hard to tell, even with all the light from the candles Derek had littered around the kitchen.

Derek looked over his shoulder. "Almost there—" He paused as his phone vibrated. He reached for it, and I found my own heart twisting. It had been weeks since I'd talked to Nate. If it wasn't for my dreams, I would have forgotten what his voice sounded like. I don't know why that thought made me sad. I couldn't be sure what part of me wanted to hear his voice again. I hated that part of me.

Derek's laughter broke my trance. I looked over at him as he typed away on his phone. He put it down then caught me looking back at him. "Sorry, my mate, Elliot, finds the best GIFs."

"Your mate?"

"Husband, partner, soul mate—"

"Soul mate?"

"Oh my, we are going to have to have the talk."

"The talk?"

"Do you want some wine?"

My mouth was hanging open, so Derek took that as a

yes. I kept cutting the rolls out of the dough we had made in a batch earlier, while he dug around in a cabinet. "So, you know how we're on pack lands?"

"Yes?"

"Well, wolves, similar to vampires, are very bond-oriented creatures."

"Bond what?"

Derek chuckled and set a bottle of merlot on the counter. "A pack isn't just important to a wolf because of the resources or protection it provides, but because wolves inherently feel a bond to the pack—like a kinsmanship. It's like being on a team, so to speak," he explained, while he fished out some glasses.

"And vampires are that way?" I asked as I cut out another roll from the dough.

He wiggled his head back and forth as he poured the wine into the glasses. "We have covens and not packs. But the bonds we feel toward each other are quite strong."

"Okay, so a pack bond is like an automatic loyalty or draw to a group of people."

"Pretty much," he said as he put the cork back in the bottle. "But mates are probably the most important bond you have besides the one you have with your inner beast. Neither of our kinds would have made it very far without mates."

"Okay . . ."

"Your mate," he said while I dried my hands off, "is your other half. The other half of your soul."

I reached for my glass as my inner voice started laughing. "Your soul? Really?"

Derek looked over at the fire. His eyes glowed slightly,

almost an amber in the brown. I'd never really thought Derek looked like a monster before now, in the dark, when you could see how unnatural his pale skin was and how hungry his eyes with the flames dancing in them looked. "You can't live without them, literally. Not like you would want to. They help to tame your demons. In your case, a beast, and you theirs. It's fate in its purest form."

"You can't live without them?" I asked. "Really?" In the back of my mind I could hear Nate snickering at the idea while also subtly asking me what I would do without him.

Derek turned slightly to me while I cut away the last bits of dough to make the rolls. His face was more serious than I had seen, a seriousness that made me pause in my task. I'd never noticed how sharp his cheekbones were before or how his pupils would expand and contract in an animalistic nature of their own. "If a wolf loses its mate, then it's very serious. Wolves, like vampires, mate for life. So when they die, it's like half of you is ripped away. Like a quilt that's had all the stitching torn out. Without them, a wolf's mind can go mad and their body can start to quit. They go rogue. Similar for us. It's incredibly rare that a wolf makes it without their mate."

"That is insane," I replied as I wiped my hands off. It was rare that animals mated for life—hell, humans half of the time went through one-point-five husbands before they found the right one. "Just one. You just get one?"

He nodded. "Just one. Of course, you can mate with another wolf if you want. But you only get one true mate. It's very hard to find your true mate. Some Weres and vampires never find their true mates, some find them early on. So many of them settle down with someone they have a connection with. It's still healthy and keeps your beast at peace. But they are not the other half of your soul. You'll always feel that missing until you find your true mate."

"And you find these people how?"

"Usually you smell them," Derek said with a softness in his voice. It was so soft though, so unnatural. He turned, and the light from the candle danced along his skin, creating an alluring honeypot for flies to become trapped in. "For us, it's the smell of their blood, but for wolves it's usually their scent."

I leaned back against the counter and took a long sip of wine, unease filling me from the conversation. "And Elliot?" I asked him.

His cheeks started to blush, making him look more human and less vicious. "We've been together almost three hundred years. Well, two hundred and fifty-three, but close enough. We're very lucky we found each other."

I started to laugh because it was so crazy to think that Derek had been around for that long. "Can I see a picture?"

"'Course," Derek said proudly. He reached into his pocket and pulled out his iPhone and scrolled a bit before handing it to me.

The man was devilishly attractive. He was probably the best-looking redhead that I had ever seen. His hair was bright red, not orange, not fake, but bright natural red. In the picture, it looked like they were in a photo booth. Derek was laughing hard at something and Elliot was doing a monkey face. I laughed at the sight. "Can I?"

"Sure, I keep all the naked pictures somewhere else," Derek teased.

I felt my cheeks redden while Derek just chuckled. I shook my head as I scrolled to the next picture. They were in the car taking a selfie. Derek was in the driver's seat, in a chambray shirt and Ray-Bans, while Elliot, who was taking the photo, had his aviators pulled up on top of his head. He had bright-green eyes and tons of freckles covering his pale skin. He had defined cheeks like Derek, but there was something almost regal about him.

"He looks wonderful," I said.

"He is."

I handed Derek his phone back and started to put the rolls we were baking on a cookie sheet. "He's doing research on some species of birds a few hours north of here, he should be back fairly soon."

"Birds?"

Derek shrugged. "He's a bit of a conservationist. He works for a university right now as a professor but does a lot of research with the conservation groups here. It could be any animal, really. He did a whole study on polar bears not long ago."

"Three hundred years?"

"It has been long and also not long at all," he added. "It's honestly hard to think of how I functioned before without him."

"So does he live here?" I took a sip of my wine.

Derek put the rolls in a drawer under the oven to proof. "When he is not working, yes, he is here with me."

"So. . . but humans don't have soul mates?"

"You don't?" Derek asked with an arched brow. "Clearly fooled me," he added with a chuckle. "Legend says the Moon

Goddess gifted us with mates so we could find our inner peace and thus find peace between our species."

"This Moon Goddess." I paused and moved a bowl to the sink. "She sounds very—"

"Fictional?" I laughed a little with a nod. Derek shrugged. "I guess at times she can seem that way."

I grabbed my glass right as the lights came on. Levi walked inside the house. He was dripping wet and furious. Derek eyed him. "It's wet outside."

"No shit." He walked to the island, opened a drawer, pulled out a dishrag, and started to dry his face off. "What have you two been yapping about?"

"Derek was telling me about mates." I immediately took a sip of wine so I wouldn't have to answer whatever question was coming next.

Levi froze and eyed Derek, who just rolled his eyes and looked back at the fire. He scratched at his neck while Levi muttered something under his breath then stormed into his room. I was opening my mouth to say something but the door slamming made me close it. Derek sighed and looked back at me, his eyes almost black. "There's a blood bag in the refrigerator, mind grabbing it for me?"

# CHAPTER TWELVE

We watched a horrible shark movie on the television while we ate our pizza. Derek and I had decided that it would be fun to have a picnic in the living room. Levi didn't care. He was just happy to be in his recliner. I've never seen anyone that happy to be reunited with a chair.

"So, this time, the full moon—" I paused. "It won't be the same, will it?"

Levi picked up the TV remote and turned the volume down. The shark was circling a girl swimming topless in the ocean. Her friends were on the shore, yelling at her, but she seemed to only have eyes for the surfer with dark hair and wild green eyes in the distance.

"It's going to come sooner," he answered.

"Sooner?" I almost choked on my wine.

Levi turned so he could look at me. "The days are shorter, which means the moon is going to be out earlier."

"But will it be like last time?"

"Somewhat," he replied. "You'll get the fever again before the pain. It's going to be harder, she's close already and she'll want to come out—"

"What if I just let her out?" I asked, the sound of a mother screaming in the background on the television drowning out the sound of rain. My hands rubbed along my thighs as tension filled my joints.

"It will kill you."

"But if—"

The shark had eaten the girl in the movie. Her friends started to walk away like she had never been there in the first place while the green-eyed boy caught a wave, completely oblivious to the red staining the ocean nearby.

I looked back at Levi who was looking right at me. "It takes three moons for a reason. Otherwise it will kill you."

I closed my mouth and nodded. "So hold her back."

He nodded. "Hold her back."

Derek took a seat next to me on the couch. "You'll know when it's too much."

"Can't you give me something for the pain?"

"No," Levi replied into his glass. "You need your mind to be sharp, and those meds will just make you sloppy. Saw a human die badly that way."

My stomach took a slight nosedive at the thought. "And if I don't make it?"

"We all have to die, Charlie girl, all of us," Levi said, and then turned the volume on the television back up, the shark's jaws doing anything but drowning out my worries.

I tried to watch the movie and put it all out of my mind, but nothing was helping. Even as I dozed off to sleep, my nerves filled my slumber and anxiety fueled my dreams. Soon enough, Nate was chasing me through the house into the little bathroom where a man with sickly golden eyes was waiting for me. He smiled, winking at Nate before he reached for me. I turned to Nate for help, but Nate's fangs were dripping with blood.

"I always liked when you ran," he said.

The thunder hammered me out of sleep.

Sweat was pouring over me while rain beat at my window. She was scratching hard at my mind, scratching at dark places both of us longed to rip out. I tried to go back to sleep but it was useless. Instead, I walked to the kitchen to get something to drink, but cold mist pouring through the front door caught my attention.

Levi was sitting outside in a rocking chair, with a bottle in one hand and a cigarette in the other. An ashtray was on a table next to him that looked more ash than tray.

Instead of getting water like I probably should have, I got a coffee mug and walked outside. He eyed my mug then uncapped the bottle of bourbon and poured some into the mug for me. I took a seat in the chair next to him, curling into the cushion while rain fell around us.

"Couldn't sleep?" I asked.

He shook his head, the end of the cigarette lighting up as the other end met his lips. "I haven't slept for years." His eyes were glowing as he looked straight ahead into the forest.

"What was keeping you up so late that you had to ruin my date with this lovely bottle of bourbon?"

Levi looked over at me for a moment, something behind those silver eyes creeping closer, as if it wanted a better look at me. "You're scared. Good. A healthy dose of fear never hurt anyone."

"Do you honestly think I'll make it?"

"I've seen stronger people die. That doesn't mean you will and it doesn't mean you won't."

World's best motivational speaker.

I took a long sip, cringing as the liquor burned my throat. The rain was starting to die down into a steady mist, but the thunder wasn't letting up. "I didn't know you had a nephew."

He side-eyed me then took a sip of bourbon. "How about this?" He flicked the ash off the end of his cigarette into the tray shaped like a salmon next to him. "You can have a question, and I can have a question?" I nodded in agreement.

He took another long drag. "How long were you with him?"

It was my turn to take a long drink. "Around five years."

"Never married?"

My gut twisted bitterly. "No." He was never going to keep that promise, I knew that now. It was just a future he used as a carrot for me, always holding it close enough to seem attainable but never truly in reach.

"That's two. I get two."

"Fine." He threw back his drink and opened the bottle.

I bit my lip. The liquid was giving me the courage to ask

the ones I would have not dared ask in the daylight. "Why does Derek live with you?"

"Long story short, my father saved Derek and Elliot's asses a long time ago. I think he feels like he's paying that back in his own way."

"How long has he been here?"

Levi paused as he poured his bourbon to think. "Eight years, I think. He's always been in the area. Elliot too. Their coven has always had good relations with the pack."

I threw my drink back. Levi laughed at what I assumed was the expression on my face. "So." He swirled his drink around, silver eyes looking over at me like they were trying to pick apart a Jenga tower. "How did you meet him?"

I wanted those memories to die. I hated that I had to repeat them. But what I hated most was how much a small piece of me wanted to hold on to them.

"He was the graduate assistant for a class I was in. I picked up a paper one day—a big midsemester paper—and he was there instead of my professor. He tried to tell me that I would have gotten a better grade if I hadn't had some issues with the structure. Which of course he was wrong about, and I made sure to point it out—"

"I'm sure you did." Levi snickered with a shake of his head, amused.

"After, he asked me out. The rest was history. We were inseparable after that."

I'd had such a crush on him in that class. I remember seeing him, this boy with blond waves and sleepy hazel eyes. We played eye-tag for weeks. I remember wanting it to be him there when I picked up my paper. He didn't just ask me to dinner, it was coffee. Then drinks, then dinner, then it was the two of us between a set of navy sheets. When I woke up to the sight of him smiling sleepily at me, I thought magic in the world was truly alive.

"And what did you do before all of this?"

The happy memory was gone at the sound of his gruff voice. "That's two questions."

"Fine." He rolled his eyes and took another drink.

I mirrored him and leaned back in the chair. "I transcribed notes and did administrative work at his father's law firm."

I had been so devastated. I had majored in journalism and had interviews at reputable magazines, but never received an offer. I had built up my résumé all through college so I would look like that person you had to have, but it had been worthless.

Nate had tried to cheer me up. He already had a job at his father's law firm and got me the position, which was supposed to be temporary. But if you tell yourself that for too long, it becomes devastatingly permanent.

"Is it my turn?"

"Yap."

The light at the end of his cigarette illuminated the tired lines on his face. I took another drink and mustered up some courage. He wasn't the boogeyman, and I wasn't the same girl he'd saved.

"Who do you talk to at the stone columns?"

He continued to stare out at the mist, this tired sadness coming into his eyes. "My brother mostly."

"And why are those there? The columns."

"To keep the pack safe," he admitted quietly.

"From what?"

Levi paused before he looked up. "From me."

I felt frozen in my seat. This thing in the back of my head quieted, as if it was as stunned as I was.

"It wasn't the first time, was it?" he asked.

It was a knife twisting in my gut. Truth ripping open the infection to let it drain. I shook my head. It wasn't the first "accident" or the first time I had been "clumsy."

"You did the right thing."

"Why doesn't it feel that way?" I asked. Because at times it still didn't feel that way. At times I still wished I was lying in his arms.

Levi was looking at the purple irises around the yard that still had droplets of rain on them. They had already started wilting. There wasn't much of them left standing. "It never really does."

"I hate this. I feel—you know, my friends told me in school. They knew something was off, and I didn't listen."

I should have listened. I should have walked away so many times before.

"You got away," he said. "That's all that matters."

I shook my head because when I closed my eyes at night it felt like he was right there. "I wish the nightmares would stop."

He sighed, looking into the night. "Me too."

# CHAPTER THIRTEEN

I didn't sleep the rest of the night. My mind raced all night long with this thing that seemed to be set on keeping me from a normal night's sleep the closer we got to the full moon. Levi had me run longer and chop extra wood, I think so I would calm down, but nothing worked.

He had me swim again as well, and for a while in the water I was able to forget about my impending doom. I found myself walking back to my favorite tree while Levi unpacked the cooler. For some reason, I felt calm being around the tree. My fingers traced a set of initials, *L. L. T.* and *L. B. T.* This thing in me came closer to look, almost as if she was cocking her head in the back of my mind.

"Charlie!"

Levi had sandwiches out with a big bag of salt and cracked black pepper kettle chips. I walked over and dove right into the bag, shoving a mouthful in.

"You look like a damn chipmunk."

I didn't care. I chased down the chips with some water then picked up a turkey sandwich and started to devour it. Leaves that were turning shades of red and orange were starting to fall off the trees. The only trees that stood strong in the fall were the evergreens. Levi told me no winter wind could sway them.

"Well, you're awfully quiet today. Not that I'm complaining."

I leaned back and shrugged. "What if I don't make it?"

"Then you don't make it," he said simply. "We're not invincible. We all have to die one day. You and me included." He took a bite of his sandwich and swallowed it.

"And if I do make it?"

He snickered. "Then you got a whole lot more wood to chop, Charlie girl."

This thing in my brain scratched at me some more but I shook it off. Right now, I didn't want to think about the thing that could very well kill me tonight.

I walked back to the tree one last time before we left. My fingers wandered over the initials again, winding down the lines of the letters *L. L. T.*

I heard the boat shove into the water then a long breath being released. "They're mine."

My fingers froze. My head snapped around. "What?"

"Let's go, you need to rest," he said, walking back into the water of the swollen stream.

She rushed forward with a million other questions, all trying to vomit out of my mouth. I swallowed them, knowing once I saw the look in his eyes that there was no more discussion on the topic. Which was bullshit. Of course he would tell me this today of all days. Probably an easy cop-out for him. Although, if anything, it was reason enough for me to push through tonight; someone had to pester his grumpy ass about this, and I doubted Derek was going to do it.

Derek did, however, feed me until all I could do was fall asleep in my room with the sound of the wind whispering in the background. When I woke up, it was dark. I peeked outside and saw only lonely stars looking back at me. My heart dropped into my stomach while inwardly I cursed myself over and over for sleeping away the last few hours of a day that could very well be my last. I looked out into the night again and spotted something tied to the bush. I looked closer and spotted what seemed like a rabbit's foot—still bloody on top from where it had been torn off the poor animal. But it was definitely the foot of a rabbit. Shaking my head at a gift that had to have come from my new "friend," I stumbled into the kitchen, where Derek had me eat a bowl of stew, but my nerves had me throwing it up in my bathroom before I could even get the third bite down. I tried to splash water on my face to calm down, but my face was already hot.

"Shit," I hissed. It couldn't be happening yet. It was too early.

I turned on my heel and ran into the kitchen. "Derek!"

Levi stepped onto the front porch with a dead white dove in his hand. He let out a sigh and waved me over with his free hand. "Come on."

I approached carefully as he pulled a knife from his pocket. He set the dove down on an end table and unfolded the Swiss Army knife then offered it to me. "We need blood."

"I thought you didn't really believe in this stuff."

"You need all the help you can get."

Reluctantly, I took the knife, then sliced my palm, hissing as the sharp blade drew crimson from my skin. I held my hand over the bowl and squeezed while he slit the neck of the dove then let it hang over the side of the bowl, neck facing the pool of my blood at the bottom so it could bleed out.

A hand touched my forehead. "You're hot." I could feel my own cheeks heat when he said the words. They felt warm and were probably pink. "Go wrap your hand up. Get in the tub."

"Tub?"

"Use Derek's."

I didn't bother to grab a rag. I just walked straight to Derek's bathroom, where he was filling the tub with cold water and ice. "Hey." He breathed out with a smile. "You're going to want to strip. Do you want to wrap that up?"

"It's fine," I mumbled. I peeled my sweatshirt and leggings off, leaving just my sports bra and bikini underwear. I wasn't a fan of being so unclothed. I could feel every blemish, every scar, and every bruise on my body as if they were glowing traffic signs, but I was also burning up. The heat easily won the war with my insecurities.

I was too fucking hot already. Sweat was rolling down the back of my neck and my forehead. I struggled not to pant and to breathe through my nose, but my heart pounding in my chest made that near impossible. "Here." Derek offered me his hand and helped me into the ice bath.

I sat down with a hiss as the frigid water nipped at my skin, but after a moment, I felt some temporary relief. "Holy hell," I groaned, leaning back in the water.

Derek poured a bucket of ice over me. "Thank you," I huffed.

"Lean forward," Derek told me. I complied and felt him slip a bath pillow behind me. "Better, yeah?"

I swallowed as the heat picked up. "It's hot, Derek."

"Do you want more ice?"

I shook my head. The water was cold enough. It stung my skin and I wasn't sure if more ice would be painful or helpful. That and we probably needed to save it for later.

Levi walked in with a chair and dragged it over next to the tub. He put his bottle of scotch down then reached forward to feel my forehead. "Go get the flowers and open the blinds up in here." He looked back at Derek with a wordless expression that sent a chill down my spine.

Derek nodded then zipped out while Levi poured himself a glass. "How bad?"

I shrugged. "Like a bad summer back home. You can cook an egg on the sidewalk sometimes."

He breathed out a laugh. "Is that right?"

I rubbed my eyes but only got salty sweat into them. I could hear Derek fussing in the room while I tried to blink the perspiration out of my eyes. But the hot drops were streaming down my face in tears, almost rendering my vision useless.

Levi picked something up then reached toward my face.

I felt a towel brusquely rub over my eyes and forehead. The sweat was gone for now and my vision cleared. "Thanks."

He reached down again and poured another bucket of ice on me. I gasped and jumped an inch out of the tub. He nodded to me. "You're welcome."

The big window in the bathroom was open. Moonflowers dripped in the blood mixture were hanging from it. There were clouds in front of her—hiding her. This angered the beast. She was clawing at me to see what we both knew was hiding behind the clouds.

Something wet started to draw along the edges of half my face. Levi's eyes were starting to glow, pupils growing wider. "Don't let her out."

He leaned back and wiped his fingers on his jeans. I looked back at the moon as a wave of heat rolled over me. I could feel her pawing at me—scratching harder. I wondered if Nate was watching the moon too. If he was up late smoking his favorite cigarettes with a glass of vodka. I wondered if he was looking at the moon and thinking of me, like I was of him. I wondered if he even cared.

The beast snapped at those thoughts. She snapped, and I jumped again. My head rolled and the clouds moved, curtains unveiling the moon shining brightly in the black sky. Levi's eyes flickered to a steady glow. There was a strange voice in the back of my mind, a howling. It was a song, a sweet serenade that turned into a cry for death or war.

Nate was laughing in the back of my mind now. His laughs were turning to howls, howls that were turning to growls, growls that sounded too real to be my imagination. Were they mine?

I felt someone shaking me, but it was so hot and my mind was so foggy. I couldn't see through it to find my way, but when the fog parted, all I was met with was pain.

It was like her claws were ripping against the inside of my face. A slap to the brain that was blending that place between pain and lucidity. Something cold was thrown on me. Something started to pierce my gums, ripping through the flesh. Levi took another sip from his cup and offered it to me. I snatched it and gulped down as much as I could until I started to choke. Derek was wiping the sweat off my brow when another wave hit me. A wave of needles.

It felt like she was stretching to stand inside my skin. Someone pulled me forward while my legs felt like they were going through a year's worth of growing pains. "Charlotte— Char!" Derek shook me while Levi watched the moon.

He looked back at me, dark pupils bleeding into the silver. "Don't let her out."

I fell back against the tub while every fiber of me tried to reel her in. Yet each time I pulled, she pushed back with a brute force I didn't think possible. Blood-curdling screams were coming from my mouth. My fingers clawed at the tub until something started to pierce my nail beds.

I opened my eyes and looked at my fingers, at the claws that were replacing my nails. I wanted to scream as they kept pushing through my fingers, but the feeling of my arm breaking had me actually screaming my head off. Levi snatched my chin and forced me to look at him. Something behind those silver eyes was pacing back and forth. "I don't want to have to chop my own damn firewood, Charlie girl."

And I was drowning.

I was clawing at the shore in waves of pain. I was trying to pull myself from the tide but it kept dragging me deeper. I blinked, and Derek was pouring ice over me; Levi took another long drink from his cup before he poured more scotch into his glass. The pungent smell of it cut through the fog and pain. I tried to hold on to it when another wave of pain smacked me.

My mother was right next to me.

The car was filling up with cold water and it was dark all around us. She was beating at the windows but nothing was budging. "Charlotte," my mother said as she looked at me. "I'm sorry, Charlotte," she told me, like she knew that it was a lost cause.

"Charlotte!" Derek slapping my cheek brought me back. I opened my mouth but a sharp cry rang through the air as something pierced my gums. He gave me a cold cloth to bite down on as Levi rested his chin on his hands, which were folded in a praying position. I sucked in a deep breath and tried to pull her back. I could feel the way she was inching closer, closer to the moon who kept calling to us from the deepness of a water I didn't want to drown in.

The car was filling up. My mother was looking around her until she found me. She smiled at me and pushed some of my hair back. "You can't let her out, baby. She can't come out."

"Mom?"

"Pull her back!"

I snapped my eyes open to find that Derek had gotten into the tub with me. He was sitting behind me, holding me steady so I wouldn't slip under the water. Levi offered me the bottle again. I shook my head as another wave hit me into darkness.

I was looking at my mother again. The water was up to her neck and she looked like she was praying. I never thought she was that religious, but in that moment, she seemed just like an angel to me.

The beast in me cried at the sight of my mother's last moments. She clawed at my skin and snapped at my hands to move but I was frozen in a frantic fear mixed with paralyzing pain. All I could do was scream. All I could do was cry out as my bones started to ache and my skin started to stretch. I clawed at the bathtub, but nothing was easing the feeling of my body beginning to contort in ways it shouldn't.

"Pull her back, Charlie girl," I heard my mother say.

My head rolled to see her clearly in the calm water. It was at her chin now. She had lifted her head up so she could get the last few breaths of air left in the car. "Pull her back, Charlotte," she pleaded desperately.

Something snapped me back to reality, and I was pulling the beast back as hard as I could. I thought my teeth would shatter from how hard I was grinding them together.

Something kick-started to life in me. Resolve was building and slowly seeping into my veins. I wasn't going to let her win, and I sure as shit wasn't going to die in a fucking bathtub. I closed my eyes and focused, carefully holding her back with everything I had until the prickling on my back stopped and the piercing in my gums felt like it was ceasing.

"That's it—you're doing good, just keep holding her back," I heard Derek say to me.

Levi leaned forward while I pulled harder at her. It was like she was snapping my soul apart, severing the fabric of it in her rebellion. For a moment I thought I had her until another wave hit me. Then I was under the water. I was looking at my mother from outside the car. She was floating with her hair like a halo around her head. Her palm touched the windshield and I found mine reaching out for her. She smiled at me, a few bubbles leaving her mouth before she looked around the dark water and shook her head at me. "You shouldn't be here, Charlotte," she whispered.

"Mom?"

She smiled and shifted away from the windshield. "Go, baby. You shouldn't be here."

Someone was shaking me as I gasped for air. Water splashed around me while Levi pulled me out of the tub. He laid me on the cool tile while pain still hummed through me. It felt like the beast was starting to fall back from her battle.

"I think you're done with the tub."

"I think I am too." I found myself laughing.

He smirked and sat back beside me, then looked at the moon. "Rest while you can," he said before he looked over at me. "It's going to be a long night."

# CHAPTER
# FOURTEEN

Nate was holding my head in his lap. He took a drag of his cigarette, letting bits of simmering ash sprinkle onto my skin. I hissed through my teeth, little fires biting me in the shape of gray wolves. "Wake up, baby," he said, taking another drag.

The beast in me lashed out at him. Claws scratched at his face and drew blood as they peeled back flesh, but Nate only laughed harder.

"I always liked it when you used your nails," he said in a lower voice with a subtle sweetness that was enough to lure anyone into the mouth of his Venus flytrap.

"Charlotte?"

Sweat was beading on my brow when I woke up. I

looked around the room. There was something different about it. Something about the details that stood out. In fact, I was absolutely sure that I could see all the tiny grains in the wood lining the ceiling above me.

The knock on the door made me wince. The sound was too loud, like a drum set right next to the bed.

"Charlotte?"

"Yeah?!" I cringed away from my own voice, which sounded shrill, my head pounding from the visual overstimulation.

A rush of air flew into the room. A melody of scents poured in and serenaded my nose. "Are you all right?"

All the layers of scents were shoving their way down my throat. I leaned my head against the cold window but it wasn't settling my racing heart down. "I don't know."

Derek walked over to me. He smelled like a strange coppery iron mix—like blood. "Are you hungry?" he asked.

"How long was I out?" I wasn't sure if I could stomach anything right now.

"Two days." I doubted that. It felt like I had barely slept.

The sensory overload was making it hard to hear my own thoughts. There were too many smells in the air. Too much sound. Too many details for my eyes to take in. Everything was too fucking much.

"Come on, you'll feel better once you walk around." I also doubted that. I wanted to curl into a ball in my bed, close my eyes, and pray that the pounding in my head would cease.

Derek was rambling off something when we walked into the kitchen. A man with bright-red hair and a face full of freckles across his cheeks set his coffee mug down and smiled at me. "You must be Charlotte?"

I put my hand over my mouth. The coppery smell pouring off him was a sucker punch to the gut. "I—I—"

Somehow, I stumbled outside. At first the cold air felt like it was calming my body down, but when the scent of the rosebushes hit me, it was all over. Whatever had been in my stomach was quickly disposed of on the pungent flowers.

A hand was on my back, then another was easily pulling me backward. "Here." Derek held out some kind of weed. It smelled like peppermint. "It will help your stomach, just chew on it. There's plenty more. It's just going to take some getting used to."

I shoved the mint into my mouth. "My head won't stop spinning," I told him weakly.

He pushed some of my hair back and looked me over again with a sigh. "You can lie down again, but I really think moving around will be best."

The mint calmed my stomach, but the beast was running in circles in my mind. So vivid, so close—too damn close—as she took in the earthy scent that I never realized he carried. Pure with a power of its own that wielded authority and demanded attention. I stumbled back and tried to steady myself against the support beam.

She was strong. A strength that scared the shit out of me. Because I wasn't sure if I had the strength to hold my own if she wanted to lose it. If she wanted to turn us into the monster that had started this whole thing.

Levi stopped at the end of the steps and looked at me. "How do you feel?"

"Is this normal?" I heaved.

He rolled his eyes with a nod. "Welcome to the world of becoming a werewolf. You should eat something. You'll feel better."

"He's right. He threw up on his father's shoes the morning scent came to him," Derek added. Levi narrowed his eyes with a low growl. "Perhaps some toast? Something easy on your stomach?"

"I don't know if I'll keep it down."

"Let's try?"

I let him help me back inside the house. My body ached worse than it had the last time, and this time I had her running around in my brain like she was on a hamster wheel.

Derek helped me sit then zipped into the kitchen. A hot cup of coffee was set in front of me. The redhead took his seat next to me. "Derek said you like cream and sugar. I'm Elliot," he said with a soft smile.

"Right . . ." Something in me made me shift away from the new man. Something she snapped at, and when she did, it felt like she was snapping a nerve in my brain. I felt something pulse over me as my chest vibrated; vomit started to crawl back up my throat.

"It will calm," Levi said, sitting down in his normal seat with a cup of black coffee in hand.

She was watching Elliot. She crept so close that I thought she would walk out of my eyeballs. She wasn't sure of this new male. I wasn't sure of anything other than that the coffee smelled like the coffee beans were crying from being roasted for too long. My fingers dug into the table; I needed to hold on to something. I felt like my brain was a small boat in the middle of a storm that was having too much fun tossing the dinky ship around.

"Charlie girl."

His nickname for me made her still. Made my mind still. I found myself looking into his silver eyes. The animal behind them was more evident than it had been before. He cocked his head and watched me while I watched this thing behind his eyes. I felt something in me sizzle—a current that rolled outward from my chest until it danced right through my fingers.

Levi sighed, as if he was looking at a giant pile of wood that he had to chop alone.

Elliot wiped his mouth with his napkin, then stood up from his chair. "I think I'll go hunting," he announced.

Derek set a plate of eggs and some toast in front of me. "You sure?"

"Yeah, I can run into The Hole later as well, pick up some supplies."

I eyed the plate. "No bacon?"

Elliot bit back a laugh and pecked Derek on the cheek then zipped out of the house. Levi just laughed under his breath. "Little shit."

"So, this is normal?" I asked. I slowly cut into the eggs, the smell of them surprisingly stirring my appetite.

"Yap."

"Is it always this way?"

"Forever and ever," he replied, eyes going to his crossword puzzle.

Derek's tongs set some bacon on my plate. He zipped to the kitchen then zipped back to take a seat next to me. "I hope you won't mind Elliot. He came in last night. Surprised me—"

"It's fine." It would be fine. He was Derek's mate; I had no reason to dislike him. He wasn't Nate. I just needed to meet him again when I wasn't puking my brains out.

"Well, you made it."

The realization still hadn't hit me. Part of me, a good part, thought I'd drowned with my mother in her car.

I think I was more afraid now of the part of me that had made it out of that water.

"I can't believe it."

"Only a few more weeks," Derek replied, his smile too fucking perfect. I never realized how easy his fangs were to spot. "I think I'm putting my money on you. Eh, Levi?"

Levi looked up from his crossword. "We still have a lot of work to do."

I swallowed my coffee. "I know."

He nodded, a tired look in his eyes. "You did well," he added, this strange gentleness to him that had both the beast and me cocking our heads. He got up from the table and walked to the front door, pausing to look back at us. "Just rest today. You're useless as much as you're puking."

"No shit," I grumbled.

"How does she feel?" he asked.

My eyes met his and I knew *exactly* what it was that he was asking. The problem was, I had no idea how to answer him. That thought in itself scared the living shit out of me.

"I don't know."

Levi held my gaze with a slow nod. "We have a lot of work to do then."

• • •

For the next few days I wasn't useful at all. It took that many days for every sound in the house to stop sounding like a clap of thunder and for the nausea to leave.

But she was still there, running around in my mind every second of the day and night. Levi said she would calm down, but I couldn't see how. When I had called Yulanda to check in I thought she would leap out of my skull. It was like my excitement to hear from Yulanda had spread to this beast in me, becoming *her* excitement that was all too real.

Poor Yulanda. I had to lie to her and tell her I was hungover from a late night out. "Honestly, Charlotte, you should get out more! You know, have a good time. Let your hair down!"

"I feel like you should be advocating the opposite?"

She just laughed gently on the other side of the line. "Absolutely not. You deserve to enjoy your life."

"Well, I will see what I can do."

"Have you heard from *him*?"

I hadn't heard from Nate, but there was no way for me to. I didn't have my old phone, and there was no way Nate could find this place, not in the fortress of magic and wolves. There was something about that fact that didn't sit well with me. The beast in me was glad, a good part of me was glad, but there also was another part of me that wanted to hear his voice just one last time.

"No. Have you?" I asked.

"No," she replied. I bit my lip as my mind raced. "Charlotte? Why? What's wrong?"

"He sent someone up here for me."

"What? Why didn't you say something?"

"I never saw him, someone else did—they saw him at a store where he was asking questions. No one confirmed it . . . he hasn't sent anyone after you, right?"

"He'd have to get through my husband and brother before they'd be able to touch a hair on my head," she spat. "Little fucker—so what are you going to do? Do you need to go somewhere else?"

I shook my head. Like I could go anywhere else. "No, I don't. I'm safe here. They never found anything and he doesn't know. We're hoping that the guy he sent thinks it's a dead end."

"If you need to leave again—"

"Yulanda, you're sure he didn't know about your brother's place?" I found myself asking, a boldness taking over me.

She sighed. "I never said a fucking thing, but you know him. He has his connections. It wouldn't be hard to find out, if he really wanted to, that my brother has property here. That's public record."

I leaned back and rubbed my temples. She was right. It was public record. We were just hoping it was such a crazy idea that he would never think it would be something I'd do. He must be getting desperate.

"Okay." I swallowed down my anxiety. There was no use letting that eat me up. "I'll lay low and let you know if anything else comes up."

"If you need to run again—"

"I'm done running." I sucked in a breath, my fist clenching. "I'm tired of running. So damn tired."

She let out a long sigh. "Then be careful, Charlotte."

"I will," I promised.

"Good," she said, yawning.

"Well, I need to go. A nap is required before the husband decides to grace me with his presence."

"Fighting again?"

"Hardly." She laughed. "You're sure you don't need money?"

"No," I said with a shake of my head. Money wasn't going to do me any good out here. "No, I really am all right. Shirley is wonderful, I'll probably start looking for a job soon."

"Well, let me know. We can always ask around for you. You know, people do so much work on computers now—we could see if someone could hire you remotely?"

"Yeah, actually," I mused. If I made it, I would need a job. I couldn't mooch off Levi and Derek. "Look, I'm not in a rush. Please don't burden yourself."

"I'll ask around my friends—see if anyone has anything. We'll keep it low key. It would be good for you to have a little extra in case you needed to get out."

"Thank you." The extra money would be good, but I wasn't getting out again. At least, not because of Nate.

"It's nothing. Now, try to get some rest and keep misbehaving for me?"

"I'll try." I laughed.

"Talk soon." She chuckled before we said our good-byes, but this time when I hung up the phone, I felt the beast in me churn. I certainly didn't want it to be the last time; it felt like she didn't either.

"Charlotte!"

I groaned at the sound of Levi's voice. "Yes?"

"Get out here! There's wood to chop!"

Levi had me chopping wood as soon as the smell of the rosebushes didn't have me puking. Derek was right. Being outside, moving around, did make all of it better.

I was lost in my chopping for what felt like hours when something behind a few cords of unchopped logs caught my eye. I paused and looked past one of the stone columns and saw the bushes move as a familiar set of eyes peered at me through them. I arched a brow as they backed out of sight behind the thickness of the limbs.

I gripped the axe and walked around the pile. The beast in me ran forward, my body buzzing with energy as I quietly crept over the grass and to the stone column.

I looked around and only saw a quiet, lonely forest staring back at me. As I licked my lips, my fingers impatiently tapped the axe and the hair on the back of my neck stood. I looked again, until I heard a whistle.

My head snapped around to see a familiar head of white hair and silver eyes smiling at me.

"Liam!" I hissed. I dropped the axe and jogged into the forest, looking over my shoulder for any sign of Derek or Levi.

"I knew that rabbit's foot was good luck." He snickered. "Fucking called it."

"Levi is going to kill you if he sees you," I hissed, ducking around a tree to where it felt like we were somewhat out of sight.

He waved me off. "Please, he'd have to catch me first," he answered with a cheeky smile. "You can totally thank me for the rabbit's foot later."

"That was you?"

"Duh, I even got you a fresh one."

"You're such a good friend," I drawled.

His smile widened. "The best. How do you feel?"

I paused as the beast in me crept forward. She cocked her head as a feeling of electricity started to sing in me; it crackled like fireworks through my veins all the way to the tips of my fingers and toes.

Liam cocked his head. "You really are moon-blood, aren't you?" he asked, a pulse rushing off him as well.

"You are too?" I answered, the breath caught in my throat.

He shrugged. "It's a family thing I think?"

I licked my lips and let out a long breath, trying to calm myself down. "Sorry, it's—this time was a lot."

He nodded. "Yeah, it's really overwhelming at first. I was sick for days."

"Really?!"

"Yeah," he said with a breathy laugh. "Literally could not keep any food down. It was awful."

I leaned against a tree as a smile caught my lips. "I thought it was me. I thought I was losing it," I added. His eyes quickly lost their playfulness. I opened my mouth and closed it quickly, inwardly cursing myself for saying something that would probably have the whole pack thinking that I really was about to go rogue. "I don't know. Okay? I—it's a lot. It's been a lot."

He gave me a reassuring smile. "It felt like he was everywhere at first. Like I couldn't just think. Everything was loud. Everything—it was sensory overload. I felt like I couldn't hear myself think for days."

"Yeah—there's a lot of that." I sighed as my brain thought back to what I had done to the poor rosebushes.

Liam ran his fingers through his hair. "Look, you look pretty damn normal to me. Honestly, I told the guys that if you were going to go rogue that you would show signs after this turn."

"And your diagnosis, doctor?"

His cheeky smile gleamed at me. "You seem pretty normal to me. Other than you smell weird."

"What?!"

His smile widened more. "Obviously kidding." He shrugged. "You're starting to smell like one of us. Rogues typically smell sick. Like a dying corpse."

"Doesn't mean it can't happen."

"True," he agreed. "Would be a huge bummer. I would still be your friend even if you were a rogue pain in my ass."

"God, I am so lucky."

"You really are," he agreed with a laugh. He stepped back and walked to another bush. "By the way, because I am the best, I brought you something."

I arched a brow. "You got me something?"

He grabbed a basket with a red-and-white checkered cloth over it. "Okay, technically my mom put it together. But I put something in here too. It was obviously my idea."

"Obviously." I laughed.

He handed it to me, fingers brushing mine and drawing a blush to my cheeks. I smiled politely.

I tried to push the blush back. As he diverted his gaze, I turned mine to the basket. Carefully, I peeked under the cloth to see clothing folded neatly on top.

"They're shifters," he told me. I put the cloth down and looked at him. "They shift with you so you're not totally naked when you shift from your human to wolf form."

A flush rolled over me that made me want to puke. "Thank you. You—you didn't have to."

"You're almost pack. It's what we do."

I looked at the clothing again. "How—I mean, I hope no one had to go out of their way?"

"My mom had extra. Dad thought you'd be the same size. If you make it, the witches can make you some more."

"Tell your mother thank you. That—this is too nice of her." I paused as a wry laugh escaped my mouth. "I probably won't even need them."

His gaze narrowed. "Bullshit." He huffed and made an eye-roll that I swore had to be a family trait. "I'll just get more rabbits' feet."

I shook my head and tried to stop the smile from tugging at my lips. "Thank you," I said again. "I better go before Levi notices."

"Yeah, I don't feel like dying today," he mused.

I stepped back and headed toward the pile of wood I had left. "Charlotte!" I heard a whisper cut through the silence of the woods.

Turning around, I paused. Liam rubbed the back of his neck, before backtracking into the woods. "I'm glad you didn't die."

This time, I let the smile win. "Thanks for the rabbit's foot."

He grinned before jogging backward, disappearing into the thick brush like he hadn't even been there to begin with.

Sighing, I headed to the axe I had dropped and picked it up. I walked around the woodpile and immediately smelled Levi. He was walking over, pulling on a sweatshirt but barefoot in his jeans. His eyes were darker. Although they always looked darker now. Or maybe it was the beast I could see behind his eyes?

He looked straight at the basket then let out a long breath through his nose. "Where did you find that?"

"The woods," I answered. Not totally a lie.

His eyes held mine for a moment that had me praying that Liam had made it a good distance from here. He grunted a nod and took out some cigarettes. "Take it to Derek."

Without question, I headed to the house, wondering how many more rabbits' feet I would need to make it through the next full moon.

# CHAPTER
# FIFTEEN

Derek was getting a fire going when I walked in. "Ah, there you are."

"I think Lander left this." It was just a basket, but in my arms, it felt like a bomb. I could still smell Liam on it but prayed that it was only me who noticed.

Carefully, I set it on the counter, then Derek lifted the edges of the cloth and picked around through the things. He set the cloth down, saying nothing, then grabbed a water bottle and turned to me with a smile.

"Listen, I think we should do something about your hair."

"What's wrong with my hair?"

I walked to the fireplace and held out my hands. Curious, I looked around for Elliot. I hadn't seen him much. Part of me wondered if he was just elusive or if he was trying to give me space over the last few days considering that when I had met him, I ended up accidentally vomiting on the bushes because of him. I felt myself flush, the embarrassment of the incident something I knew I'd never live down.

"Well," Derek said while he started to pull the clothes out of the basket, "I mean, unless you like this streaky look? I can trim it too? It's a little choppy."

I rolled my eyes and sighed. "We need dye."

"I sent Elliot into The Hole this morning to get some things, including that. He got a few different colors on my instruction," he said while wiggling his brows. "I think we can mix two and get the color of your roots. If that's what you want?"

"The Hole also has hair dye?"

"It's like a general store but it's friendly to nonhumans and humans alike."

"How do you know?"

"By the color on the doorframe. Yellow is for both humans and nonhumans. Red for nonhumans only, and green for humans only. The Hole has a yellow doorframe."

I nodded slowly as my thoughts drifted back to Elliot. I wanted to get to know Derek's mate better. Derek had been more than kind to me; he had been a key part of me surviving this nightmare. And I had come to realize that he was someone that I truly felt was a friend. A friend whose partner had to be a stellar person if they were with Derek, because knowing Derek, he would never settle for less.

"I'm sorry about earlier this week with him. I feel bad. I just—"

He snorted out a laugh. "Elliot's never caused anyone to vomit upon first sight. I thoroughly enjoyed that." I narrowed my eyes. Derek waved me off. "It's fine, really. Now, come on. Shower off first but don't get your hair wet."

I rolled my eyes. "Fine, then."

"Want something to drink?" he asked while I headed to my bathroom.

"Whatever you're having!" I called back.

After I rinsed off, I walked to Derek's bathroom, where he had set bowls up on the counter along with two steaming mugs.

"Ready?"

He pulled some gloves on then reached for a trash bag he also had on the corner. "Planning to kill someone?" I asked.

"Not today." His lips turned into a crooked smile while he had me lift my arms so he could pull the trash bag over me. A slit in the top for my head to pop through and two slits on the sides for my arms.

"That one's for you." He motioned his chin to one of the mugs.

"Just coffee?"

"Well, whatever else sounded good," he added, running a brush through my long hair. "Booze and coffee are always a good choice."

I took a long sip then sighed in contentment. He was right. Whatever liquor he'd put in the coffee only drew a sappy smile to my lips. "That's good. Really good."

"See? I told you blood isn't so bad." I spit all the coffee into the sink while Derek roared with laughter.

"Oh—" A growl rolled off me before I started to laugh at myself. "You shithead!"

"Take a seat." He continued to laugh.

I let out a playful huff then sat back down, my not-bloody boozy coffee in hand. Wordlessly, he slathered a brown goop carefully over my head, making sure every strand was coated with it.

"So, Levi never really mentioned Lander before."

"Mmm." He hummed.

"He's never really mentioned the rest of his family before either."

"Have you ever asked him?" I bit my tongue. Derek shook his head with an inquisitive brow. "Like I said, he's not the boogeyman, Charlotte."

"For the most part," I grumbled into my mug.

Derek rolled his eyes and kept on painting my head before wrapping it up in plastic. He pulled the trash bag off me then handed me a towel. "Oh, Char, when did you do that?" His fingers touched the scars on the back of my shoulder.

"It, uh—it was a while ago—" Why was the truth so hard still?

"Am I interrupting?" Elliot said, poking his head out from behind the bathroom door.

Derek dropped the subject to greet his mate with a kiss that was all but chaste.

Elliot pulled away then looked at me. "Hello, again. Feeling better?"

"I'm so sorry," I sputtered. "I—well, I feel—"

He stepped closer to me. "It's fine." He laughed. "I never realized I was that repulsive before."

"You're not," I quickly replied, my cheeks whiplashing into a blush once I realized what I had said. But it wasn't a lie. He had perfect thick red hair secured by a bandana, and a face full of freckles that made him easy to smile at. It also helped that he had on a black shirt that read *Bite Me* under his vest. "I didn't—"

He burst into laughter, clapping his hands after. "And the truth comes out!"

I felt like sticking my head into the sand, then let a laugh fall out of my lips.

"It's a pleasure to meet you when you're not puking." The color drained from my face again when I realized how ridiculous I must have looked with my hair wrapped in plastic and a trash bag over my body. My fingers picked at it nervously while I shook his hand. "Oh, don't worry, I've seen far worse."

"Derek's told me so much about you," I said as he took a seat in the free chair across from me. "I was wondering if I was ever going to meet you."

"You'll be seeing a lot of me." A mischievous grin crept up his lips when he looked back at Derek.

"Well, go on, tell Charlotte what you did," Derek teased.

Elliot shrugged before looking at me. "Well, I don't have classes this semester, which makes things easier," he replied. "But I may have told them that my cousin was having a baby and well, you know, since she's having twins and her husband ran off, she will need quite a bit of help. They gave me family leave, so, considering everything, I thought I should take it."

Derek stared wide-eyed at Elliot before he burst into laughter.

"That's horrible!" I bellowed. "They believed you?!"

"Compulsion, darling. Always works like a charm," he replied deviously as Derek padded over to him, taking a seat on one of his thighs.

Derek pulled the bandana off Elliot's head and pushed some of the hair back with a sigh. "We're going to have to do something about this. It's too damn long."

Elliot rolled his eyes then placed a sweet kiss on Derek's cheek. "Fine, but let's get that condom off her head. Poor thing," he added with a chuckle.

Derek shook his head then slid off Elliott's lap to check out what was happening with my hair. "Looks streak-free," he added before he started to carefully peel the plastic off.

Elliot took a long sip from Derek's mug. "Bloody hell, are you trying to get her drunk so she doesn't realize the back's purple?!"

"What?!"

Elliot almost fell out of the chair laughing. Derek just shook his head and reached for my mug, taking a long sip for himself. "All winter, Charlotte. Do you see what I've been cursed with?"

"Oh, come on now, you love me, darling."

"I do," Derek agreed with a nod. "But you're getting a bloody haircut."

• • •

Elliot was sitting on a barstool at the counter, a perspiring bottle of some local IPA in his hand. He took a long sip then leaned back in his seat.

"Can you believe it?" he asked with a mock glumness. "He maimed me, Charlotte. How could you let him do this to me?"

I rolled my eyes and continued to help Derek with our homemade calzones. Derek tossed a slice of bell pepper at Elliot, which he caught in his mouth. "It could be worse," I offered. My fingers ran through my new short dark locks. "I like this, though."

"Oh, don't I know it," Elliot teased. "And the short looks good on you. You're like a little pixie."

Thunder cracked outside. Rain was dribbling against the windows. Derek left me to continue rolling out the calzone dough while he pulled inside filling from the refrigerator. I looked back at him and froze. The countdown calendar with its tiny red dashes through each day stared back at me. There was only a little over one week left.

Levi walked inside and took his wet jacket off. He stepped out of his boots, nose slightly in the air as his nostrils flared. Elliot arched a brow. "Fun time?" Levi just rolled his eyes. "Come on, Levi, didn't you miss me?"

"It smells like a vampire lovefest in here."

Elliot lazily shrugged. "Sorry, Levi, but you know what they say: absence makes your dick grow harder."

A growl sounded from Levi's chest while both of the vampires roared in laughter. I was trying not to laugh, but once Derek started there was no stopping it. Levi muttered some curses under his breath on his way to his room. "What are we having?!" he called.

"Calzones!" Derek called back.

I was still smiling as Derek's faded. Elliot turned to look at the doorway, brow arched as Lander strolled forward in navy sweatpants and a long gray thermal.

He hovered behind the screen door then waved at Derek. "I heard there were calzones?"

Derek arched a brow. "Lander, long time."

His silver gaze cut to Elliot. "It's only been like two months."

Elliot chuckled and waved him in. "Come on. Levi went to change."

Derek shot Elliot a nervous glance before looking at Lander. "To what do we owe the pleasure?"

"Came to see this one," he said, nodding to Elliot. They grasped hands and quickly hugged before Lander took a step back to look at me. "And check on this one."

"Still in one piece," I told him.

Lander arched a brow and took up the stool across from me. "Are you ready for the next full?"

I was opening my mouth to answer when footsteps stopped my words.

Levi paused at the edge of the kitchen, his gaze shooting directly to Lander. "To what do we owe the pleasure?"

Lander sighed then and tipped his chin toward the counter. "Figured I would stop by for a quick drink."

"Sure did," Levi grumbled before he looked over at me. "Where are your socks?"

I looked at my bare feet and shrugged. Levi rolled his eyes then walked out of the kitchen, curses echoing in his wake.

I rolled my eyes and started to place some pepperoni inside my calzone. Lander looked it over. "You're a real chef there."

"Flattery won't get you anywhere," I shot back.

Levi chuckled as he stepped back into the kitchen. "Here." He chucked a pair of socks at me. I set them down as he walked to the cabinet, eyeing the case of beer on the counter. "Elliot, is that good?"

"Very. Brought another six-pack for you too." Elliot paused and eyed Lander. "What do you want?"

Lander nudged his chin at Levi. "I'll have what he's having."

"There's also wine in a decanter in there," Derek added as he chopped a bell pepper.

Levi held Lander's gaze for a moment before looking at me. "Charlie girl, what are you having?"

I looked over my shoulder, fingers covered in tomato sauce. "Wine, please." Levi nodded and pulled two glasses from the cabinet while I went back to my task.

"So, Elliot, how's the research?" Lander asked.

"Good. A lot of good numbers in the populations. Next year I'm applying for a grant to go farther north so we can do some research on polar bears again."

My brows shot up. "Polar bears?"

Elliot nodded with a warm smile before he turned a playful gaze to Levi. "They can get a bit cranky, like someone else we all know and love."

Levi set a glass of wine next to me, his eyes locking with Elliot's mischievous green ones for a moment before they looked at the socks on the counter then back at my feet. "You don't need to walk about barefoot when it's this cold outside. It's going to dip around zero later."

Inwardly, I felt this thing in me smile. I put on the thick tube socks that were way too big for my feet but were warm, which was nice on the icy wood floors. Levi nodded to me in approval before taking a long sip of his wine.

He handed a glass to Lander, leaning on the edge of the counter. "Are you staying for dinner?"

"Is that an invitation?"

"Why not? The more the merrier," Elliot said with a cheeky grin.

Levi grumbled under his breath and walked back into his room. Lander winked at me playfully then eyed the calzones. "I like extra sausage."

"Then you can get over here and make one," I told him, earning me a loud laugh.

We ended up camping out in the living room and watching some Western Elliot loved on the television, with six different calzones scattered on the coffee table. I helped myself to another gooey slice with fresh pepperoni from a local butcher and ricotta that made my mouth water.

Elliot whispered something to Derek that made him laugh from deep in his belly. I shook my head and went back to my calzone. The sound of their laughter, though, took me to a time when it was just Nate and me on the couch eating Chinese takeout while we watched bad movies so we could make out the whole time.

The beast in me snapped at those memories but I shoved her away. I knew better, but seeing the two vampires together in the kind of love that I thought I knew only made the memories flame to life. Memories of how we used to be.

"Any news at The Hole?" Lander asked.

Elliot stilled. His eyes flickered to me. Levi caught his gaze. He narrowed his silver eyes at Elliot. "She deserves to know," Lander said.

My ears perked up. "Know what?"

Elliot wiped his mouth. "At The Hole—they have a little restaurant there. I was waiting on them to ring me up and heard a man asking about you."

My blood turned cold as ice. "What?"

Elliot sighed then smiled sympathetically. "He was looking for a woman who fits your description. Driving a beat-up 4Runner. Said he was hired by the woman's husband to find her."

The beast in me charged forward. I could barely contain the growl that rolled out of my chest. "What did he look like?" Dear god, had Nate found me?

Elliot leaned back in his chair. "Short bloke, a little pudgy. Balding—had never been in cold weather before," he added with a laugh. "Barely had what could be considered a coat on."

While I felt some relief that it wasn't Nate, that didn't stop the unease from growing in my gut.

Lander wiped his mouth and looked at me. "I already have someone tailing him."

"Why not let Derek or Elliot handle it?" I asked, trying not to sound desperate.

Lander leaned on his forearms. "Well, since this is the second human up here looking for you, we wanted to see if we could figure out a little more as to what your boyfriend—"

"Ex," I snapped. I looked away and at my glass. "He's my ex."

"Has the guy been seen anywhere else?" Derek asked, breaking the silent tension in the room.

"Staff said he had been asking around at other places," Elliot replied. His gaze narrowed. "We're going to have to handle that soon."

"If I die, you can't let him have my body," I found myself saying. "Cremate me. Bury me somewhere out here. Bury me next to the fucking woodpile, but you can't—" My voice cracked. I felt the tears building in my eyes as my fists clenched. "He can't have me again."

"He's not coming near you," Derek stated, his eyes growing dark.

Levi leaned back in his seat, his silver eyes holding mine. "We need to call the attorney. Have him cook some shit up."

Lander took a sip of wine, carefully eyeing his brother. "And what if they want a body?"

Levi shrugged. "Say she fell off a goddamn cliff. We can always have some of your coven go down and compel him."

"I'll volunteer for that," Elliot said with a dark smile.

"Attorney?" I asked.

Lander leaned forward, resting his elbows on his knees. "For humans who turn who had past lives and whatnot, we've had one of the pack attorneys fake their deaths. Car accident, wild animals, drowning—doesn't matter. Usually creates something that explains there not being a body. Either they turn into a missing person who is declared dead after so many years or they're just declared dead. They do that, then they create a brand-new identity for the new were or vamp so they can go out into society, if they need to, without being traced.

"We can't have anything coming back to the pack. All of us, well, we're more or less living on bullshit. I think I've 'died' and had a new identity made a dozen or so times—I've lost count. Keeps the pack safe and keeps you safe."

Levi cleared his throat. "If you don't make it, we'll have the attorney spin something. Bury you somewhere out here. I personally agree that the woodpile would be nice."

I felt a grin pull at my lips. I wiped my eyes with a nod, but it didn't help the uneasy feeling in my stomach. "He won't stop looking," I told Levi. "He won't. He'll send more people up here."

"Winter will be here soon and no one will be able to snoop," Derek pointed out. "Too much snow. All the roads will be closed."

I shook my head because I knew Nate all too well. "He won't stop."

He would not stop until he had the answers he needed, which meant harming anyone who got in his way—including the pack. While I was not technically pack, I wasn't about to let Nate ruin innocent people's lives because of his selfishness.

I wasn't about to let him expose Levi and Derek.

"We'll think of something," Derek said. "You just worry about the next full moon."

"I can go out with the scouts," Elliot offered.

Lander nodded. "Go and compel him. Easy story. Say no one has seen her. Let's see if we can't get them to look elsewhere for her."

"He'll send more people, Levi." I pushed back.

"Let's deal with one bridge at a time," Lander gently responded. "If we can get him to start looking for you in another state, then that buys us enough time to think of something long-term."

I closed my mouth, my heart racing as my beast paced. Elliot looked over at me. "Don't worry, love. I'll send him home. In one piece too," he added with a wink.

I reached for my wine, which wasn't helping my nerves. Wiping my mouth after a long sip, I looked over at Elliot. "Any sign of rogues? Any rumors?" I asked.

Levi went rigid in his chair. Elliot eyed him before looking at me. He shook his head. "No, and if there were, you would know."

"It's a big deal," Derek said. "Like I've told you."

But I knew if there were rumors Derek would try to protect me by not telling me.

Elliot tossed an arm around Derek's shoulders.

Lander shook his head. "Nothing so far. Although they are usually very sick. Very easy to spot. Our neighbors haven't seen anything either."

"But I don't understand . . . the wolves that attacked me. They looked sick but they weren't—they were organized. Planned." I sighed. "It feels like these rogues could hide in plain sight."

Levi's jaw clenched. His hand tightened around his glass.

Lander nodded. "Yes, but after looking into it, we decided they had to be recently rogue. Meaning they weren't that far gone."

"But how did they get that way? They really seemed

normal, minus their eyes. Honestly, Lander, they seemed pretty high functioning to me."

Lander took a longer sip of wine. "I know. I'm still looking into it."

I arched a brow. Levi looked like he was about to burst from his skin while Derek took a convenient sip of his drink.

"One problem at a time," Levi grumbled. He stood up from his recliner, icy eyes looking right at Derek before his wintery gaze was trained on me. "Just worry about not dying first."

I shut my mouth then nodded. There was no use getting worked up over something that may very well not happen.

Derek watched Levi walk back into his room and slam the door before he took another long drink. Elliot looked at his glass then smiled gently. "Another?"

"Yes, please."

"You're drinking more blood."

"All right, Mum," Derek teased, diffusing the atmosphere in the room but reawakening old memories that I wanted to stay dead.

Lander stood up, eyeing the mist coming down outside. "I better head out. My mate is going to be pissed I missed dinner and even more pissed when I tell her I had a calzone."

I stood and walked with Lander to the door. He stepped outside and turned, looking past me first then directly in my eyes. "You're all right?"

"Why wouldn't I be?" He arched a brow. I crossed my arms over my chest. "I am as good as I can be."

He stepped back with a nod. "I'll check back again."

I nodded with a wave, and in an instant Lander was

gone into the darkness of the night and only mist danced on my cheeks. The outline of the waxing moon peeked through the rain clouds, and I found myself finding more comfort in that than the thought of another sunny day.

# CHAPTER SIXTEEN

He would expose the pack. I knew this. I knew if he kept sending people to look for me, that I would be the undoing of the pack.

Nate wouldn't settle until he either had me or a body. No fake death certificate would do, no matter how much Derek wanted me to believe that it would solve things.

I hated how easily my fingers dialed his number into my dingy burner phone. I hated this wine for making me feel bold. I hated the fear that he created in my stomach. And I hated the part of me that missed the way he used to hold me.

But that part of me was quickly stomped out when I thought of Nate anywhere near Derek or Levi. Nate may be human, but his wrath was as vicious as Levi's teeth. They were my friends. The first set of friends I had had in a long time, and I wasn't about to let Nate and his sickening wrath reach them.

He needed to end this hunt. He had to end his hunt. But the little voice in my brain also wanted—hoped—that for the first time in his pretentious-ass life, he would say, "I'm sorry." That, after everything, he would realize how bad he fucked up and finally admit his wrongdoing and respect my wishes by leaving me the hell alone.

There was over a thousand miles between us and still my fingers shook like they used to before he would come home. My heart was raging while a cool sweat brewed on the back of my neck. The phone rang a few times before he picked up—neither of us saying anything.

Outside, it was cold, but I had been smart enough to bring a blanket. The moon was out, watching me. The last thing I wanted was someone else to watch me make another stupid mistake.

"Hello?" The breath I was holding fell out of my lips at the sound of his voice.

"Nate."

"Charlotte?" I had no idea how to reply. Part of me wanted to curse his name and part of me wanted to cut my heart open so he could see the shameful veins that still loved him. "Charlotte, is that you?" he added, a firmness in his voice I knew too well. It was the sting behind the sweet.

"Yes, it's me."

He was silent for too long. I thought he would hang up. I wished he would because in that moment I was much too weak to do it. "I don't know what to even say, Charlotte. What do you want me to say?"

After everything, he had nothing to say? "Is that the best you can do, Nathaniel?"

"I haven't heard from you in weeks and now I get a call from a random number in the middle of the fucking night? Yeah, I have no idea what to say."

"You could say 'I'm sorry,'" I hissed, hoping the anger would hide the sorrow.

"I think we both know that it's a little late for that."

"Fuck you!" The beast churned in me. Hair on my arms started to stand while a small fire crackled to life. "You almost killed me—"

"Charlotte . . ."

"You almost fucking killed me, and you don't think I deserve an apology? Seriously, is that normal for you? Attempted murder, but it's fine, right, Nate?'"

"Is that what this is about? Did you leave just to see if I would care?"

I almost laughed. "You know why I left, Nate."

"Do I, Charlotte? Do you even understand what you did?"

*Not really, no, to be honest.* I was about to turn into a werewolf and still didn't understand what the hell I was getting myself into. But with Nate—oh, I knew exactly what I'd done. I'd left him. An act that, if he had it his way, I'd be marching up to a guillotine for.

I looked up at the moon, which was starting to get heavier in the sky, the glow around it almost calming. "I know damn well why I left, Nate. You do, too, whether you want to admit it or not."

Because I did. He was hammering nails into the coffin holding what little was left of any feelings I had toward the relationship—toward him.

"What do you want? Are you coming back?"

"No," I snapped. "I'm not. And you need to stop looking for me, Nate."

"Then what is this, Charlotte?"

We spent five years together and he couldn't even apologize. Five years and nothing. Our love reduced to the tone of voice that he used when he thought something was a waste of time. I leaned forward in my chair, my body ready to burst. Anger and frustration bubbled in me, nipping at the lid that was starting to come loose around my soul.

"Charlotte?" It was the same tone he had used that night, when I thought it was him who would end me.

"You need to stop looking for me."

He laughed. It grew colder as the wind outside picked up and cut right to my core. "You're a fucking idiot if you think I'm going to let you walk away. If you want to end it, you can come and tell me it's over yourself."

"Don't fucking tempt me," I found myself hissing. My chest vibrated as she snapped her jaw in the back of my mind. I could feel her anger toward Nate, and toward me. I disappointed her. That in itself killed me.

"Baby, just come home." He used the voice that used to work all the time. The same voice that made me step away from the door and back into his arms time and time again.

"I'm not coming home, Nate. You're wasting your father's money."

"Fuck you, Charlotte—"

I hung up the phone.

The peaceful quiet outside was screaming at me—exposing me and stripping me down to the ugly rawness I'd kept hidden. The need to scrub my own skin off returned, as did the feeling of his fingers caressing my shoulder—a gentle reminder that those fingers weren't so gentle.

Snow was starting to fall but I could barely see it through the tears. My throat tightened, and my chest ached.

I'd thought he was going to put a ring on my finger. I'd thought I was going to have his children. How had I put my future so willingly into someone who so easily discarded it?

Was he looking because he actually cared? Did he even worry? Wonder if I was alive or dead in a ditch? Or did he just sit on his ass while his intern blew him, throwing away what we had one orgasm at a time.

My chest squeezed at that last thought. At how pathetic I must have seemed to him. The beast in me snapped at these thoughts, but all I wanted to do was let the familiar tide of pain pull me back out to sea. I shoved her down while the pain in my chest shoved back. Tears fell as I struggled to catch my breath, gasping like a fish out of water.

"Charlotte?"

Elliot walked slowly over to me. I shrank back as shame rolled over me. How long had he been there?

He knelt down so he was eye level with me. "Bit cold out here, yeah?" He rubbed his hands together. "You should come inside."

"Please don't—"

"It's not my business. But I can't let you freeze out here. Sorry, but we have a strict no-freezing policy."

THE BITE

"I—Derek—"

"It's not my business or his," Elliot repeated.

I placed my burner phone in his hand. "I'm sorry."

Elliot tucked it quickly back in his pocket. "Hey, it's okay. Nothing to be sorry for."

"I fucked up," I found myself whispering.

Elliot nodded to himself. "We all fuck up from time to time. If we didn't, well, things would be less interesting. Do you want me to take care of him for you?"

A laugh bubbled through the tears, but one look at Elliot made me suspect that he was semiserious. "No."

"Okay, shite, let's go. It's bloody cold."

• • •

The next morning, I found myself cozied into Levi's chair with a giant quilt tucked around me. Elliot was snoozing on the love seat. I didn't remember getting here, but I did remember that Elliot insisted I warm up by the fire before I went to bed.

I started to wonder if it was going to be this way forever. If I would always be tied to Nate in some way—unable to stay away, even when everything in me screamed not to pick up a fucking phone. I wish I could just erase his number from my mind.

How could he not be sorry? It wasn't like I was a one-night screw. I was important—or at least I thought I was, wasn't I?

He would never let me go. That was the more terrifying

part of it. He would never stop. Not until one of us was dead.

The hairs on the back of my neck rose as the feeling of a steady, pulsing current made its way through me. Turning, I saw Levi leaving his bedroom. He slowed, eyes looking at Elliot before he looked at me. "Get up, we have work to do."

I didn't know if Nate had tried to call me back. I never asked for Elliot to give the burner phone back to me. Part of me wanted to ask; part of me was too ashamed to ask. I knew that right now, it was too dangerous for me to have that phone in my hands again. But another part of me, something that had been buried for a long time, didn't care. That part of me was a fire brewing every day, a dragon with teeth that wanted to rip apart the phone and my memories of him.

While it did scare me, it also was something I was glad for, especially on days like today, when I was sure that Levi was trying to kill me.

"Now go on, hit me. Don't worry about breaking my pretty face."

"Go on, Charlotte, he definitely deserves to have his teeth rearranged." Derek chuckled. He had a juice box in his hand that I was sure had blood in it.

Levi scowled at Derek then looked back at me; clearly his patience was starting to wear thin. "Charlie, hit me."

All I could think about was that night. In my ears, I could hear the sound of Nate's fist meeting my face. There was no calling it an "accident" now. It was there, black and blue on my face, looking back at me the next day.

"Charlie," Levi said, and I could feel the scar on the side of my leg from when I'd "tripped" on Nate's bougie oriental rug and fallen into the corner of an end table with a glass top. He'd told the nurse that I was always so clumsy, especially when I was in a rush.

The scar felt like it was burning on my leg. I wondered how long I would have to lie about it. Even if I made it through this mess, would I ever live to speak my truth?

I shook my head at Levi. "What's the point of this again?"

"So you don't get eaten up by a bunch of wolves," he replied, digging into his pocket for his pack of cigarettes.

"I don't see why—I mean, why not use your words?"

Both Levi and Derek broke out into deep belly laughs. I felt a rumble escape my mouth. The beast inside had not only grown stronger, but more vocal. Apparently, she didn't take this teasing or my discomfort well. She was annoyed with me. It felt like we were always at these strange odds with each other; at a crossroads where I felt torn in two.

"Come on, Charlie," Levi said, a taunt in his eyes even though his words were calm. Nate used to do that. He had a tone he saved for when we were in public that was the red flag for me when I hovered too close to disapproval.

I shook my head, the phone call playing over and over in my mind. "No." With that I walked away.

My throat tightened again as the words *What do you want me to say?* ran through my mind like a bad ringtone.

I stumbled through the forest until I found myself leaning against a tree while treacherous tears tried to fight their way out of my eyes. I was so damn angry at Nate. But I was angrier at myself. I was so much better than calling him— the beast in me agreed—but it was hard to fully believe it when the shame in me still reminded me that I had called him. Why did I have to have so much wine?!

"Charlotte." There was a gentleness to Levi's voice that scared me.

Quickly, I wiped my eyes, hoping he wouldn't notice. "I *don't* want to talk about it."

"Wasn't going to ask," he replied, leaning against a tree a few feet away from me while he took a long drag from his cigarette.

I didn't want to cry in front of him, but I was losing the war with my eyes, and my nose was starting to run. I wiped my face with the edge of my sleeve.

"You're better than this, Charlie girl."

"I don't want to talk about it."

"You sure about that?" My throat clenched, and I felt the ugly crying face coming on. "Charlotte?"

I couldn't answer. I felt myself start to shake. I could feel it coming. I could feel the fear for my life mixed with the painful yearning for a past life that was gone. Levi sighed and dipped his head so he could look me in the eye. "You're going to make a small pond right there if you keep that up."

"Oh! Fuck you!" I growled.

I had no idea what I was shouting, but in three steps he had tossed his cigarette down and was over to me, and in one step I was beating at his iron chest with everything I had. There were things I said that I knew I didn't mean, but I just wanted someone to hurt as bad as I was hurting in the moment. I didn't want to feel alone.

He wasn't hugging me. He was just trying to keep me from hurting myself. Eventually my arms gave out and my knees buckled. He was holding me up before he carefully knelt us down in grass lightly dusted by snow. I was crying against his sweatshirt, sobbing until it was just a mess of whimpers and growls.

He pushed me back and carefully wiped some of the wetness away from my cheeks. "Why did you call him?"

"How did you—"

Shame sucked me into the quicksand. Of course he knew. He always knew. I shook my head but Levi dipped his farther so I couldn't get away from him. "Why did you call him?"

"Because . . ." I hated the answer, the true answer. I hated it but I knew I had to say it; I had to stop lying to myself. "Because I still love him." My shoulders shook as more sobs came. "I fucking hate him too. I wish he would leave me alone. I just—what's wrong with me?"

"A lot," he answered. My head snapped up to look at him, shock dripping over my face, but he just shrugged. "You were with him for a long time, it's reasonable that you feel the way you do. There's nothing wrong about that. He, however, is a real piece of shit."

"Did you hear?" I rushed the words out.

"No, but I could have guessed as much. Man doesn't do what he did without being a real fucking bastard."

I bit back a sob. "He—he didn't even care. He didn't even say sorry! He almost killed me!" My fists clenched over the memory of it. "And he just said, 'Well, what do you want me to say, Charlotte?' Who the fuck—and—how did I—"

"Charlotte, he's a piece of shit." Levi pulled his sweatshirt off, leaving him in a long-sleeved gray T-shirt, then held it open for me. I slipped into it and found myself feeling better. "Sometimes bad shit is going to happen, and you're not always going to be able to tie it in a cute bow and walk away from it."

"Is that what you did?" I asked, instantly regretting the words.

He sighed and eyed me. He wasn't angry or annoyed; if anything, it looked like he got it. Oh, he got it more than Derek ever would. "I've screwed up enough to tell you that you're going to have to find a way to tie your own pretty bow and move on."

"How?"

He shrugged and helped me up. "Figure it out. It's not wrong to still care about him—piece of shit. He sounds like a sniveling bitch." He paused and took another cigarette out, lighting it up, then taking a long drag. "You're not always going to get a clean break."

I wiped my eyes then nodded at him. I could feel the thing in me moving quietly, like she was afraid her footsteps would break the resolve I had left. "I hate this."

He offered me the other end of his cigarette. I shook my head. He sucked on the end of it for a moment, pausing before letting a large cloud out of his nostrils. "I know," he sighed tiredly.

After one last drag he tossed the cigarette down and stomped it out, then cracked his neck. "Now hit me. Come on. Don't forget to do your hand like I showed you, I don't want to deal with a damn broken hand of yours." He watched me while my heart raced. All I could think about were the fists of someone else racing toward me. "You know you're not him. This doesn't make you the same person."

"I don't see why I have to do this."

"I'm not telling you to go around picking fights, but you're going to have to learn to fend for yourself."

"But why do I need my fists to do that?" My voice was hot. This thing in me was scratching at my brain.

"Sometimes you don't," he conceded. "But if you live, you're going to be living in a world of wolves and, at the end of the day, there is a beast inside of them that doesn't always understand pretty words." He shrugged at me. "We're not heathens, but one day some dumb wolf may come at you and you'll have to be able to beat its ass instead of running the other way. You don't run. You start running and you'll never stop."

The beast in me was pawing harder now, almost like she was trying to tell me that she agreed. I sighed in defeat. "Fine." Because he was right. I wasn't going to run from any more monsters.

He rubbed his hands together and rested them at his hips. "Now hit me. Square in the nose."

I closed my eyes and tried to focus on my beast. She was aching to get out, begging for blood. She wanted to prove that we weren't weak. But mostly, she wanted to prove to me that I could trust her. A new energy buzzed through me. I felt my fists tighten. The cold air hummed around me. Before I knew what I was doing, I walked straight to Levi, pulled my arm back, and nailed him right in the nose.

He staggered back, holding a face that was now trickling with blood. Derek gave me a slow clap of applause as he walked up. He leaned against a tree, with a soft smile on his face.

My mouth dropped at the sight of Levi's blood. I wasn't sure if I had royally fucked up or made Levi proud.

"Dammit, that was pretty good for a girl." He cracked his nose back into place as he uttered a string of curses under his breath. My mouth dropped more.

Something fanned the flame in me. "Well, maybe if you practice enough, you could hit like one too."

*Where the hell did that come from?*

Derek covered his mouth to muffle his laughter before he started to slow clap as he walked over with Elliot in tow. "Bravo, Charlotte."

Levi's brows rose high. There was a pleased look on his face, along with traces of what looked like relief. "Well, hell," he grumbled before he walked toward me. "If you can do something good once, you can do it twice. Now do it again."

Almost instinctively, I threw a blow at him, but he leaned out of the way, stepping around me—out of sight. I whipped around to see him standing behind me. A sly smile was on his lips. "Hit me."

I threw another blow, this time with my other fist. He leaned out of the way, moving like he was the wind, out of my line of sight. I turned, punching in the air toward him, but he caught my fist, which looked like a child's wrapped in his hand. He pushed my hand back. I stumbled backward while he slowly stalked around me.

His eyes pulsated with a glow. The beast in him was close. Power radiated off him in waves that made goose bumps run over my skin. I looked at his feet, something in me pushing me to move. I found myself mirroring his motions, not sure if I was doing the right thing, but it was better than being a sitting duck.

The wolf in me was pacing, her animalistic nature

licking through my veins, scratching and snarling to be let out. She was pawing harder now, wanting to come out and play, but I was afraid of letting her get too close. I didn't want to be a monster.

"You're going to have to learn to trust her," Levi told me. "This is what you're going to be. Do you want to spend the rest of your life afraid of yourself?"

"I don't want to go mad."

"That's only going happen if you don't learn to work with her—you have to learn to trust her or she and every other wolf out there will eat your ass up."

She was quiet. It was like she was trying to show me that he was right. That she was on my side. I didn't want to be afraid anymore. I didn't want to be the girl who could be easily discarded.

I didn't want to lose myself again.

My eyes closed, and when they opened, I ran toward him, lunging with a fist aimed at his ribs. I wasn't sure what I was doing, but I was letting this thing in me drive me.

Levi blocked me with ease, hands grabbing me and tossing me across the ground. "Shit," I hissed while clutching my side.

I jumped up. Levi was walking toward me and something crackled to life in me. The feeling of it was addictive; the adrenaline on my tongue mouthwatering.

He stepped toward me but somehow I sidestepped him and threw another blow. He blocked it but almost instinctively I moved my fist out of the way and slammed another into his chin.

*How the hell did I do that?*

He stepped back and stared at me in shock while I stared at my own fists. A deep-rooted nature was taking hold of me. My fingers itched to be thrown again and my toes curled in anticipation.

This beast rumbled inside me but I was too consumed by Levi to be perturbed by the sound rolling off my chest. He stepped toward me and swung. I dodged his fist but when I did, I fell into his trap. A hand reached for me and grabbed me, then tossed me across the grass.

A groan fell out of my mouth along with the air that had been knocked out of my lungs. Something prickly started to poke through the back of my neck, small needles making their way through my skin.

"Get up, Charlie," I heard him say.

A hiss came out of my mouth as the prickling became more painful. It spread down my back and behind my legs. My gums ached while my vision swirled. The clawing was rampant. She pawed at my brain while I tried to seize control of her.

"Charlie?"

A whimper fell out of my mouth. The prickling started to spread through my whole body. I tried to pull her back, but a pain in my abdomen began to swell. I groaned and clawed at the ground, but it was hard to breathe through the pain clouding my senses.

"Charlie!" I couldn't answer him. My gums felt like they were about to explode. The pain in my abdomen wasn't subsiding.

Suddenly, I was flipped onto my back and silver eyes

bored into mine. I tried to catch my breath but it felt like no matter how much air I gulped, it wouldn't be enough.

"Push her back."

"What?" I gasped.

"Push her back," he calmly ordered. Derek cradled my head in his lap, his hands pushing the hair out of my face while Levi held my gaze. "Push her back."

I closed my eyes and retreated to the place where she was. She was angry. She wanted to protect us and show this male that she wasn't going to be so easily tossed around. I felt like I was tearing myself into two. I tried to pull her back but she lashed out angrily at me.

"If you can't work with her, then this shift is going to eat you alive."

I didn't want to let another being rip me apart. I wasn't going to lose my mind, not to this beast.

She was snapping at me again but I shoved her back and pleaded with her. Tried to reason with her. I didn't want to die; I doubted she did either. She was seething. Our time would come when she could have at Levi but right now, we had to worry about living—about surviving.

It felt like we were at an impasse until I pushed her one last time, this time reminding her that I wouldn't stop. If I had to sit here and do this for hours, I would. I didn't want to die. Not when I had worked this hard.

I felt her cock her head at me. It felt like if she could smile, she would have. She stepped back, calming down within me. The prickling in my gums ceased and the pain in my abdomen diminished.

My eyes fluttered open to see both Derek and Levi looking at me like I was about to melt away. A wariness in both of their eyes scared the shit out of me.

I rubbed the sweat off my brow while my heartbeat started to simmer down. A long breath fell out of my lips. "What was that?"

"She got too close," Derek answered.

"What does that mean?"

Levi stood up and brushed his pants off before walking away. He looked back with an eye-roll. "It means nothing."

I blinked. "Nothing?"

Derek helped me up and brushed the backs of my legs off. I winced when he brushed over the side of my hip that had slid across the cold, hard ground.

"We'll get something for that," he told me.

"What—this doesn't mean nothing!" I whisper-hissed to Derek while Levi walked back toward the house.

"Come on, Charlie girl!" he called. "You have wood to chop before it gets dark!"

"You're stronger than you give yourself credit for," Derek added. He turned and zipped ahead to fall into step with Levi.

I didn't know what that meant. I didn't know what kind of strong he was talking about.

Usually when someone said you were strong they meant that you were channeling your inner pop star of the moment with flawless brows and perfectly puckered lips, ready to spit venom on whoever dared subtweet you. Strong women were contoured masks made up of layers of filters, like a puff pastry baked to a crispy perfection. But inside that pastry, it was ugly. It was rotten and broken. But of course, that wasn't for anyone to know, because you were strong, weren't you?

"You all right?" Elliot strode up from the forest. Blood stained his mouth even though it looked like he had tried to wipe it off.

The beast in me snapped with a power that made me jump. She was the strong one. The one who wanted to tear Nate's face off instead of kiss it.

She snapped again, this time at my own monologue of self-deprecation. I wanted to be better for her—for myself. I didn't want to be the wet blanket she would have to drag through this world.

"I didn't tell him," Elliot said quietly.

He didn't have to tell Levi for Levi to know. "I know."

He picked up my hand and looked at the broken skin across my knuckles. Blood was starting to peek through the split pores. "It will heal."

"At least that will."

His eyes snapped to mine before they found scars on my shoulder. The marks that would never fade. "Wolves find scars to be almost like ornaments. The more the merrier. They're going to think you're the fiercest warrior of them all."

I shook my head, my eyes dropping to my feet. "I don't deserve that."

His fingers reached under my chin and tilted my gaze to meet his. "Oh, now, we can't have that. People who survive what you have—you're a fighter, darling. Through and through."

"A fighter who is still fucking scared." I paused with a sigh. "I'm scared, Elliot."

His eyes twinkled as a smile tugged at his lips. "People will tell you to face them, 'conquer them.' They don't have the demons we do. When our monsters come for us, we become the monsters they fear."

I started to shake my head, but Elliot's fingers moved my gaze back to his. "A brave man dances with his demons, a strong man becomes one of them." I let out a long breath, nodding. "I compelled that gent. You're safe, for now," he added, his fingers falling from my chin to give my shoulder a comforting squeeze.

I stepped away with an uneasy feeling. "For now?"

"'Course, my little monster. He thinks you got eaten by a bear. He's going to get a fake report from the authorities next week."

"I don't want to be a monster, Elliot."

His fangs descended while his lips curled into a dark smile. "It's a little late for that, isn't it?"

# CHAPTER
# SEVENTEEN

I couldn't think of anything to use as a signal that would not be suspicious to Derek or Levi, except a small pillow with a bunny stitched onto it, which I thought was poetic, so I put it on my windowsill as soon as the night fell. For hours, I waited; it seemed silly—it could take days for Liam to notice . . . unless he came by regularly. It was a thought I played with, but a hypothesis proven true when I heard clinking on the window.

Peeking around the blinds, I jumped back as small pebbles bounced off the glass. Silver eyes stared at me. I walked back to the window then mouthed, "Hold on," to him.

Sneaking out of the house made me feel like I was in high school again. I half expected to see my mom waiting in the living room with an amused grin on her face, the same one she always had when I created a new way to sneak out the front door.

Instead, it was just silence that breathed back at me. Carefully, I opened the screen door so the rusty hinges would not give me away. I closed the door with what could be considered bomb squad–approved care before darting across the lawn and over to the bushes in front of my room, where familiar silver eyes on a familiar black wolf watched me.

Liam trotted over to me and licked my hand, then turned and darted into the forest. I looked behind me and trotted after him, my eyes able to see surprisingly well in the dark as I curled and turned around trees.

Once we were past the stone columns, he jumped into the air, bones cracking and joints shifting until he was standing in front of me in very human skin. Human skin covered by black tights that did not leave much to the imagination. I looked away while he jogged behind a tree.

"What are you doing?"

"Burrows!" he whispered. "We've got them all over. They have extra clothes. Sometimes supplies." He stepped back out in a matching set of Pepto Bismol–pink sweats that were too short for him. "Sometimes we don't get the best options. We're always pranking each other with horrible clothes."

I covered my mouth, stopping the laugh, and bit back a smile. "I'm glad you saw the rabbit."

"The rabbit is our code now," he answered, taking a seat on the grass.

I walked into the moonlight and sat across from him. "The rabbit knows all."

He snorted a quiet laugh and leaned to the side, resting on his forearms. "So what are we gathered for?"

I shrugged. "I think I needed a friend who isn't Levi. Or Derek. Or Elliot."

"Mother hen driving you up the wall?"

I narrowed my gaze at him.

He shrugged. "Love Derek. Love the guy. Good as gold. Elliot is badass, though. Savage man."

I sighed and picked at the grass. "My ex is looking for me. He sent people up."

"I know." My gaze snapped to his. Liam sighed with an apologetic smile. "I heard Dad talking about it. He sent my friend's mom, our head tracker, to look into it. Sounds like Elliot compelled him?"

I shook my head. "Won't matter. He'll just keep looking." Liam cocked his head. "You know he wouldn't even apologize? He almost fucking killed me and he couldn't even say sorry." I scoffed a laugh. "I had never been to the ER until I met him. I had never dealt with police until I met him. And apparently, it's all my fucking fault."

"You want to kill him?" He shrugged casually. "I know a guy."

"Is his name Elliot?" I laughed.

Liam shook his head. "Death is way too easy for that bastard."

I nodded in agreement. "It is. I just don't want him to send more people here."

"You can't go back."

"I'm never going back," I said, a growl vibrating over my voice.

Liam sucked in a breath and shook his head slowly. "For the record, I never want to piss you off. Your eyes look nuts when you're mad."

"Nuts?"

He nodded. "Like a hurricane or a winter storm on the bay. Nuts, but still pretty."

I bit my lip as a blush crawled over my cheeks. An uneasy feeling settled in my gut. I had no business flirting with Levi's nephew in my current situation. The thought of someone touching me, even Liam, made my skin crawl.

"Charlotte?"

"Sorry," I answered quietly. "My mind wanders."

"I'm sorry," he said.

"For what?" I cocked my head.

"For whatever happened before. Whatever drove you to us. Dad said you were in bad shape." He paused. This time his eyes flickered to the grass. "I'd fucking kill him if I ever saw him."

I shoved back the feelings that felt so enticing yet so dangerous. I looked away then quietly stood up. "I should go."

Liam nodded. "Yeah, not sure if Levi's up. But we'd better not push our luck."

"Not without a rabbit's foot."

Liam jumped up with a big nod. "That's for fucking sure. I'll get you some more before your shift."

"You don't have to."

He tossed his hands up. "We're friends. And you need all the extra luck you can get, wild one."

He wasn't wrong there. "Just try not to decimate the rabbit population."

He stared at me for a moment, opening his mouth before he closed it. His hand went to his hair again, feet backpedaling to the forest.

"Check the woodpile tomorrow," he told me.

I bit my lip with a nod. This time, it was my turn to disappear into the forest.

# CHAPTER EIGHTEEN

There was another basket waiting behind the woodpile. I set the axe down and carefully walked to it. Various jars of herbs and what looked like yoga pants were folded into it. A smile bloomed on my face.

No one was in the forest around me, at least from what I could tell. I took the basket back inside, where Derek and Elliot were making noodles from scratch for lasagna tonight. "This was outside."

Derek wiped his hands on his apron and zipped over to me. He took the basket and peeked under the cloth, which had little blue flowers stitched around the edge.

Elliot winked at me while he cranked the pasta machine. Golden dough came out the other end in thin strips. "Well?"

Elliot asked over his shoulder. "He always makes me do the dirty work."

"Only because you're so good at it," Derek murmured, eyes looking at a piece of stationery before they snapped to me. "More shifters, from Claire. Lander's mate."

"That was really nice," I said, taken aback by the kindness of someone I had never met. She had already sent me a pair of her own. This was too much.

"She even put in a few books for you too."

"We should make an extra pan and send it to her," Elliot suggested.

"I want to help." I leaned against the counter. Derek went back to the ball of dough resting in a snowfall of flour. "She didn't have to do that. She doesn't even know me."

But Liam did. I knew this was his doing.

"Pack looks after its own," Derek replied. "But I am sure that a thank-you note and a pan of this won't hurt either."

"I'm not pack, though."

"Yes, but you're Levi's charge," Elliot added. "Finish chopping?"

I shook my head. "I didn't get to start, I saw that." I motioned my chin at the basket.

"Well, after you finish, help us make this. Elliot is really only good with the noodles," Derek added with a cheeky grin.

"Lots of experience," Elliot replied, a sly smile creeping up his lips.

Derek rolled his eyes. "Cursed, I tell you."

Elliot shrugged innocently. "What? You like my noodles? Or noodle, should I say?"

My cheeks flushed while my feet started to backpedal. "And I have wood to chop."

I turned and headed back to the woodpile that I had come to hate less but that still didn't have me springing out of bed each morning. After I finished with the log pile, I showered before I helped Elliot with the lasagna. He banished Derek to sit and drink his wine while we assembled it. Elliot was apparently an expert lasagna assembler, per his own words, and he let me sneak bites when Derek wasn't looking.

"This is right? Right?"

Elliot looked at where I was smoothing out a ricotta cheese mix of fresh herbs and sharp parmesan cheese. He nodded. "Yeah. Doesn't have to be perfect. Just try to make sure the lumps are gone and all the sides are covered."

"Want another drink?" Derek asked me.

"Trying to get me drunk?"

I wished they would. I didn't want to think about what would come the next day.

Derek rolled his eyes. "We would never entice you to misbehave. Right, Elliot?" he asked, walking to the refrigerator.

"Oh, us?" Elliot said, a dramatic hand flying to his chest. "Never."

Derek shook his head, a coy smile on his lips. Before he opened the refrigerator, he reached for the red marker and marked another day off the calendar. The last day before tomorrow—the full moon.

My fingers froze. Nausea crept in. Elliot gave me a side-hug. Derek smiled softly. "It's going to be fine. Look at you, you've worked so hard—"

"Levi said it may not matter."

"Well, one thing you'll learn is that sometimes, Levi is full of shit," Derek countered sharply. He pulled out the red wine and carried it over to me. "Oh shit—" He zipped back to the refrigerator and pulled out another bottle then shrugged at me. "That one had blood, sorry. Unless you want to try?"

"Nope!"

Elliot laughed as he scooped ricotta off my spatula with a finger. "Hey!"

He shrugged. "A little trouble is always good for you."

Derek poured some more wine into my glass. "You're going to be fine—look, you're going to be fine."

"How do you know?"

"I don't, but if you were a racehorse, I would be putting my money on you."

I went back to my task. Elliot looked at the calendar then picked up his glass and took a long sip. "You know, I think it's going to be a Blood Moon tomorrow. Actually"—he paused and pulled out his phone, scrolling until he nodded to himself—"yup, Blood Moon. I forgot it was that time of the year," he added, eyes looking outside where fresh snow was starting to fall.

He leaned his head in his palm. "It always comes earlier than we anticipate."

"Is that bad?"

"Is what bad?"

"The Blood Moon."

Elliot shrugged. "It's an honor to be able to shift on a moon like that. Lucky, I think. Don't you, love?"

Derek nodded. "You'll be fine," he said, but it felt like he was trying to convince himself more than me.

All night it felt like he was trying to convince himself more than me that I would still be here after tomorrow. He gave me extra helpings of the lasagna bursting with flavors of gooey cheese, sweet tomatoes, and fresh basil that danced around my tongue. He argued that I would need the extra weight for winter. He even made me tiramisu, his mother's recipe. He said it wasn't a special occasion, but to me it felt like the Last Supper.

Levi didn't say much. It seemed like he drank whiskey more than he ate. I tried to ignore it and just focus on myself—on living. But it was hard when the solemnity of the situation shadowed your every step.

There was no sleep at all that night. I tossed and turned while my thoughts ate at me like ants. Eventually, it was too much. The room was hot, my thoughts too constricting, and the sheets too suffocating.

I found myself walking out of my bedroom to the kitchen. The front door was open, but the screen door was closed. Levi was outside drinking and smoking up a storm, while heavy clouds slowly released a light mist into the night sky. Rationality told me to go back to bed, but my gut had me grabbing a coffee mug and blanket then walking outside.

He didn't move or look at me. Then he took a sip from his glass and leaned back in his chair. "Can't sleep?"

"No." I took a seat in a rocking chair on the other side of the small end table where a fish-shaped ashtray was becoming a mountain of gray.

He opened the bottle of Jack Daniel's and poured me a healthy amount. "Well, happy drinking, Charlie girl."

The bottle was almost gone. There was something more rigid than usual about tonight. He threw his glass back so I tried to do the same, but almost choked on it. He grumbled some curses under his breath then poured more whiskey into my mug.

"What do you think?"

"About what?" I asked before I tossed another drink back. Maybe if I drank enough, I would fall into a dreamless sleep where Nate couldn't find me.

"You know what."

"I don't know."

He looked over at me, eyes lightly glowing like the moon. "Yes, you do."

"I don't want to die," I admitted.

He nodded, the pupils pulsating in his eyes. I felt this thing in me crawl forward, making her presence known in the conversation. "She doesn't either."

"She could get me killed."

"She could," he agreed.

He poured some more whiskey into our glasses before he took a long drag of his cigarette. He looked like a dragon blowing smoke out of his mouth, and for a moment I wouldn't have been surprised if there was fire too.

"Did you ever think about running before?"

I sank in my seat. There was no getting out of this. "Question game?" He eyed me then nodded in concession. "Yes, but I never could follow through."

"Why?"

"That's two questions."

"I know."

I took a sip from my mug. "There's a laundry list of reasons to answer that. I was scared, I didn't have a good enough plan, I thought I could make it work—I thought I could fix it. I wanted to fix it, I thought I could help us find the people we once were. I was so stupid."

"You did the right thing."

"Thanks," I replied, my voice smaller than I wanted it to be. "My turn?"

He opened the bottle and poured more whiskey into his glass before reaching across the table and pouring some more into mine. "Yup."

"Do you think I'm going to die?"

He rubbed his tired face. "It's not about what I think."

"Answer me." He looked over at me, face leaning on his palms. "Please."

"I don't know," he told me honestly. "You're a stubborn little shit. I'll give you that."

"At least I have that going for me."

"You do," he added with a dark chuckle. "You do have that."

"I get another question."

"I know." He sighed.

"You rarely mention your brother," I said. He looked over at me from the corner of his eye, almost like he was waiting for the inevitable. "You said last time the columns were to protect the pack from you. Why?" He leaned back and took another long drag. "You—you're an asshole. But you don't seem—"

"Crazy?" He let out a dark chuckle. "Oh, I went crazy. Real good and crazy. Some nights I still do." I didn't open my mouth because I could see he knew that I wasn't backing down from this. If I was going to die tomorrow, then what did I have to lose? "It wasn't safe. I wasn't in control of myself. It was more to protect the pack than me." He took a drink. "It's my turn."

"Okay."

"You never thought about running to any family?"

"There's no one left but my uncle, and I—I was too embarrassed," I admitted. "My uncle, Benji, well, he and Nate never got along. We drifted apart. Benji and me. I mean, I knew he would always be there; it was just hard with Nate. I haven't talked to him in years. I have no idea where he even is these days." I took a long drink from my mug, the whiskey washing away the fear that held back my words. "If I make it, I would like to see him again. He's all the family I have left."

Levi grunted in agreement. He opened the bottle then poured some more whiskey into each of our glasses. The mist was letting up enough for us to see a ghost of the moon behind the clouds.

"My turn?" He nodded. "What happened to you? Why seclude yourself?"

"She died. They died," he answered quietly, almost so quietly I thought I could have imagined that he said it.

I didn't open my mouth. I didn't dare push further while he flicked the ash off his cigarette into the tray. "Do you remember what Derek was talking about the other day, about bonds?"

"Yes," I replied.

He nodded to himself, swirling his whiskey in his glass. "How did I know that you were going to ask me this?"

"Because you know everything?" I tried to tease.

He laughed, almost sadly, then nodded into his glass while he took a drink. "Around eight years ago I told her not to go—my mate," he said, answering the question on my tongue. "She took our son, only nineteen, with her. She'd promised her brother that we would go to this cookout they were having at his pack. I had to stay here. I had things I couldn't get away from with work. I was going to come later. She went ahead with Lucas. That night, when I was supposed to go over there, we were under attack. It was just a few rogues, nothing a few grown wolves couldn't handle. But as soon as we handled them, two more groups just appeared.

"All the packs close to the mountain were attacked that night. We had no idea how bad, they figured out a way to stop us from linking." He tapped his temple. "Communicating. I couldn't hear her calling me. I couldn't hear my son."

He paused. His eyes looked at his mug. My chest was so tight I thought I would shatter with the slightest touch. "Someone finally got a hold of Lander's cell phone. They told him to bring everyone, but it didn't matter. When we got there, it was a fucking bloodbath. They slaughtered men, women, kids. Tore them up like animals," he snarled. "They killed her brother, the head of that pack, his mate, and their oldest son. And they took her from me. They took her, my son, and the baby in her belly."

My hand was over my mouth. What could I even say to that? We both sat there quietly. The mist turned into snow around us. The whiskey unable to relieve the heaviness.

"Levi, I'm so sorry."

"She loved these fucking rosebushes," he murmured. He

nudged his chin behind us. "That's my son's room. His old room."

"What?"

"The one you're in." He took a drag. "I wanted to die. I went crazy. I don't remember the first year after or really much of the one after that. But I guess, as you know, we don't always get what we want in this life."

"I'm sorry," I found myself half whispering.

"Me too," he said before he took a long drag.

"And your initials on the tree . . ."

"Lander's better for the job anyway."

I opened my mouth and closed it. The snowflakes were heavier, and the whiskey enticing me to prod, but I hated seeing him like this.

"Change of subject?"

He let out a sharp laugh. "Please."

I took a long drink, my mind still spinning and half wondering if I would even be able to sleep in my room tonight. "So tomorrow—" He laughed again and looked over at me, brows raised a little higher. "What's the plan?"

"Don't die."

"No shit." I rolled my eyes. "Will it be like last time?"

He poured more whiskey into my cup. "Worse," he answered. "You'll get the fever, like last time, but it's going to be so hot that you're going to want to rip your skin off. Don't do that."

"Right," I replied sardonically.

"And you'll start to shift. Bones will move, things will crack into place. It's not a fast process, takes a long time. We have adrenaline that Elliot was able to get just in case."

"Adrenaline?"

"In case you get close to dying we can shoot you up with some to give you an extra boost."

"Jesus." I let out a hot breath then took a long sip. "Sounds like it's going to be fun."

"Oh, you're going to have a damn ball, Charlie girl."

"How long do you think it will take?"

He wiggled his glass back and forth. "Well, for born wolves, anywhere from four to six hours. It depends. Humans I would say the latter end of that. I wouldn't try to rush it. Too fast and it will kill you, and too slow and it will also kill you."

"So, what—what the hell do I do?"

"Figure out where your Goldilocks is. Work with her—she doesn't want to die, but you have to work with her. You'll know when it's too much and you'll know when you need to push harder." He started to crush his cigarette out. "We have plenty of water, ice, blankets. Tomorrow you need to try and rest, save up your energy."

"Okay." I breathed out.

"Well, that's a damn miracle."

"What?"

"You agreeing with me," he grumbled. He reached for another cigarette.

"If I live, you have to quit smoking."

"What if I told you I liked it?"

"You can't like that. It smells like death."

"Death ain't bad."

"If I live, no more."

He held my gaze, fingers toying with the fresh cigarette.

"Fine." He put it on the table next to his drink. "You should attempt to sleep. You're going to need it."

I was too wired to sleep but he was right, I needed to try. I stood up but almost fell backward. Apparently, I wasn't at Levi's level of whiskey drinking.

"Easy." He walked to me and held out his arms. I tried to push them away and walk on my own, but I almost fell on my ass again.

"I didn't realize that—"

"You're a lightweight?"

Before I could argue he picked me up. I wanted to grumble at him but I let it pass. At the moment, my bladder was more important than arguing with him.

"Levi?"

"Yap?"

"Can you drop me off at the bathroom first?"

"I'm not a damn taxi, Charlotte."

"Please?"

He hissed something of a different language under his breath, then dropped me off at the bathroom. After I was finished, he just picked me up and carried me to my bed, where I scooted under the covers.

My vision was swimming from the alcohol. When he walked away, it looked like he was walking sideways. He returned and put a large glass of water along with a bottle of Advil next to my bed. "Drink this. Take some tonight and tomorrow morning."

My fingers slipped on the lid of the bottle. "How many?" I asked.

He rolled his eyes and opened the bottle for me. He

poured two into my hand. I swallowed the red pills then chased them with the cool water.

"Hey, Levi?"

"Yap?" he replied from over his shoulder.

"Thank you."

He paused at my door, this strange softness about him. "Eve. Her name was Eve."

# CHAPTER NINETEEN

I didn't know if anything had felt more horrible than the hangover I had. It took me almost twenty minutes just to physically get out of bed because I felt like I was either going to throw up right there or have to crawl to the bathroom so I could properly use the porcelain throne to throw up.

I somehow made my way into the kitchen; really, the only reason my legs moved was because they were set on following the faint scent of bacon. Elliot was flipping pancakes, a cup of coffee in his hand, while Derek walked around the porch religiously waving burning sage. Levi was outside draining a doe into a metal bucket on the front lawn. He had it tied at its back feet so it could hang upside down from a thick tree limb. His arms were covered in red, the sight of the crimson making my stomach slightly churn.

"Hangover?" Elliot asked with a sleepy smile, red hair tied back in his usual blue bandana.

"I feel like Levi's wolf ate my brain, regurgitated it, then tried to stick it back in my head." I groaned.

"Sleep?"

He smelled like the woods after a hard rain, which looked like it was coming for us outside. "Will it rain?"

"Probably snow," he mused. "Hungry?"

"A little."

"You should eat." Before I could open my mouth, he had a hand out in front of me with a cup of coffee in it. "Most humans don't make it this far, Charlotte," he said. "Besides, Derek and I need a third person for our Halloween costume. So don't die. It would put a damper on our plans."

A breathless moment passed before laughter erupted between us. Elliot hugged me to him while I wiped my eyes with my free hand.

"Elliot, what have you done?"

"I just told her she couldn't die because we need an extra person for Halloween."

Derek opened his mouth and closed it a few times. "Okay. He's not wrong." He paused while I covered my mouth to stop a laugh mixed with a sob from coming out. "You're going to be fine," he said, zipping over so he could hug me. "Now, we are going to feed you because you're going to eat, dammit."

"Fine, fine." I laughed.

"Where's Levi? Levi—"

"Right here," Levi grumbled. His forearms were covered in blood that was turning the bottom of the sink red. "You're going to burn those." Levi motioned his chin toward the pancakes.

"Dammit!" Elliot hissed. He zipped back to the stove and quickly flipped the pancakes.

I took a seat at the table, taking a long sip of coffee and trying to ease my mind. If I hadn't known any better, it would have been like another normal morning here. In this place that felt more like a home than the one I'd known for years. Than any I'd had before that.

Levi's eyes found mine and in that moment everything became real. It wasn't just an ordinary Sunday morning. It was the day that could be my last. The hourglass of my life turned over, and I was all too aware of how fast the sand was slipping through it.

"How is she today?" Derek asked as he set a plate of what had to be the world's fluffiest pancakes in front of me.

"Quiet." She was both quiet and vivid at the same time, silently moving through my veins like she was already a normal part of my blood.

"We're going to throw some blankets outside and set you up there tonight, so you'll have more room," Levi explained, scrubbing the blood off his arms and into the clean sink.

"We've got plenty of supplies, but if you think we need more I can run out to The Hole again today?" Elliot offered.

Levi nodded. "Double-check, we don't want to run out of ice."

"More ice?" I asked. My fork stabbed nervously at the food on my plate.

"You'll be real glad for it later," Levi replied. "The minute the moon calls for her, she's going to want to run right out."

"Gradually," I said more to myself than to him. A mental note to help me pace myself.

Levi nodded. "Exactly."

"How will I know when it's time to really shift?"

"You'll just know," he answered, his eyes softening. I squirmed in my seat.

"And today?"

"Rest," he replied, drying his hands on a towel. "If she gets restless, we'll figure something out," he added before walking back outside to the deer he had hung up on a low limb, blood draining into a bucket.

Derek smiled, desperately clinging to his facade of calmness. "Movie day?"

I nodded to him then started to work on my pancakes. My appetite drained away like the blood of the deer outside, much like my own calmness throughout the day. A movie was a great idea until it wasn't. Every little thing in the movie seemed to remind me of what was coming, and the beast in me was pacing with a jarring giddiness, stirring so much it gave me a headache.

Thankfully, Levi took me outside to chop some wood. I didn't think I would ever be thankful for that log pile, but it was keeping my mind busy and wearing her out enough so she would stop her incessant pacing, which was a struggle to control the rest of the day. Levi kept me doing small chores to take my mind off things, but nothing worked.

Derek tried to make me eat a light dinner. I forced

myself to get something down, but my nerves gnawed at my stomach. I ended up puking on the rosebushes.

The light from the day waned, the coolness of night turning into a bitter cold with the darkness, but I wasn't cold at all. Elliot had offered me a jacket a few times, but I waved him off. He sat with me while I watched Derek and Levi from the porch as they set up some blankets with coolers next to them in the middle of the lawn. Ice in a large red one and medical supplies in two smaller white ones with extra towels and lamps. Derek also set out bowls of burning herbs—what smelled like sage—around the blankets while Elliot poured a circle of salt around them.

"What was that about?" I asked Derek as he walked to me.

"We can't take risks tonight." He watched as I wiped some hair out of my face. "You want a jacket?"

I shook my head. Levi had a bowl of blood in his hands. We didn't say anything. He handed me the knife, and I cut my palm then squeezed blood out until he told me to stop. I wasn't sure about this Moon Goddess, but I prayed that whatever we could do to please her would work.

Levi got another bowl and tossed some moonflowers in it then started to burn them while Derek dipped his own bouquet into the blood and hung them from the porch. I tugged at my long-sleeved shirt. The clouds hid the moon, but I knew she was there. It was like I could hear her faintly humming to me as the night waned on.

I didn't even realize it was happening until a bead of sweat rolled off my forehead and onto the floor. Derek zipped to me and put a hand to my forehead. "You're hot."

Levi looked up from his task. The look he gave me only made the dread in me surge. "Go change, Charlotte."

Derek followed me into the house then handed me the shifters, yoga pants, and a sports bra that Claire had gifted me. He left me to my dark bedroom, the night sky hidden behind the closed blinds.

I wanted to crawl under the comforter and pretend that this was all a bad dream. I threw the clothes on before I had second thoughts. As I looked in the mirror, I felt my scars laughing at me. All the exposed skin only welcomed an insecurity that I did not need present today.

I shoved those thoughts back and instead walked back to my window and pulled the blinds up. There were three rabbits' feet tied to the bush outside my bedroom window. Three white rabbits' feet cut off right before the knee, still dripping with blood.

A smile tugged at my lips. I wasn't sure what Liam was to me. I knew it would take a lot of time and work on myself before I could stomach someone being intimately close to me again. But he made me want to try—want the option. That was all I wanted: options instead of being pushed into a goddamn corner.

Derek knocked on the door, startling me while I tied my hair back. "Come in." The words stumbled out of my mouth.

He walked in with a sweatshirt in his hands, one I had seen Levi wear. I took it and tried to say something, to say thank you for everything, but only broken words came out. He hugged me then kissed my cheek. "You'll be fine, yeah?"

"Sure," I answered, and slipped the sweatshirt on, letting

out a deep breath as I straightened it and smoothed out wrinkles that weren't really there.

When I walked outside, Levi was waiting on the steps with a bowl of the blood paste in his hands. "Take that off, you won't need it." A droplet of sweat slithered down my neck. I opened my mouth to protest but Levi gave me a look that froze my tongue in place. "There's more important things to worry about right now, all right?"

I took the sweatshirt off and handed it to Derek before I said something to Levi I'd regret. Levi stepped toward me and dipped his fingers in the paste.

"Does this really help?"

"It's supposed to," he answered, drawing the half circle around the edge of my face before he drew strange markings on both of my shoulders. "Go on. Get in the middle of the blankets." I took a step forward, but his hand around my wrist froze. "Don't cross the salt line once you cross over."

"Why?" The look he gave me yanked the breath out of my lungs.

He released my wrist. "Just stay on the blankets. Go on."

*What the fuck?*

I walked to the blankets where the sage practically gagged me. I wanted them to take it away, but I reminded myself that I needed all the help I could get, so I would just have to suck it up.

I sat down and Elliot zipped to me with a water jug in hand. "You'll want to start hydrating."

"Hydration is key," Levi added, pulling a plastic chair inside the ring of salt, a cooler beside him. He reached inside and pulled out a bottle of beer while I tried to get comfortable on the blankets. But the heat was starting to make everything uncomfortable. My skin felt sticky, and the air felt like quicksand sucking me down to the hot core of the earth.

Levi offered me some of his beer. I shook my head and chugged more water.

"Suit yourself."

I wanted to rip the yoga pants off, but I had no desire to be naked in front of three men. Derek handed me a new jug of water. He wiped some of the sweat away while Elliot handed me a new bag of ice.

But the heat rose to a point where the baggies of ice weren't lasting long. Elliot kept trying to get me to drink water, but I could feel it sloshing in my stomach. The heat was making me feel bloated, and I was half afraid that I would pop if I drank any more.

Inside, I could feel her impatiently pacing back and forth under my skin, which felt like it was melting off. I didn't even notice Levi sit next to me. He grabbed a towel and tried to wipe the sweat from my face before he gave up and dumped a bucket of water over me instead.

"Thanks," I panted, sounding more canine than human.

"Here all night, Charlie girl."

"Good." I meant it. I didn't want to do this without him even if I didn't want to admit it to him.

The heat rose. I felt like my blood would start boiling. I could barely see straight—or hear my own thoughts. Derek put more ice around me while Elliot checked my vitals, vigorously writing them down in a black notebook. "You're doing fine," he told me with a soft smile.

Levi dumped another bucket of water on me but nothing worked. It felt like the water just evaporated once it hit my skin.

My fingers clawed at the ground, my mind trying to hold on to thoughts and not this fire burning in me, but it was impossible when my toes felt like hot coals about to combust. Derek had me drink more water but I choked. The panting was rapid now, inhuman. I was trying not to think about it, but the sight of my chest rising and falling like a dog's sent my mind into a frenzy.

"Let's play a game, Charlie girl," Levi said as the vampires got more ice out of the cooler.

He had me rest my head on his thigh so he could wipe sweat out of my eyes and give me water. "Which one?" I huffed out.

"The lying one. You're first."

"Now?"

"Now is as good a time as any."

"Shit." He wiped my brow with a cool cloth while I struggled to think. "She scares me, this shift scares me, and I really hate chopping wood."

He barked out a laugh and dumped a bottle of water over me then leaned back and grabbed another from Elliot. "You love chopping wood and you know it." He held the bottle to my lips so I could gulp it down, moving it away when I started to choke on it.

"You're an asshole!" I coughed, water spitting out with my words.

"Okay." He chuckled. "I actually hate smoking, her mother made that quilt that's lying on your bed, and I think you're going to die, Charlie."

My vision was blurry, but I could still see his silver eyes cut through the blur, the truth in them so evident that it was the only clear thing in my hazy brain. "You don't think I'll die."

"It's not about what I think."

"But it helps." In that moment, it clicked in me. Something raw wrapped its arms around me and shook me furiously until the fog parted. "I don't want to die," I said through the pants. "I'm not going to fucking die."

"Good," he replied with a pleased nod.

I blinked, and when I opened my eyes, I saw the moon. She was red in the sky, full like she had drunk a heavy filling of blood as she looked at me. I could hear Levi saying something to me, but all I could think about was how beautiful she was and how I so badly wanted to touch her.

I blinked again, and this thing in my mind raced forward. Levi wiped my brow. He opened his mouth to say something but was interrupted by my screaming.

My arm had cracked, contorting into a bad Barbie limb. More cracking sounded while she called to me like she was my mother calling me home.

It had begun.

I was shifting.

# CHAPTER TWENTY

It sounded like a rabid animal dying a slow death. Screams were mixed with desperate howls, echoing in the chambers of my brain, burning a memory that I knew would forever haunt me.

The moon was calling to this beast in me, and the beast was desperate to appease her. Everything felt like it was spinning out of control. I couldn't stop myself from answering the moon's demands, and I sure as shit couldn't stop this beast inside me. I realized that Derek was right; we were slaves to the moon.

Cracks.

Sickening sounds originating from random parts of my body. My arm broke again into a position that scared me more than the pain, while my foot felt like someone had taken an iron fresh out of the fire and stabbed it. My gums blazed as fangs angrily ripped through the flesh. Levi rolled up a cold cloth and had me bite on it.

"Morphine?" Derek asked.

Levi shook his head. "She'll be too loopy."

Elliot scribbled something in his notebook. "You're doing fine, Charlotte—"

A wave of cracks rolled over me. It felt like the beast in me was just under my skin, trying to stand up. I was blinking hard, trying to calm myself down, when my leg broke, fracturing slowly like ice shattering in spiderwebs across a frozen lake.

The beast in me was howling for the pain to stop, but one look at my arm made me shake my head. There was no stopping it.

This had to be punishment for the shit mistakes I had made time and time again. Fate was a vengeful bitch. Because this shift was dragging on, and I wasn't sure if I could last for hours in this kind of torment.

Elliot threw a bucket of water on me. The cold felt better, but it was fleeting. Because as soon as I caught sight of the moon again, it was like she was pulling me out with the tide. Another wave, another set of cracks, and I was back to a place where Nate's laughter was dancing around my mind.

It felt like his fists were fracturing each of my vertebrae over and over again. I hunched away from the pain into the only position my back would let me lie in. I felt more cold rags on my body while Nate laughed harder. The beast in me tried to bite him, claw at him, but her actions just made me whimper from the pounding they brought to my brain.

"Look at me. Hey, look at me." Levi's eyes were glowing the brightest I had ever seen them. "We both know you're too goddamned stubborn to let something like this beat your ass."

I gasped for air. "How much longer?"

Levi looked at the sky then down at me. It was the first time I'd seen him unsure of what to say. "Don't worry about that."

Another wave caught her and swept her up in an angry current. She rushed forward, almost like she was about to hurl her way through me. I gritted my teeth and tried to pull her back—tried to save both of us from being caught up in this uncontrollable desire to respond to the moon.

But more cracks came and the fingers on my right hand were like delicate piano keys creaking. I took one look at their new disfigurement and vomited on the grass next to me. Derek wiped my mouth while Levi moved me away from the vomit. Elliot pushed some of my hair back and looked me over. "Well, at least it wasn't because of me?"

I wanted to laugh with him, but the beast clawed at me, yanked at my resolve like he had yanked me around one time. He'd been in the mood, but I hadn't. He was never gentle when he was like that.

She was desperate, snapping at the memory. She clawed at me to get out, the memory of him forcing me over the couch too much for her. She wanted to save me—save us—but this was something that would always be with me. She couldn't save me from the past.

"Stop it!" I pleaded with her. She cocked her head at me,

as if in shock, while I cringed at the memory of his nails digging too deeply into my hips.

The moon pulled us, tugging at the fibers holding my soul together. The beast howled at the sight of her in the sky and yanked at me. She wanted to drag me into the sky because for a moment, I think she thought that the peaceful lure of the moon could save us.

"You're better than that, Charlie girl." I could hear Levi's words dancing around in my head.

She was whimpering in the mess of confusion. She didn't want to fight me but she didn't know what to do with this spell over us. I was trying to reach out to her when another wave came, bringing a blanket of needles with it.

A million of them pierced the skin of my back. I screamed into the wet cloth while Elliot wiped my back with another rag that had turned bloodred by the time that he was done.

"Fur," he murmured to me.

Levi sat next to me, the scent of whiskey invading my nose. He held a glass up to my lips.

I drank it down in two large gulps then let him pour me another glass that I tossed back in one gulp. It burned the whole way down to my stomach, dulling my limbs with the comfort of soft blankets, if only for a short-lived moment before another wave of cracks came.

It felt like Nate had taken one of his fancy cigarettes and welded my ribs into a new constricting position. The spots behind my shoulder from his "accident" burned hotter at the memory. Inwardly, I felt her snap at me in frustration before she snapped at the sound of Nate's laughter growing louder in my brain.

Derek placed a hand on my forehead. "She's burning up, Levi."

A low growl resonated with a vibration next to me. "Get more ice. It's all we can do."

"She's fine. She's doing fine." Elliot's voice was struggling to be calm in the calamity.

Another wave of cracks came.

Nate's hands were working their way up me. She snapped at him while this thing grew between us. A rope tethering me to her. Nate looked at me, hazel eyes laughing before his mouth did. She hated that. She hated him. She jumped at him in the dull memory, her teeth biting toward him. The sound of them clinking together pinballed through my eardrums.

Another wave of cracks.

I knew she hated him for what he had done to me. I hated him for what he had done to me. I hated me for letting him do what he had done to me.

She wanted to protect me, but this wasn't working. This was going to get us killed. This just sent us faster on a merry-go-round gone wrong, where every face I saw was his and the music I heard was the sound of my own screams.

Another wave of cracks.

My face had been shoved into the wall. He loved to play rough. He thought I enjoyed it, too, but this time all the little bones in my face fractured. Rearranging themselves from the impact.

I opened my eyes and his hazel eyes were looking right into mine. He was a black hole, and I was such a fool not to see it. He nipped my lips. His quirked into something vile. "It feels good doesn't it, baby?" he whispered.

"Fuck you!" I spat. His laughing had gone too far.

Another wave of cracks.

Something smacked my cheek then smacked it again. I opened my eyes and Levi was slapping my face, saying something to me in slow, robotic motion. The beast in me was whining, pacing, begging for me to do something.

I could hear Nate whispering to me to just lie down and take the pain.

Another wave of cracks.

I was a dried-up Christmas tree lighting into a frenzied fire. The sea of pain was trying to drown me. It was harder to breathe, my ribs had rearranged more, collapsed, so it sounded like a death wheeze coming out of my mouth. My fingers ached but they weren't really fingers anymore. I screamed my head off as the knives punctured my nails, hands turning into paws and fingers turning into claws. My toes fared no better. But I dared not look at them. I didn't want to vomit again.

She was begging to be let out, pushing harder at the inside of my skin. He watched me from behind the line of salt. He cocked his head and snickered at me before he casually started to walk the salt line. The beast almost lunged at him as he lingered in front of the moon. I yanked her back because it felt like she was about to burst out of my skull.

Something smacked me across the cheek again. I blinked, and Levi was looking right at me. His silver eyes were marinating in anxiety. "You can't fight her."

Another wave of cracks came.

I could hear Levi telling me not to fight her, to work with her. Nate was watching me again with a look that dared me to cross the salt line. She was howling at me and ramming at the inside of my mind to come out. She wanted to show Nate her teeth, but I just wanted his laughing to stop. I just wanted him to stop but he never stopped when I asked him to.

My eyes opened and my mouth gasped for air, while the voices around me all called out my name. Levi was saying something to me again. He tossed cold water on my face, snapping me back to reality. "Stop fighting her," he told me.

"I don't want to die," I wheezed.

"Then let her out."

Another wave of cracks came.

She wanted to jump out right then, but I yanked her back until it was the two of us dancing in the dark. I didn't want to die. I didn't want to keep falling down the black hole that felt darker than Nate's soul.

I couldn't fight her. I knew I couldn't fight her. I didn't want to. She nudged me to move, and in that moment, moving felt like a life raft thrown to me.

Weakly, I rolled to my stomach and let her push me forward while I clawed at the blankets. My legs tried to move behind me while bones shattered with every movement.

The moon looked like a heart pulsing in the sky, and for a moment I swear I thought I could hear it thumping as it drew me closer. A clawed hand reached out and shredded the blanket while it dug into the ground to pull me forward. There was more cracking, but I didn't care. All the pain felt the same now, and I had to keep moving. She pushed me forward because it was either move or die. I hadn't come this far to be eaten up by a fucking fairy tale.

Nate was kneeling down. I took another step, grasping the ground while she coursed through me with an anger that felt too damn good to be real. I took another step, and it wasn't just me stepping, it was me and her—us. With each step it was like she became the breath coming from my lungs and the heartbeat thumping erratically in my chest.

Another wave of cracks.

Black spots came into my vision. Nate was shaking his head at me. "You're a monster, Charlotte," I heard him say.

I felt my tongue lick over my fangs before something ripped through my chest in a vibration that made him stumble back. "I am," I answered. I lunged at him and yanked him down the dark hole, ripping him apart piece by piece as blackness swirled around me.

For a moment I thought I could hear my mother again. For another moment I thought I could hear my father. I was floating in a painless peace that was tempting to stay in, but I wanted to live. My hands clawed at the walls of the blackness, desperate to find something to hold on to so I could pull myself out of the darkness.

It was in that moment that I grabbed something. It felt like a rope that this beast had tossed to me. I could hear Nate screaming at me as he fell down the dark well, but his screams faded as she pulled me closer to the light. She pulled, and with each step she took, it was like our DNA was being sealed together. I reached for her, and I swear I could feel her fur between my fingers while I held on to her with everything I had.

She was intertwined and interwoven with every fragment of my being, and in that moment, I felt our hearts beat as one and our souls seal themselves together. I realized that I could never be without her. She was just as much mine as I was hers. She was my beast, a part of me, as was the blood that ran through my veins. She was the beacon of hope that I never realized I wanted or needed, but right now she was the fire that was keeping us from perishing.

I took one last look at Nate. He was still falling, yelling horrible things at me. The beast snapped at him, but I pushed her back. He wanted retaliation, and he wasn't worth that. She stilled while I tried to pull us out of the darkness. There was one last wave that drew a groan from me. I felt the cool air around me. I prayed that it meant that we were close to the end of this misery.

The pain was dull, but it felt like the tides had calmed around us. Something wet brushed my cheek. I thought Levi was throwing water on me, but it felt rough. I tried to swat it away while my eyes opened.

Someone was stroking my fur. The moon was still ready to bleed out into the sky, but I didn't care. All I could think about was how good the fingers felt running through my fur.

*Fur.*

I raised my head and looked up to see Derek staring down at me with a teary-eyed smile. He opened his mouth a few times before closing it. I felt my brows raise at him, begging him to say something. Elliot was squatting next to Derek. He leaned back with a laugh, then fell back on his ass. "Bloody hell, Charlotte," he said with a shake of his head.

Something nudged my face. A large silvery wolf—Levi.

I moved my head to look at the rest of my body. The paws in front of me were almost black, but the warm brown undertones told me otherwise. I had paws and a tail. I was a wolf. And I wasn't dead.

*I had a fucking tail.*

I was still here. I was alive, in the middle of the salt circle, while the moon's red rays blanketed us in the cool night breeze.

Derek started to laugh. "Try to stand up."

My shaking legs weren't sure what they were supposed to do. Levi moved his head under my belly and helped me lift myself until I was standing at my full height. I wobbled, still unsure of how to use four legs. Levi moved his head away, leaving me on my own while Derek stood beside me with his hands ready to catch me. Elliot just smiled and held his phone up. "Just recording the moment."

My beast and I took a step forward, relishing the feeling of the cool night breeze sweeping through our fur. We took another step on the cool grass, which felt like a pillow under our paws. I took another step, and this strange muscle memory kicked in. I took another step, and it was like breathing.

Levi motioned his head toward the forest, a strange smirk on his snout. He turned then darted into the darkness. Without question, I chased him, instinct kicking me into gear.

Running in this form was even better than in my human form. It was like the energy of the forest was coursing through my blood and driving me to run after the trail of Levi's scent. It smelled like rain about to fall, alongside that feeling you get when a chill sweeps over you. It was a breathless reverence that his aura demanded.

He was waiting patiently for me in a clearing. I trotted to him, taking everything in around me. I didn't think my senses would get better, but I was wrong. The picture my fine-tuned nose and eyes painted was that of a world so much more elegant and magical than the one I once knew.

My ears heard everything. Every breath the forest took. I could hear the flap of the birds' wings before they flew away, I could smell the little squirrels keeping a watchful eye on us, and I could see the rabbits hopping away to the safety of holes hidden to the human eye.

I trotted past Levi straight to the little stream, and my beast practically threw herself in. We heard Levi rustling in some bushes behind us while we gulped down our weight in water.

After she was finished drinking, we turned and found him leaning against a tree in old jeans and a sweatshirt, barefoot on the forest floor. He was staring hard at us. I cocked a brow at him until I felt a pressure in my mind. A stabbing that made my beast whine while we pushed it back.

He rolled his eyes. "Stop fighting it."

He looked at me again, the pressure coming back. Instead of pushing back, we let it pass. At this point, both my beast and I were too tired to fight anything.

A wall fell down in my mind while something electric crackled to life. "*Charlotte?*" Levi's voice said in my mind.

My eyes went wide. I had to be losing it. "*Charlie.*" The gruff voice called in my brain space again.

"*Yeah?*" I answered inwardly, to this new strange mental ether we had now connected.

My mouth hung open. Levi shook his head with a tired laugh.

I wanted to know more about how this telepathy worked,

but all the questions were too much for my tired brain.

"All right," he said out loud. "Shift back. You're exhausted."

I looked down at my paws. I was exhausted; he was right. My wolf didn't want to shift back, but we couldn't deny how tired we were. However, getting back to two legs felt like another mountain to climb over.

Levi just sighed. "Just imagine yourself in your skin."

There was no way it was that easy. I huffed and closed my eyes, trying to imagine myself in my previous form. I felt like a moron. There was no way it was going to be this easy.

A few moments passed. I was sure that Levi was just screwing around with me. I was afraid I would be stuck like this indefinitely, but I focused harder, tugging on something while the image of my two legs came to mind.

The cracking started again, followed by the rippling of my skin. Screams and agonizing groans silenced the forest. I wanted to take a break halfway through it, but Levi wouldn't let me; he sat next to me and kept telling me to push through.

Cold air rushed over my wet cheeks. Calloused hands picked me up from the ground and carried me. Through wet lashes, I could see Levi above me, walking quietly, deep in thought.

"I'm not dead."

"Thought you almost were there for a minute."

"You have to quit smoking."

He rolled his eyes. "Fine."

"I'm not rogue."

Levi let out a long breath. "You're not rogue."

"I'm normal though, right?"

"Charlie girl, there's not much about you that's normal."

"Levi?"

"Mmm?"

"Thank you." I breathed out, a yawn following my words.

He looked down at me with tired silver eyes still glowing as the beast in them came closer to look at me. "For what?"

"For not killing me."

He nodded solemnly and kept walking. "Sleep, Charlie girl, you need it."

# CHAPTER
# TWENTY-ONE

The smell of bacon and coffee woke me from the grave. There were four Advils on the nightstand next to two huge glasses of water. I took the medicine and washed it down with both glasses of water.

Walking proved to be more than a challenge. I had to hold on to the wall for support as I made my way slowly down the hall. The only reason I kept on was the smell of food. My whole body trembled with each step. My muscles spasmed, and my stiff joints had me practically hobbling. My beast grumbled inside me. We both felt like we hadn't eaten in ages.

The beast.

I almost fell when I could feel her moving in me. It was

so natural; the organic way she ingrained herself into me was impossible to deny, yet the innate way she was pulsing through my veins paralyzed me. My eyes fell down to my quivering hands with an inner dread that the cracking would start again. I was so sure, looking at my fingers, that the bones would start to break.

"If you watch it long enough, I heard that sometimes you can grow a sixth finger." Levi lowered his paper enough so I could see the smirk forming on his lips. The dread started to dissipate while annoyance took its place. "How do you feel?"

*Like I fucking clawed myself out of my grave, Levi, thanks for asking.*

"Charlotte?" Derek walked over to me with his signature warm smile and hugged me like I was glass ready to shatter. "Go sit. I'll bring you a plate."

"I can get it."

"You can barely walk without holding on to the wall. Go sit." Begrudgingly, I gave in and shuffled to the table, which seemed much farther from the kitchen than it usually did.

My legs burned when I sat down while my lips struggled to hold a whimper from escaping. Levi didn't look at me; all I could see was the big paper, a crossword puzzle half filled out on the back staring back at me. I felt like I could feel him smirking at me, though. I wished I had laser vision to burn through his damn paper.

"Have some vitamin C, you need it." He lowered his paper, picked up the pitcher of orange juice on the table, and poured me a glass.

"Thanks." His silver eyes were watching me, the beast in him coming closer to look at us. I felt my own wolf stir.

She was crawling on her belly, trying to creep quietly without detection. But there was something different about him that I didn't notice before. My eyes found a vein in his neck. It pulsed right as this strange energy whipped out at me, snapping like an electric whip between us. I jumped, barely concealing a whimper.

"Here you go, Char," Derek said, setting the plate of bacon, eggs, and pancakes in the shape of wolves in front of me.

"Thanks," I said over my shoulder, my eyes lingering on him as he walked back to the kitchen.

It was so obvious how easily a human could fall into a vampire's trap. Derek used to be a human to me, who sometimes had fangs and a strange blood mustache that I liked to convince myself was wine, but he wasn't human at all.

Carefully, I turned back and took a sip of coffee. "Well, well, well." Another breeze of coppery sweetness approached me. Elliot sat down at the table with a smile. "Looks like Sleeping Beauty is up. I can't believe you, Charlotte," he said with a mock scold while I started to cut into the pancakes. "You left me with these two on my own for four days! Four days, Charlotte, how—"

"*Four* days?" I almost spat out my coffee.

Levi turned the page of his paper lazily, like it was a normal morning. "You went through Extreme Makeover: Werewolf Edition. It's expected."

"It's normal," Elliot added.

Derek set a plate in front of Elliot then took a seat on the other side of me, a cup of coffee in his hand. "How do you feel, then?"

I felt Elliot put the back of his hand on my forehead.

"Fine, everything hurts."

"No shit?"

A low growl from my inner beast reverberated over to Levi. He just chuckled at me, and in a way his assholish nature made me feel normal again.

Elliot leaned back in his seat with a tired smile. "I think you're going to be fine. Your vitals look good. You're going to want to take it easy for a few days. Your body is still adjusting, so you'll probably, more or less, sleep through the next few days."

"How does she feel?" Derek asked.

"Everywhere. She's everywhere, like she's always been here the whole time," I found myself saying.

"She's strong, Levi," Elliot mused.

Levi just grunted, neither agreeing nor disagreeing.

"But I'm normal, right? Nothing is wrong, right?"

Levi took a bite of bacon. "Besides being a pain in the ass? No."

"You're fine," Elliot assured me, although I wasn't convinced. With my brain scrambled, it was hard to be convinced of anything. "What would you like to do, Charlotte?"

I hadn't thought about that in the previous weeks; surviving had been my only goal. Only concern. What did I want to do?

"Charlotte?"

"What happens now?"

"You need to rest, so I was thinking we could have a movie day? The Wi-Fi is sketchy, but we do have plenty of DVDs, and—"

"No, I mean, what am I supposed to do now?"

Levi folded his paper. His eyes looked tired, like my question reminded him of all the sleep he had lost.

"Come on, Charlie. Let's go for a run."

"Right now?"

"Yes, right now," he answered.

"Char, the shifters are on your bed. I can put them in the bathroom if you don't want to walk that far?"

My eyes hadn't left Levi's form, which was now walking down the steps and onto the lawn. "I'll be fine." Which was a dead lie. I practically cried walking back to my room, my beast wailing inside me. Everything felt like it was frayed, hanging on by flimsy duct tape.

Levi looked up at me in surprise, like he had expected me to need to crawl outside. I didn't blame him. I was surprised my bones hadn't given up.

"All right, try shifting."

"How?"

"Just let her come out like you did your skin. Just think of your fur. Think about the change from where you are now into your other form, and call that forward."

Simple enough according to Levi.

"Right . . ." I felt like more questions were not in the cards for me today.

The beast in me was ready, but memories of the Blood Moon made the hair on my arms rise. Levi sat back on his heels. "It's going to hurt until you're used to it, but you won't get there until you do it over and over again."

"Is that what you did?"

"It's what you'll do when you don't look like you're about

to shit yourself. Now come on. Putting it off only makes it worse."

"Fine," I huffed.

I closed my eyes and let her come forward. There was something different about her, something careful. She pushed but she wasn't charging. Inwardly, I could feel that she knew how breakable we still were, a notion she held close as she pushed some more—the shift taking over me.

In the middle of it, I thought I would pass out. My screams and the sound of cracking were a nightmare I didn't want to relive. I tried to walk again like I had during my first shift, but ended up flailing around in the grass until fur rolled over me and a muzzle sprouted from my face.

With a heavy breath, she shook out her fur then looked at Levi.

"Well, that wasn't so bad."

I opened my mouth, but nothing came out, only whines and angry-sounding growls. I had done this before, but trying to think in my tired brain about how that had worked was like trying to find a needle in a pool of molasses.

"Just talk. You'll feel it, like you're turning a dial to find the right radio channel."

I sat back and closed my eyes. My mind felt vast until a humming called me to it. An energy I couldn't have missed even if I'd wanted to. I reached out, touching it with the fingers of my brain, instantly feeling something click.

"*Levi?*"

He rolled his eyes. "*Congratulations, you can annoy the hell out of me in both forms now.*"

He jumped with ease into the air. His bones quickly

cracked into place and fur moved over him like a wave as the transformation rolled over him with ease. I tried to control my envy when he landed gracefully on the ground on four paws.

*"How long until it doesn't hurt?"*

*"It always hurts, you just get used to it,"* he replied, darting into the trees.

My wolf leaped after him. She had so much more energy than I did, and I was happy to let her have temporary control of the situation. When she ran it was like she was practically flying. She was so graceful, careful not to step on the dried leaves or fallen branches, easily falling into a silent swiftness that both impressed and unnerved me.

Levi twisted and turned through the trees. It was a struggle to keep up with him, but my beast was relentless even with the pain still humming through us. Considering his size, the way he could snake around trees and out of the way of boulders that jutted up angrily from the ground was more than impressive. It didn't seem real.

We ran until the land became stark with unforgiving inclines. A few times I would slip or pause for a break, but Levi would nip at my legs until I would start to run again.

I followed him until the canopy of the trees thinned out so a cool, snowy rain mixed with mist could sprinkle onto us. A harsh wind ran through my fur, bitter and carrying the sound of ice breaking with it. Levi shifted to his skin, wearing long black pants that I assumed were shifters. He jogged to a bush where he dug around in some kind of burrow.

"One thing to know," he said as he reached his arm into the hole. "We have these burrows all over the pack. There's usually some supplies and clothes inside of them." He pulled out a pair of sweats and tossed them to me before reaching back into the hole.

My eyes closed and my mind tried to find that fuse I needed to set off so I could shift back to my skin. Eventually, I felt the ripples comb over me before the cracking started. Birds flew away as sickening sounds rolled off my lips while my skin took over me. My hands clung to the ground as I caught my breath.

Levi held the sweatshirt open for me and helped me carefully slip into it. "It only gets easier if you keep doing it."

"Right." I was still skeptical that was true. This pain felt like the kind that never left you. Always lingering around to bite you at the right moment.

He helped me up, then held open the sweatpants for me. My fingers clung to his shoulders, my legs like noodles ready to give out. "Easy," he said while I disjointedly stepped into the pants. "After I first shifted, my father had me shifting over and over, every day, whenever he would say, until I could do it without thinking. We'll get you there eventually."

He stood me upright then stepped away, waving a hand for me to follow. It was like a thousand little knives were stabbing at my calves when I stepped forward. Levi pulled sweatpants and a long-sleeved shirt on over his shifters, while cracking sounded in the sky. "Levi?"

"Walk it off." He walked past me and farther up the hill without a glance back.

My beast groaned until I heard what sounded like thunder. I looked around but the sky didn't have a storm cloud nearby. Curiously, I made my way up the hill to where Levi was sitting, using every swear word in the book as I climbed.

"Levi—" I was cut off by the sound of something shattering and groaning.

We were on top of a cliff that bordered a lake. The water below was foggy but still the most vibrant color of turquoise that I had ever seen. Big chunks of dusty ice floated in it and dotted the beach below us.

The glacier the ice was falling from started to groan again, almost like it was trying to wake up and stretch its arms after a long sleep. It was a whimsical shade of frosty blue with ridges so sharp yet so aristocratic that part of me thought it looked more like a painting than something real.

"This is beautiful," I said, walking past an old tree stump to where he was sitting.

"She's been receding a little more in the last few years, but not as bad as others," he replied over my whimpers while I tried to sit.

"I've never seen one before." I paused, sucking in a sharp breath while I adjusted my legs out in front of me. "It's so loud."

"Mhmm," he hummed. "It's shifting, there haven't been many big pieces that have fallen off lately, but usually you can catch a few smaller chunks."

"Do humans know about this?"

"That glacier and lake are on human territory." I looked over at him as a tired smile tugged on his lips. "They can't see us, but we can see them. Can't you feel it?"

There was a strange wave coming off the glacier, an energy rolling toward me. The hair on the back of my neck stood and my nostrils flared as the scent neared me. "It smells like burning sugar."

"Magic," he said as the glacier began to rumble again. "We can't necessarily see it, but it's there. All of it smells a little like burning sugar, but the scent is unique to the witch or group of witches who cast the spell."

"What do the humans see?"

"Hills and a forest. The park rangers think this is private property. It is, but they can't see the wolves on the other side of the magic."

"But before? When I was attacked? Was that protected?"

Levi shook his head. "It borders our land."

My mind wandered off, remembering the tracks that disappeared into the mud when I first met Levi. Levi watched me carefully before smiling. "You didn't even see me coming, and you wouldn't have."

My heart skipped a beat. "But the clearing you sent me to?"

"Not protected land," he admitted.

"What about if humans try to cross the border?"

Levi shrugged. "It happens. Some packs have some deterrents—one pack has a path that will magically appear to take the human out of the pack land. It depends. But no harm comes to them. Usually someone on patrol finds them and escorts them out. If they saw something they shouldn't, we try to deal with it as carefully as possible—it's why we need the vampires to help us since they can wipe their memories."

The glacier groaned again, small fragments of it rolling down the steep side and into the water, the ripples making their way to shore. I turned to look at it, my mind drifting away from the conversation and onto watching the ice fall into the milky water.

"I come out here a lot," he admitted. "Always have. Sometimes it feels like the only place I can fucking think." He looked tired, and not from a lack of sleep. He looked like whatever future he was staring at exhausted him.

"What's going to happen now?"

He was quiet for a while before he turned his head to look at me. "What do you want to happen?"

"What do you mean, what do I want to happen?"

"Yes, that's exactly what I mean." He laughed to himself. "You're a stubborn little shit, you know that?"

"Do I have to join the pack?"

"Do you want to?" he asked. "No one is going to make you do anything."

"What am I supposed to do?"

He rolled his eyes. "If you keep living life the way you think you're supposed to, you're going to find that you end up pretty disappointed."

And I was. I had helped build a life, brick by brick, and it had only crumbled. I had done everything right, all the boxes on my "supposed-to" checklist were filled out. Constantly, I metered myself to make sure that this list was carefully balanced—every woman does, it's what we're "supposed" to do.

Because you have to be fierce, but not to the point where you're shoving feminism down everyone's throat. You have to be beautiful, but you can't be intimidating. The goal is to look like you just woke up with those puckered lips ready to open wide and sharp cheekbones that look elegant even when they carry black-and-blue battle wounds. You have to be fit, but you can't be that fit—not to the point where your strength is emasculating, but enough that justifies the need to live off overpriced meal replacement shakes.

The game is to keep checking boxes off your list until you die. Go to college, have a kick-ass career that you can blog about, get married, pop out some kids, stay fit and hot as hell so your husband won't lose interest, pick up some hobby you can also blog about, only ever shop at Target, never forget your nail appointment, and never let your gray hairs show. Ever.

I had no idea what my list was even supposed to be now, but I did know that I never wanted one ever again.

"There's no going back now. If you do it, it won't be the same."

There was no denying that. I felt the beast in me hum in the back of my mind in agreement. Levi was right. I needed to decide what I wanted for myself.

"And the pack?"

"Is here if that's what you want."

The cool wind bit at my lips. My beast stirred while my mind wandered in circles around what a new life with the pack could mean.

"There's some business I need to take care of first."

Levi turned his gaze to mine, silver eyes locking me in place without resolve. He said nothing. Neither of us needed to. He nodded to me, understanding in his eyes, and let me step away from him and the cliff.

My paws carried me home quicker than I would have liked. Derek and Elliot were out of the house, the silence dancing around me. I swallowed whatever was bubbling in my gut and strode into my room; to the closet where the shoebox tucked in the back corner was along with the duffel bag I had carried here so many weeks ago.

I fished out the phone and powered it on. My fingers paused for a moment, hesitation daring me to drop the phone and leave it behind. But this was something I couldn't leave behind. To go forward, sometimes you had to go back.

My fingers rushed over the number and lifted the phone to my ear. Dull rings sounded over and over along the hollow line until finally, the line was picked up.

"Hello?"

"Nate," I said, the words escaping on my breath.

"Charlotte?"

I sucked in a breath. "It's me."

He let out a breath, silence creeping over the line. "Charlotte—what is it this time?"

"You were right," I said. "I'm coming home."

"You're coming home? Baby?"

I blinked hard and let out a breath of my own. "I'll be there in a few days."

"I'll be waiting."

# CHAPTER
# TWENTY-TWO

Mr. Dawson was a pudgy man who had too many plants on his first-floor balcony. He always told us they gave him privacy. Now I realized it just made it easier for him to peep on people without getting caught.

Before I would not have noticed him watching me with his beady brown eyes from between the leaves of his morning glories, but now I could more than spot him. The scent of day-old cologne and smoked oysters hanging on his skin smacked me in the face the minute I stepped out of the car.

He sat up in his chair, holding his paper up like he was actually reading it as I stepped up to the call box for the condominium. His eyes watched me, brows furrowing slightly like he was confused. I knew he wouldn't recognize me now. He would have recognized the frail, bleach-blond, tan ghost of myself. But now? Now I am a stranger to him.

"Visiting?" he asked as I buzzed the call box.

"I am."

He set his paper down in his lap. "Friend? Family?"

Was he always this nosy? From the corner of my eye, I could see him checking my ass out. The beast in me wanted to snap at him. I couldn't blame her.

"It's Nate," I heard from the call box speaker.

"It's me," I answered.

"Thank god," he breathed. "See you soon," he finished as the door buzzed open.

Mr. Dawson's brows raised. "You must be the new girl-friend. Lucky Nate," he teased.

Funny how before he only watched. Scrutinized. Never showed an ounce of friendliness.

"Lucky him," I agreed, before stepping inside.

The whole building was as I remembered it. Shiny marble floors that led to a shiny elevator where an attendant waited inside. "Which floor?"

"Top. Penthouse. Nathan Lane."

The attendant looked over at me. He nodded politely. "Of course, miss," he answered before hitting the appropriate button.

My beast cocked her head at him. We didn't miss how he angled himself away from us, or how he pressed himself into the corner.

The doors dinged opened, cueing the attendant to let out the breath he was holding. I nodded politely and stepped into the foyer. The private foyer where only one door waited for me.

I smoothed out the cream blouse tucked into my jeans and stepped forward. My brown leather stiletto boots clicked along the floor like a clock ticking away the seconds of the day.

My nostrils flared. I could smell him before the door even opened. I could smell the whole apartment the minute I stepped out of the elevator. My eyes easily spotted the little bit of bright-pink lipstick still smudged on the edge of the door as I stepped up to it. Someone forgot to clean up their recent mess.

Before I could knock on the door, it was opening, whether I wanted it to or not.

His scent hit me hard, almost forcing me to take a step back. He smelled about as hollow as he looked. There was a breath of scotch lingering on skin that I could have sworn at one point was golden, but now looked as dull as the pastel-blue Polo he wore. The ends of the jockey emblem were actually starting to fray, much like the ends of his hair, which no longer looked like the kind of strands that Rumpelstiltskin himself would have treasured.

He didn't say anything. His eyes trained on me with the hunger of a leech.

"Hello, Nate." I arched a brow. "Are you going to let me in?"

"Your hair."

My fingers twirled one of my dark strands. "I needed a change."

"It suits you."

"Are we going to have this conversation outside?"

His eyes started to harden. Losing his edge never went over well. A smile forced its way onto his lips. "I'm so happy you're home," he breathed, stepping forward to hug me with arms that I knew were far from gentle.

My hand shot out to his chest. "We need to talk, Nate."

His hands went up. "Charlotte, you've been gone for over three months. I thought you were dead. Can you blame me?"

I bit back a smile. "Let's go inside."

He nodded and stepped aside.

I stepped into the condo that I used to constantly fret over. That I used to constantly redecorate and scrub clean even though we had a maid. I used to worry about what would happen if Nate ever thought that I couldn't give him a perfect home, and I would stay up at night anxious about the things guests would say if one thing was out of place. I never wanted to be the girl gossiped about in the ladies' room at the country club, but now I was sure I was their number one favorite thing to talk about.

The beast in me crawled forward. I could see her scrunching her nose at the scents around her. The smell of pleather from the sectional we'd overpaid for, the candles from an organic store that reeked of too much lavender, the hints of perfume that was sickly sweet—too sweet to be anything I would wear—and of course the smell of liquor. My eyes could easily spot a stain on the carpet that Yulanda would never get out.

"Nothing's changed. I waited for you."

I arched a brow and walked to the couch. Because

everything had changed. The pictures of us were gone. I had littered the place with them. They were the closest thing to a happy relationship that I ever got to, and not one of them was left.

"I can see that."

"So?"

"So?" I asked, sitting down on the couch.

Nate tugged at his collar. A habit he did when he was nervous, although he would never admit it. "Charlotte, where the fuck were you? What—where the fuck did you go?"

"You should know. You paid a pretty penny for that P.I."

He looked at the ceiling, hands on his hips. "Fine," he admitted with a sigh. He strolled to the wet bar and pulled out his favorite handle of scotch. "Can you blame me? You just left. There was no trace of you anywhere. I thought—fuck—I thought you died, Charlotte!"

I cocked my head. "You were worried I died?" I shook my head with a chuckle. "Nate, you almost killed me that night, and you were worried I died?"

My beast licked her teeth. She wanted to sink them into the artery we could spot pulsing in his neck. His heartbeat was picking up. It wasn't time for her. I gently persuaded her to settle. Her fun would come soon enough.

His jaw ticked as he poured a healthy serving of scotch. "You're right. I fucked up, a lot. Okay? I really fucked up—I've been going back to therapy since then." He picked up his glass and took a long drink. "I—it's why I sent someone to look for you. I knew I fucked up—I know I did. But I couldn't stand the thought of something happening to you. Out there, in the woods, by yourself? Charlotte, the thought of what happened to you has kept me up for nights. I fucked up."

He walked back to the couch and settled, eyes holding mine like they had done so many times before. The same story. The same excuses. The same "therapist" that never worked. I doubt he ever saw one unless you counted one of his favorite bartenders.

I shook my head. "What happened to me doesn't matter, and it's not your business, Nate. I didn't come here today to come home. I came here to tell you that I am done, and that I want you to let me live my life—and for you to call your people off."

His fingers clutched the glass, the liquid in it beginning to quiver. "Charlotte, this is your home. Those people you're shacking up with up there? Whoever they are, they are not your people, Charlotte. Our lives are here. Your life is here with me, baby," he murmured, scooting closer to me.

I shook my head again. "Your life is here, Nate. Your life. Not mine."

He took another swig of his drink then set it on the glass coffee table in front of us. The same table I had been shoved into the night before I left. "Charlotte, just stay for a week. This is your home. You just need to be home, and you'll see," he said, sliding closer to me. "It's you and me. It's always been and it always will be."

His hand reached for mine. I snatched mine away before his dirty paws could even graze it. It took everything I had to keep the growl from tumbling out of my throat. I stood and stepped away from the couch.

"I want you to leave me alone and call your dogs off.

Otherwise, I am going to ship this to every reporter in California and to the right law enforcement agencies, where your friends won't be able to save you."

I turned and tossed him the Jumpdrive I had tucked in my pocket. He snatched it, fingers uncurling as he looked at it like it was a live grenade.

My feet gracefully carried me to the bar. I took out my own glass and poured whiskey into it. "The fuck is this?" I heard him hiss.

"This is one copy of many. It's a copy of all the ways you and your father and your friends at that firm have been hiding your tax dollars from the government and laundering money for overseas clients. It's all there. All the records anyone would ever need in order to put your ass in jail for a long time."

I took a sip of my whiskey. The beast in me started to pace, because we could see the "I miss you" facade starting to fade. I was ready for it, because if his sweet talking didn't work the anger would come next.

"What overseas clients?"

I leaned against the wall and swirled the ice around in my drink. "Don't play dumb, Nathan. We both know you loved to fuck the girls they brought over—I caught you with that Russian girl in your dad's pool house once. I should have left you then, and that's on me."

He ran a hand over his face as a sickly smile twisted on his lips. "Baby, you're so cute. Seriously? What is this game?"

I rolled my eyes and took another drink. "The game is that you're fucked, Nate. Royally fucked. You're fucked if you don't leave me in peace. Although I think you may be fucked in general."

He cocked his head. "And what about you? You know and haven't said anything. That makes you an accomplice."

I smirked, holding in a laugh. They'd have to fucking find me first, and I doubted they would.

"I'm serious, Nate." I set my drink down on the cart next to me. He stood, fists clenched at his sides. "I'm done. I'm out. I want to be left alone and in peace. That's all I ask. I don't want anything else."

"You're going to just walk out of our lives? After everything? After everything you've put me through these last three months?!"

His angry side was coming out, rage seeping through with each step he took toward me. I didn't move. No, I let the beast crawl forward and held my ground.

"I loved you! And you left! You left and I thought you were dead! And now you have the fucking audacity to come here and blackmail me?! Are—did you get your small-ass mind brainwashed out there?! Did you hit your fucking head?!"

"A few times," I answered casually. "But my mind has never been clearer."

His brows furrowed almost as if the rage was going to crack through his skin. For a moment, I wondered if he was some type of monster that Levi had forgotten to tell me about, but then I realized that he was just a man. A sad, insecure man who was losing his grip.

"You're not blackmailing me. You're not leaving. You're staying here where you belong. If you think I'm going to let you walk out of that fucking door again, you're wrong. Dead wrong."

A smile pulled at my lips. "That's where you're wrong, because you are going to let me walk out of that door. I'm done, Nate. Leave me in peace."

I pushed off the wall and moved toward the door. Nate's hand shot out to grab me. I ducked under his arm and stepped around him as the momentum of his motion caused him to stumble.

"The fuck?" he breathed, turning to me.

I cocked my head. "You don't want to do this with me, Nate."

"You? You should know better than to fucking try this with me, Charlotte."

"Try what?" I asked airily. "What am I trying, Nathan?"

He reached for me again, his long bony fingers like prongs trying to snatch me. Again, I ducked before he could reach me and stepped around him. My foot struck out and caught one of his, enough to make him stumble into the bar cart.

When he turned this time, I knew the game was over. Gone was the golden boy I once used to worship. The ghoul that used to haunt my dreams was in his place.

He lunged for me with a strange growl of his own. My arm shot out and shoved him back by the chest right as a fist hurled toward me. My own hand caught it as a growl rumbled over me. The beast was close now. I could feel her under my skin, itching to sink her teeth into him. Nate's eyes went wide as I shoved him back by his fist into the wall.

"What the fuck!" he cried, before he made one last attempt with his fist.

I blocked it then caught his other hand by the wrist, easily snapping it. The cry of a dying rabbit wailed out of his mouth. He took one more step toward me but my hand shot out and snatched his neck instead—pinning him to the wall.

The glow of my eyes reflected in his. His free hand clutched his broken one to his chest, but the minute his fingers twitched as if they were going to try one more time, I let another growl vibrate from my chest in warning.

"What the fuck are you?"

"That and the rest of my life are no longer your business. I am walking out of here and you will not follow me or send anyone after me again. Are we clear?"

"You're a fucking monster."

A laugh bubbled out of my lips. "You're right, baby, I am a goddamned monster, and right now, you really don't want to piss me off any more."

I gave his neck one final squeeze before shoving myself away from him. His free hand shot to the bar cart to hold himself upright as the sound of my heels carrying me to the front door filled the empty space.

"I'll call the cops! I have friends, you know!"

"And tell them what?" I laughed, turning to look at him. "That your girlfriend's the boogeyman?"

"And blackmailing me!"

"Ah! Yes, can't wait to hear you explain that. Especially when they want to hear what I have on you."

His mouth closed. There was no longer an argument for him to win. I took one last look at the home I used to love. I knew if I went out on the extended balcony that I would feel the ocean breeze on my cheeks, smell the salt air, and be caressed by the warm sun that could never make any bruise he ever left better. I always thought these walls would hold our relationship together, not trap me in it.

"Bye, Nate. Remember our deal," I said, turning to the door that I should have walked out years before.

• • •

The elevator door chimed open. I stepped from the car, the attendant refusing to look me in the eyes, and out the doors, where Mr. Dawson was still on his balcony. I could spot him watching my hips from the corner of my eye.

"Quick visit?" he asked from behind the safety of his newspaper.

"He didn't last long," I called over my shoulder.

He lowered his paper with wide eyes. I smiled sweetly before skipping over to the cherry-red Mustang convertible that Elliot had insisted we rent. Derek opened the door to the backseat for me. "All good?"

I hugged him as a long breath of relief rolled out of me. His arms gave me a gentle squeeze before releasing me. Eyes sparkling pride, he smiled wide at me.

"Let's get out of here," I said.

He laughed and helped me into the car. Elliot started the engine, then turned to face me. "You're sure you don't want me to have some fun with him? We may need a little snack before our flight?"

Derek pulled his seat belt on while scowling at Elliot, who shrugged casually. "What? It's like a two for one here."

I buckled my belt and shook my head. "You don't want any of his blood. It's rotten." That, and Nate wasn't going to risk coming after me now. Elliot and Derek could have compelled him, but the thought of him living with himself— living with a new monster in his head—well, that was sweet revenge at its finest.

Derek nodded in agreement. "Home, then?"

"Home," I agreed. "I think Levi is right. I think too much sunlight's bad for you."

Elliot sighed and shifted the car into Drive. "Fine. I checked the flights and we have a few hours, which means we're trying that restaurant I found online last night."

"Have it your way, then," Derek teased.

"Oh, I will," he answered with a devious smile. His eyes looked in the rearview mirror as we pulled out of the parking lot. "You good, Char?"

I nodded. "More than good."

# CHAPTER
# TWENTY-THREE

The minute my feet stepped out of the car and onto the lawn of the cabin I had come to call home, I felt my whole body relax. All the weight I had been carrying was left behind, and the crisp mountain air along with the smell of the fire burning in the fireplace started to breathe life back into me.

I jogged up the stairs and into the house, my eyes searching for Levi. His scent was everywhere, but it wasn't fresh. "Where is he?" I asked Derek.

He stepped next to me and set my duffel bag down. Elliot walked in behind him, eyes scanning the room. "Well, he was here a few hours ago. His scent isn't that dull."

I took a step back and headed out the door. "Charlotte!" Derek called.

"I'll be back!" I called over my shoulder.

My fingers quickly peeled all my clothes off, down to my shifters, before I let fur take over my skin. My paws hit the ground, hauling me to the place where my gut told me he would be.

Zipping through trees and curling around boulders had never felt more freeing. My beast surged forward as if the forest was powering her to move faster. Birds fluttered next to us, almost in a race as we started the upward ascent where the air was a hair thinner—crisper. Sounds of easy thunder sounded in the distance, but I knew it wasn't from a storm.

I could smell his scent dancing on the air until it turned into a full-blown trail leading me straight to the cliff. Shifting back to my skin, I pushed through some trees until I stepped onto the cool grass where Levi was sitting on the ledge, watching the glacier in the distance.

"So, this pack," I said, breaking the silence as I walked over to him. My hands skirted over the old tree stump that still stood proudly to guard the area. "What do I have to do?"

He looked over his shoulder as I neared. His mouth wouldn't say it but I could see the relief in his eyes. "You kill him?"

I laughed under my breath. "No," I answered. I took a seat next to him and let my feet hang off the ledge like his. "Wanted to."

"Why not?"

I shrugged. "He's not worth it."

Levi held my gaze for a moment before nodding in agreement. "He's not."

"He won't come looking. Not anymore," I told him.

Levi shook his head. "Lander could have handled that."

I shrugged. "I needed to."

The glacier groaned in front of us; a decent-sized piece of ice was looking like it was about to fall off. A breeze picked up and swirled around us, dancing as if it was carrying an unsounded joy with it.

"What do I have to do?"

"Chop a lot more wood." He laughed at my lack of amusement with his response then looked back at the fragmenting glacier before us. "Pack life isn't easy. It's not glamorous. But if it's what you want, then it's yours."

"So, I'll be swimming more, I assume?"

He chuckled darkly, with a surprised look that had hints of relief. "No, first you'll be practicing shifting so you don't look like a dead fish flopping around each time you do it."

I rolled my eyes. The glacier cracked some more. I wanted to sit here forever, fall asleep to the sound of its thunder.

Being thrown into a pack of wolves didn't sound like a joy, but I knew eventually I would have to step out of the haven that was our lodge.

I looked back at the glacier. After all this time, it had endured. Thousands of years and some, it'd endured.

My beast stirred in me again. If there was one thing I knew, it was that I had her. Ice fell from the glacier that sounded like it was hissing from the pain. It plunked into the blue water, sending ripples around the lake, disturbing the shore.

"I'm glad I'm home."

A moment passed before I heard him let out a long breath. "I am too," he murmured.

I turned to look at him. His hair looked less wiry today, and clean. Like he had actually washed it properly and put a brush through it. His eyes caught mine, exhaustion still heavy in them.

"Can I ask you something?"

He looked at me from the corner of his eye. "Well, go on, not like I can stop you."

"Why didn't you kill me?" Because if there was one thing I'd learned, it was that Levi didn't give a shit about the law. Not really. Here, he was the law—whether he wanted to admit that he thought that way or not.

He was quiet, eyes watching the ice fall into the murky water. "Because I didn't want to."

I bit my lip and turned back to the glacier. "So, I'm going to be part of the pack?"

He nodded. "You're going to be part of the pack, Charlie girl."

# TO BE CONTINUED . . .

# ACKNOWLEDGMENTS

There are so many to whom I owe a great deal of thanks to. I know I am going to miss people here, regardless, so thank you so much to everyone who helped make this possible. A dream is just a wish until you have the bravery to make it happen. I would have never made this happen without the abundance of support from my family, friends, and the team at W by Wattpad Books.

First, thank you to the W team! To Jennifer for being the world's most amazing editor. I sincerely cannot thank you enough for your kindness, patience, and ability to grasp my vision so quickly to help make it a better reality. To Deanna and Monica for keeping me on track with deadlines and taking a chance on this book. Thank you all so very much.

Kelly, Alex, and Ali—this would have never happened without you three. I am honestly not even sure where my writing career would be if our paths had not crossed.

To Bex, Will, Lauren, and Steph for supporting me in more ways than you'll ever know.

Lastly, to my family for always believing in me and always pushing me to try. Thank you, Mom, for being the best cheerleader and thank you, Dad, for never letting me quit.

# ABOUT THE AUTHOR

Z.W. Taylor grew up in Texas, where the stories are as big as the hair that seems to float around Dallas. Writing was always a hobby, and a good story was something she never stopped chasing. When she is not writing, she's wondering why her coffeepot sounds like a boggart when it gurgles, debating whether or not her cat is plotting against her, and constantly filling blank pages with many ideas for the future.